PRAISE FOR
THIS IS WHERE WE DIE

"*This Is Where We Die* is a cutthroat elimination thriller with a gloriously grisly premise and to-die-for cast of suspects. I devoured it in one sitting and immediately added it back to my TBR to read again. Wickedly funny, delightfully chilling, and propulsive to the final word."

—Dana Mele, author of *People Like Us* and *Summer's Edge*

"A devious, page-turning thriller full of terrible teens doing terrible things."

—Alexa Donne, Edgar Award–nominated author of *Pretty Dead Queens* and *The Ivies*

"*This Is Where We Die* is a locked room thriller at its finest. This twisted slasher tale of revenge gone wrong or right, depending on how you look at it, had me questioning absolutely everything and everyone."

—Trish Lundy, author of *The One That Got Away with Murder*

"From the very first page to the final twist, *This Is Where We Die* is an absolutely wild ride, a modern take on Agatha Christie's classic

And Then There Were None like you've never read. He's sophomore effort is not one to be missed!"

—Liz Lawson, *New York Times* bestselling author of the Agatha series

"Twisty, shocking, and at times brutal, He's sophomore novel is an unputdownable, whip-smart take on Agatha Christie for today's YA reader."

—MK Pagano, author of *Girls Who Burn*

"I inhaled this dark, chilling, and incredibly suspenseful read in one sitting. With tension radiating off the page, distinct perspectives, and clever twists, *This Is Where We Die* is a stunningly fresh and modern twist on the locked room murder mystery that will leave readers reeling in the best way. Absolutely impossible to put down!"

—Kelsea Yu, Shirley Jackson Award–nominated author of *It's Only a Game* and *Bound Feet*

"*This Is Where We Die* is a delightfully twisty and deliciously twisted take on a locked room mystery that feels both timeless and totally fresh. He has carved out a space in the thriller genre all her own, with breathtaking pacing, high-stakes drama and dark humor that made me laugh out loud even when I still had the chills from a gruesome reveal the page before. I'm already itching to read this again."

—Meredith Adamo, author of Morris Award finalist *Not Like Other Girls*

PRAISE FOR
PERFECT LITTLE MONSTERS

★ "Quick reveals and suspense drive the propulsive, Hitchcockian plot to an ending sure to leave teen mystery fans amazed at He's careful structuring of the story."

—*Booklist*, Starred Review

"He adds grit to a plot built on familiar high school mystery elements via the intertwining narratives, which dispense information in lightning-quick intervals that will keep readers on their toes all the way to the shocking conclusion."

—*Publishers Weekly*

"This tense and twisty thriller will keep readers looking over their shoulder."

—Natalie D. Richards, *New York Times* bestselling author of *Five Total Strangers*

"Fast-paced, dark, with a twist that satisfied my evil side, He's debut is a showstopper!"

—Jesse Q. Sutanto, bestselling author of *The Obsession* and *The New Girl*

"*Perfect Little Monsters* is a viciously shocking examination of bullying with an ending that will leave you floored. A riveting debut you won't want to miss!"

—Chelsea Ichaso, author of *Dead Girls Can't Tell Secrets* and *They're Watching You*

"With characters you'll love to hate and a twist that you won't see coming, Cindy R. X. He's debut thriller, *Perfect Little Monsters*, is a book that will keep readers up all night. He deftly weaves the past with the present to create questions you'll only think you know the answer to. A shocking delight."

—Jessie Weaver, author of *Live Your Best Lie* and *Lie Until It's True*

"A dark, voicey, and inventive debut from an explosive new talent. Prepare to be captivated from start to pulse-pounding finish and blown away by the many twists and turns. *Perfect Little Monsters* is at once a fast-paced thriller and a thoughtful, incisive look at the impact of bullying."

—Laurie Elizabeth Flynn, author of *The Girls Are All So Nice Here* and *All Eyes on Her*

"*Perfect Little Monsters* is a heart-pounding, harrowing, and twisty tale about the legacy of bullying and cruelty and its devastating consequences. An extraordinary debut from an extraordinary talent."

—Alex Finlay, author of *Every Last Fear* and *The Night Shift*

ALSO BY CINDY R. X. HE

Perfect Little Monsters

This is Where we DIE

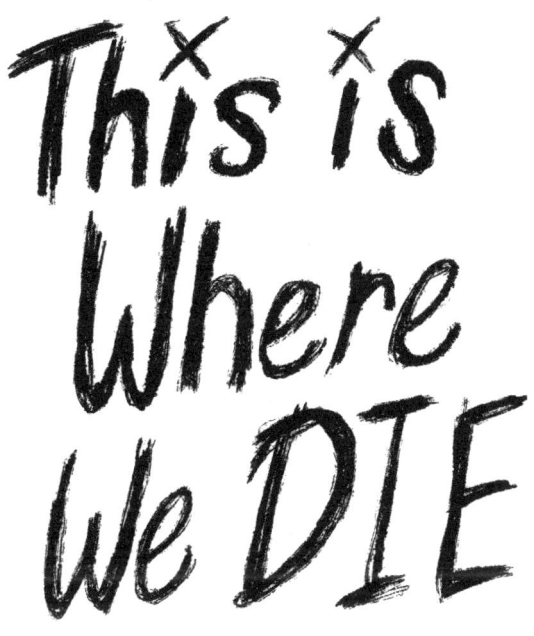

CINDY R. X. HE

Copyright © 2025 by Cindy R. X. He
Cover and internal design © 2025 by Sourcebooks
Cover design by Nicole Hower
Cover images © Silas Manhood/Trevillion, Sharoncudworth/Getty Images, Soren Hald/Getty Images, Mads Perch/Getty Images, Dave G Kelly/Getty Images, Cyndi Monaghan/Getty Images
Internal design by Tara Jaggers/Sourcebooks

Sourcebooks and the colophon are registered trademarks of Sourcebooks.

All rights reserved. No part of this book may be reproduced in any form or by any electronic or mechanical means, including information storage and retrieval systems—except in the case of brief quotations embodied in critical articles or reviews—without permission in writing from its publisher, Sourcebooks.

No part of this book may be used or reproduced in any manner for the purpose of training artificial intelligence technologies or systems.

The characters and events portrayed in this book are fictitious or are used fictitiously. Any similarity to real persons, living or dead, is purely coincidental and not intended by the author.

Published by Sourcebooks Fire, an imprint of Sourcebooks
P.O. Box 4410, Naperville, Illinois 60567-4410
(630) 961-3900
sourcebooks.com

Cataloging-in-Publication Data is on file with the Library of Congress.

Printed and bound in the United States of America.
VP 10 9 8 7 6 5 4 3 2 1

A NOTE TO THE READER

This novel contains themes and/or mentions of alcohol consumption, anxiety and anxiety attacks, depression, drug abuse, starvation, food trauma, miscarriage, off-page cannibalism, suicide, murder, and death.

If you feel that any of these subjects may trigger an adverse reaction, please consider not reading this book.

Here comes a candle to light you to bed,
And here comes a chopper to chop off your head,
Chop, chop, chop, chop, the last man's dead!

ISLA

We're going to die here.

The thought settles in my head. Curls itself around my brain, sinks its fangs in. Now that it's here, it doesn't leave.

I press myself closer to Will for warmth, tug the thin blanket more securely around us. Will's dark blond hair is almost brown now from the grease. I'm so used to the stench of our unwashed bodies that I almost don't smell it anymore. It's so cold I can't feel my toes. Maybe I'm going to lose them. It's an alarming thought, and I wriggle them frantically to try and bring back feeling into them. It's the middle of the day and the thermometer on the wall reads negative ten degrees Celsius. I think Emily said that's around fifteen degrees Fahrenheit. I guess it could be worse: if it weren't for the snow outside trapping our body heat in this stone hut, like some kind of accidental igloo, we'd have frozen to death by now.

Then again, the snow packed outside is why we're trapped in here in the first place.

Like Will and me, the rest of our small group is also huddled together on the icy stone floor. Charlie and Vera. Emily and Sadie. Ant and Tom. Everyone's starting to have the same look: hollow eyes, gaunt cheeks. The same shocked expression, like nobody can believe this is really happening.

At first, we passed the time telling stories and making jokes. It helped distract from the gnawing hunger in our bellies, and I guess we were still hopeful that someone would come looking for us soon.

We stopped talking a few days ago. Tom has even stopped moaning about his broken leg, which is a relief because I don't want to keep being reminded of it. To look at the horrifically odd shape of it.

We don't move anymore, either, unless it's to go pee in the corner or, when we're thirsty, to scrape some snow from the slit-like opening set high in one wall. We may be trapped, but at least the blizzard and avalanche deposited enough snow that we can at least reach it from that opening. I heard that dehydration is a horrible way to die, so I guess we're lucky in that way?

Although right now it feels like it might have been better to have died within the first few days. Or better still, from exposure, if we hadn't found this tiny mountain shelter shortly after the blizzard hit. This death trap.

The hunger is all I think about.

I've lost count of how long we've been trapped here. Thirteen days? Fourteen?

In the beginning we sometimes heard helicopters, but they sounded far away. Or maybe we just imagined them. It's hard to remember now. My mind keeps wandering. It's getting harder and harder to focus on anything.

I wonder if the rest of the world already thinks we're dead, buried under the snow.

There's a strange sound. A kind of keening, like a wild animal in distress. It's Vera. She's whipping her head back and forth, her black hair in her face, her mouth stretched in a grimace, a high-pitched sounding *eeee* coming from it. Charlie murmurs something to her in a soothing voice as he holds her, but she shakes his arm off. "They can't find us," she shrieks, her eyes almost bugging out of her emaciated face. "No one is coming. Don't you all get it? *No one is coming!*" She laughs, a shrill, hysterical sound that has me clenching my teeth and leaves me colder than ever. Then she starts screaming, pulling at her hair, scratching her own face. *Jesus.*

Charlie grabs her arms. "Vera, no—someone help me!"

Ant gets up and grabs Vera too. The two of them pin her to the floor as I just stare in shock. She's sobbing, banging the back of her head on the stone floor. "Gonna die gonna die gonna die—" she chants.

"No," I say. *No.* Seeing her like this makes something click in my head. I don't know what's going to happen, but I know one thing. "We're going to survive. I'm not dying like this."

SADIE
EIGHTEEN MONTHS LATER

The graduation gown is hot and itchy, and the mortarboard keeps feeling like it's going to fall off no matter how many times I adjust it. The auditorium is too small for the entire senior class and their families. It's way too packed, and I'm struggling to breathe. But I keep the smile plastered on my face as I train my eyes on Principal Bailey—or Baldy, as all the students call him behind his back—up on the stage and pretend not to notice all the usual eyes on the six of us.

It's the last Friday of high school, ever, I tell myself. *Just this graduation to get through. It'll all be over soon.* And then I won't have to see any of them ever again.

The six of us stand closely together, like we always do. We have no choice but to stick to each other. To put up a united front. Together, we will take our secret to the grave. That was what we agreed to do. Our friend group disintegrated for a while after the incident. It was too hard to keep seeing each other, at least for me, so I tried distancing myself. I tried to hang out more with other theater kids. The problem was, my new friends kept asking me what happened, *exactly*. I was constantly afraid I'd say something, accidentally leak what really happened. It made me realize that it wasn't going to be possible to have new friends here, not in this school. It was either become a loner or get back together with the old group. So that's what I did. At least we never, ever, talk about what happened.

Of course, I could have chosen to be like Charlie. I eye him, standing at my right. Like me, Charlie distanced himself from the rest of us. Unlike me, he never tried making any new friends. But it feels like an invisible tether kept pulling the six of us back together. So now he's a part of us but also not quite, keeping to himself on the periphery of our group.

Poor Charlie Rogers never stopped spiraling. His brown hair is as unkempt and greasy as usual. Like he hasn't washed it in days, not bothering even for graduation. He was kicked off the soccer team earlier this year after he got caught sneaking booze to school for the third time. He looks stoned right now; his hazel eyes dilated and bloodshot, the lids half-closed. As I watch, he takes a small bottle out of his pocket and takes a sip. I doubt it's water.

"It is with great pleasure that I stand before you today to introduce our valedictorian," intones Baldy, clearing his throat, and I tear my eyes away from Charlie and back to the stage. His bald head gleams under the glaring fluorescent lights, and he adjusts his tie like it's strangling him. "With a stellar grade point average of four point oh and an unwavering commitment to their studies, this individual has exemplified academic excellence, dedication, and leadership throughout their high school journey."

In front of me, Isla preens.

"Please join me in acknowledging Isla Claythorne's exceptional achievements and welcoming her to the podium to deliver her valedictory address," finishes Baldy with a huge proud smile.

We clap dutifully as Isla makes her way up onstage. With her shiny, bouncing blond curls and pink lip tint, she looks like Barbie: the traditional, perfect, overachieving student body president edition (not Margot Robbie's self-aware version). The one who already made it to Yale on a full scholarship.

An image of her crouched animal-like on a stone floor, gnawing on a bone, flashes involuntarily in my mind.

I shudder, shove it quickly away. Even though just a few seconds ago I found the auditorium too warm, I'm suddenly cold. I fish for the little bottle of Valium in the pocket of the graduation gown, uncap it with trembling fingers. Pop a tablet in my mouth and swallow it dry.

An elbow nudges me on my left. "Hey," says Anthony Martinez—aspiring DJ, party animal, and notorious player—winking at me. "Gimme one too, won't ya? It'll make this whole thing"—he twirls his finger—"less boring."

I roll my eyes at him. "You're not getting your grubby hands on my Valium, sorry."

Ant rolls his black eyes back at me then looks down at his phone. He has on wireless earbuds, and he resumes swiping through TikTok videos. Guess that's one way to pass the time during all the speeches.

Just behind him, Emily Chang sighs. Her large doe eyes are fixed on Ant's back, the usual look of forlorn, unrequited yearning on her face. Emily's into art, algebra (and all other branches of math), and Ant, even though it's obvious to anyone with eyes that he's put her firmly in the friend zone. I've always wondered what she sees in him, but never asked.

Ant nudges Will, shows him a video on his phone. I'm just close enough to hear what Ant is whispering. "Hey man, look at this. It's trending all over TikTok and Insta."

The popular and athletic Will Armstrong, captain of the soccer team, has always been the de facto leader of our group. He even stands up straighter than the rest of us. A blond Ken to Isla's Barbie, except, to everyone's surprise (and to her eternal mortification), he dumped her a few months ago. His dark blue eyes flicker to Ant's phone screen. "An island? What about it?"

"Not just an island. *The* island, the one that everyone's been talking about for the past year. Come on, you must have heard about it. Even *Charlie* must have heard about it, right, Charlie?"

Charlie sighs softly, then gives a half-hearted shrug.

"The one south of Martha's Vineyard, with that glass

mansion?" says Emily as she inches nearer to Ant. "The one that's allegedly secretly owned by Timothée Chalamet?"

"I heard it's actually secretly owned by Harry and Meghan," I can't help but chime in.

"Okay," says Will, now also drawn in, his attention piqued. "What about it?"

Onstage, Isla stops midsentence to shoot a deadly glare at us for daring to be doing anything other than paying rapt, complete, adoring attention to her inspiring speech, and Ant puts his phone back in his pocket. But when she continues speaking, he whispers under his breath, "It's up for rent, man. To anyone who can afford it."

"Oooh," breathes Emily, making googly eyes at Ant. I suppress an exasperated sigh. She always makes the same googly eyes at him no matter what he's saying, as long as he's talking in her direction.

Charlie's lip curls back derisively. "So? What's that got to do with you, or us?"

But before Ant can reply, Isla is back, and she is not happy. "What. Is. So. Interesting?" she says through gritted teeth with a smile that's totally screaming, *I'm going to kill all of you.*

"This," says Ant, totally unperturbed as he takes out his phone and shoves it at her.

Isla frowns at first as she stares at the TikTok, but then her expression clears. "Oh, Christie's Island. The one that's secretly owned by Taylor Swift. Oooh, she put it up for rent?"

Around us, our classmates must be listening in, because all of a sudden, everyone is on their phones googling Christie's Island or looking it up on social media, and nobody is paying attention to the poor guest speaker onstage offering us their words of wisdom.

"So?" I say, even though I know where this is going.

"Okay, maybe this is a dumb idea, but…why have our graduation party in this dumb auditorium this weekend, when we can have it *there*?" says Ant.

It's true; it *is* kinda boring our school organized the graduation party to be in the auditorium.

Emily has her own phone out now. "Wow, there are ten bedrooms, and it comes with a valet, a housekeeper, a private chef, and a fully stocked bar." She looks up at us. "Talk about lush. It must be so expensive."

Ant shifts his weight excitedly from foot to foot. "Is it, though, if we all split the cost? If everybody shares a room, it can take twenty of us. Or even more, if some of us sleep on the couch. Think about it, man." He looks at us with wide eyes. "Our own private island."

Will rubs his chin. "How much is it, anyway?"

Isla passes Ant's phone to Will, who does a mini double take when he looks at it, then shakes his head. "Even if we all split the cost—the entire graduating class—we can't afford *that*."

That's not strictly true. *One* of us can afford it. I shrink back a little—try to sort of fade into the background—but one by one, their heads swivel to me. "It's not expensive for *you* though, is it?" says Isla, always the first to speak up, never embarrassed to ask.

Why am I not surprised? Because this has always been our group dynamic. I pay for their things, and in return... Actually, I don't know what I get in return. The chance to feel like I'm fitting in?

"Oooh, that would be *amazing*," says Emily dreamily. She's probably already imagining herself sharing a room—one with a romantic sea view—with Ant.

Isla's right; I can afford it. But it's annoying the way they keep turning to me whenever they need someone to fund something. They must think my trust fund is bottomless. I always pay for everything. The limos for prom. New computers for the lab.

A ski weekend in British Columbia.

"Are you really doing this? Renting the island for whoever wants to go?" says some girl breathlessly. I think her name's Kate. Or is it Cathy? Hey, there are 245 seniors, I can't know every one of them.

"Wow, that's really generous of you," says another guy who might have been in my Chemistry class. Joe? Jake?

I try to protest. "But what about the party organized by the school graduation committee? Won't they be pissed if we—"

"Nah, why should they care if a few of us don't show? It's not like they paid to rent some place." says Isla.

I narrow my eyes at her.

"This is, like, a once-in-a lifetime opportunity," she continues, probably imagining herself rubbing shoulders with Taylor Swift, or whichever celeb really owns the island.

I suppress another shudder, because I've heard those words before. *A once-in-a-lifetime opportunity.* Who was it who said it the last time? Was it also her? Or Will?

"It *does* sound like it'd be fun," says Will.

"One last blowout party before college," says Ant.

Charlie just shrugs, his eyes still unfocused on something in the distance.

"I think you're right," says Kate/Cathy. "That it's really Taylor Swift who owns the island. God, can you imagine? *We might get to meet her!* I *love* Taylor."

Me too.

I exhale. "Fine. I'll ask my dad's PA to check if it's still available for this weekend."

One last blowout party, and then I never have to see these people again.

—*Did you hear about it? What happened in that mansion? On that island?*

—*Oh my god, yeah. Those teens from Boston Academy, right? On that luxury island? The one that supposedly belongs to some celebrity? It's all over the news and blowing up on CrimeTok.*

—*Such a tragedy.*

—*Always a tragedy when they die so young.*

—*Does anyone know what happened? Was it some kind of accident?*

—*Apparently, it was a massacre.*

—*So horrible. And right after they just graduated too.*

—*Imagine being free from the hell that's high school, at last, and then dying immediately after.*

—*But what happened exactly?*

—*I heard that they were murdered.*

—*Murdered by who?*

—*That's what they're trying to find out.*

WILL

The entire morning felt surreal—the way my parents' faces glowed with pride when I was on the stage accepting my diploma—and the fact that this chapter of my life is almost finally over. Now that the graduation ceremony is finished and people are slowly starting to trickle out, the electric hum of excitement—the kind that only comes with the end of something monumental—is starting to subside. I'm surprised to realize suddenly that I'm already a little nostalgic for the four years I've spent here. In these classrooms, these hallways, and especially on the field, where I really shone.

But enough of being nostalgic. This isn't an end; it's a beginning. With my full athletic scholarship to Michigan State, my future is as bright as they come, and I'm ready to make my mark on the world.

"We're so proud of you," Dad says now, his hand grasping my shoulder firmly. I'm taller than him now, so he has to reach up.

Beside him, Mom beams and nods. "Ready to go home?"

I glance over at where Sadie is standing in the corner of the auditorium, her phone held to her ear, other seniors who have managed to shake off their family already starting to gather around her. "Actually… Could you give me one second? I have to talk with my friends."

"Of course. We'll wait for you outside by the car," says Mom.

As I make my way over to Sadie, who must be making her call to her dad's PA, I see that Isla, Ant, Charlie, and Emily are already there. It's been a while since we all did something together outside of school, and it's kind of exciting.

Not that we don't do things together. We're an unbreakable unit in school, more than ever after that horrible incident. First of all—as we are all aware of—we've had to put up a united front. But more than that… What happened changed us. Marked us. Bound us together even more tightly, because it's not the kind of thing anybody else can relate to. I guess that's why, even though I don't need to be reminded of things I'd prefer not to remember, we're closer together than ever.

I still had to break up with Isla though. I mean, other than the fact that we're heading off to different colleges—long-distance relationships are just too much work and too hard on everyone involved (why put a damper on the college experience when there are endless possibilities?)—it just got to be too much. Don't get me wrong; I still think she's hot. I sneak a sideways glance at her. Especially when she does her hair and puts on makeup like today.

She must feel my eyes on her, because her cornflower-blue eyes meet mine and she gives me a cool, knowing look, her lips turning up on the right side. *Regretting it yet?* her smirk seems to say. Alright, maybe I do sometimes, just a little. Maybe we can get together again one last time this weekend on the island, just for old times' sake. I raise an eyebrow at her, and she flushes slightly and turns away.

Ant is right. Why have our graduation party here when we can have the world's most dope-ass party ever on a celebrity island? We'd go down in history, be the envy of every high school kid in Massachusetts, if not the entire country. It's the kind of thing that can make you social media famous. Open up all kinds of doors. Invaluable when you're not born with a silver spoon in your mouth like some people. I glance at Isla again, who is touching up her lip gloss while listening to Sadie talk to her dad's PA on the phone. Knowing my ex, these must all be thoughts that have already crossed her mind too.

"…so could you just check if it's available for the weekend?" Sadie worries her lower lip with her teeth, twirls a lock of her light brown hair around her pale fingers. "Yeah, this weekend. And if yes, I want it, for me and my friends. Uh…maybe from this evening, up to Sunday afternoon? I know it's very short notice, sorry. Let me know. Thanks, Elle."

"Dude, this is going to be so awesome," says Jake, a guy with freckles and an unruly mop of dark hair, who was the left fullback on the soccer team and who I know loves a good party as much the next person.

"I'm crossing all my fingers and toes!" says one girl, who I've maybe seen once or twice in the hallway.

Gotta admit, it's such a power move, booking a celebrity island for the weekend right at the very last minute on a Friday. Several other seniors are staring at Sadie, their mouths gaping open in awe. Everyone knows she's rich—even though she hates that they do—but sometimes we forget just *how* rich. There are a few other people in this school whose parents are millionaires, but Sadie is in another league. She and her younger brother are already in line to inherit their family's pharmaceutical billions. Must be nice not to have to worry about winning a scholarship to college, because you can just buy your way in anywhere. Not that she even has to go to college.

I shouldn't complain though. If it weren't for her family's wealth and connections, there'd have been many more questions asked. Probably an inquiry started. But her family lawyer and PR team took care of everything, so we got to go back to our lives as usual, as if nothing happened.

We don't have to wait long to find out if we got the island or not. After five minutes Sadie's phone rings, and there's a collective holding of breath as she answers. She brushes her hair out of her face distractedly as she hears what her dad's PA has got to say. "Oh, we got it? Cool. Thanks, Elle—"

There's an explosive burst of sound as people start cheering and whooping. Isla's face is flushed, Emily is jumping up and down, Ant is grinning from ear to ear, and I'm smiling too. Even Charlie looks a bit less depressed than usual. Ant and I high-five each other. Wow, this is really happening. The island that's been all over social media the entire past year, and we're going to party there this whole weekend.

Isla sneaks me another look. Alright, I guess we can hook up, for old times' sake. I haven't dated anyone in a while, she's still hot, and enough alcohol will probably silence the more troubling memories of what she was like in those final days.

Sadie shushes all of us and continues talking on the phone. "How are we going to get there? Ah, okay. Could you arrange them? Yeah, tomorrow morning is good. New Bedford? Oh. Okay…" She pauses, listening.

Then her voice drops slightly. "The chopper? Oh, I…I guess that's a good idea. No, you're right. Better than me getting on a boat. Tonight? Why…? Oh. Yeah, um…okay. Text me the details. Thanks."

Sadie hangs up, then looks around. "Okay, everyone, listen up! The island was available this weekend, so we got it!"

Everyone cheers again. "Sadie's the real MVP!" someone yells.

"Elle—my dad's PA—says she'll arrange for speedboats to pick us up from New Bedford," continues Sadie, blushing a little. "She's handling the logistics for everything, so those who wanna go, can, um…write your names and contact numbers down—anyone got a piece of paper?—and I'll pass it to her so she can text you all with the details tonight, and the exact departure location and time for the speedboats tomorrow, Elle says probably at around eleven. Okay?" People start cheering, but Sadie holds up one hand. "The thing is, there are ten bedrooms, so that puts a limit on how many people can go. Like Ant said, if we all pair up and share rooms, that means a maximum of twenty people."

"I don't mind sleeping on the couch," someone pipes in.

"I can sleep on the floor!" someone else shouts.

"Oh. Then twenty-two, I guess," says Sadie with a doubtful air.

People start jostling to get their names down on the piece of paper being passed around. But Isla tilts her head at Sadie. "What was that you were saying to Elle about a chopper?" says Isla sweetly. "Are *you* going directly by helicopter?"

"Uh…yeah." Sadie fidgets, pulls at her collar like she's too warm. "I get seasick on boats. But not in our chopper—I'm used to that—and I sit up front. So Elle suggested that for me."

Sadie suffers from the worst seasickness. Freshman year, on a trip to visit the Statue of Liberty and Ellis Island, she spent the entire time on the boat puking her guts out in a paper bag. I've never heard her getting sick in her family's helicopter though.

Isla taps at her phone again. "According to Google, New Bedford is an hour and fifteen minutes' drive from here, and then…how long to the island by speedboat?"

"Um…I think Elle said around forty-five minutes—"

"Right. So two hours, not including allowances for traffic

or waiting at the harbor. And how long does it take directly by helicopter?"

Sadie is starting to blush. "Elle said an hour," she mutters.

I can see where Isla is going with this. I repress a smile, sit back, and watch her do what she does best, which is *get what she wants.*

Sadie squirms under our gaze. "But, um, my dad's using the chopper tomorrow so I'm going tonight."

"So whoever goes on your family's chopper will spend an extra night there, before everyone else arrives?" Ant grins. "An extra night of debauchery and partying."

I see where Sadie's thoughts are going though, because I'm thinking the same thing. *Do I really want to be there with just them, after the last time?*

We haven't been alone, just the six of us, outside of school, since the incident.

But this isn't some isolated mountain in Canada. This is a warm island south of the Vineyard, with a mansion fully stocked with food, drinks, a valet, and a freaking private chef. This is *paradise.* There isn't going to be some freak snowstorm to trap and bury us. And everyone else will be arriving the next day.

"How many people can the chopper seat?" asks Emily, glancing at Ant again.

"I… Our chopper *can* seat a maximum of six passengers," says Sadie finally and very reluctantly. "I guess it shouldn't be a *problem*—"

"Guess we're going to get a head start on the partying!" says Ant.

"Yay!" says Emily.

"Thanks!" says Isla.

Hell. "I don't mind a ride too," I say.

One by one, we turn to Charlie. He's still gazing into the distance, at something only he can see.

Poor guy. He hasn't been the same since the incident. Actually, I'm not sure if we're still friends. He's here, but sometimes, I get the impression that he's barely tolerating us. I guess that's fair enough.

Still, he can't continue spiraling like this. All that moping. He has to stop being so self-destructive. Besides, he wasn't the only one who lost someone. I lost my best friend too. Shit happens. You just have to pick yourself back up and keep going. He should be happy and grateful he's still alive, like the rest of us.

I wanna tell him all that, give him a good come-to-Jesus talk, but things have been awkward between us recently. I know he suspects it, but despite what he thinks, I wasn't the one who told on him to Coach and got him kicked off the team.

Still, I feel a little responsible for him. I was his captain, after all. I should have realized how bad his drinking was getting, did something more to help him. Look at him now: scholarship gone, future down the drain. And unlike Sadie, Charlie doesn't have rich parents to help prop him up.

What he needs is a good distraction. "Coming with us, Charlie?" I say. Maybe Ant and I can talk to him later tonight.

Cheer him up a little. Tell him it's not too late to turn his life around (even if it probably is).

Or at least, to take a shower.

"Sure. Why not?" He digs a small flask out of his pocket, uncaps it, and takes a swig. Like he truly doesn't give a shit anymore. "Just the six of us tonight, huh? It'll be just like old times."

EMILY

"You're really excited about this, huh?" Mom laughs as our car finally turns into the long driveway lined with pretty red maple trees that leads up to the house in Milton that Sadie calls home.

I still my jittering right leg and shove my hands under my thighs on the car seat so I stop chewing at my nails. I've been bouncing off the walls all afternoon since it was confirmed we got the island for the weekend, and that we're going *right now, this very instant*. It's so wild that we'll be sleeping in a luxury celebrity mansion on a private island, this very night. And I get to do it with my best friends. It's so good that Charlie is coming too. I've missed having him around.

We were supposed to meet at Sadie's place at 5:30, but I'm running late because after rushing home and taking a shower, I spent too much time trying to decide what to wear and what to pack. Even though it's only for the weekend—and Sadie warned us that in order for everyone's stuff to fit in the helicopter's luggage hold we could each bring only one soft medium-sized bag—packing was still hard. Nothing I had was good enough. Pretty enough. Attractive enough. Especially when Isla and Sadie have the most amazing wardrobes.

Look, I do know how pathetic it is to dress for a guy, alright? But I just can't help it. It might be our last weekend together. My last chance to move out of the friend zone.

Ant isn't aware that I like him. I've tried hinting, but he never got it. It's not his fault; we've just been friends for too long. I've thought about how to tell him, but always ended up chickening out. Yeah, it's been annoying to watch him hook up with one girl after another, but at least he was never serious with any of them. I guess that isn't surprising; it's hard to get close to someone who doesn't understand what we've been through.

It was after what happened that I realized I had feelings for him. He was there for me then, taking care of me. And after, when we were finally home. Like the night when I hated myself so much and wanted to end it all. He wanted to come over—sneak into our apartment, stay the night—just to make sure I was okay. But we both knew my mom would go ballistic if she found out, so he just stayed on the phone with me the whole night, cracking jokes to distract me, to keep me sane. He fell asleep sometime around three in the morning, and me too shortly after, listening to the comforting, rhythmic sound of his breathing. The next morning, thanks to him, I felt okay again.

None of the others would believe it if they knew; it's not a side of him he shows to many people.

Anyway, I finally settled on a sapphire-blue velvet minidress that I'd bought when it was on sale and that I've been saving for a special occasion. It's perfect for partying on a celebrity island (I hope), and I paired it with a pair of silver sandals and dangly silver earrings that Mom lent me. Surely he'll look at me differently when he sees me in this. I usually live in jeans, and I know Ant likes legs, so I ignore the way the minidress makes me feel a little uncomfortable (how on earth do people sit in these without flashing others?).

Our car finally pulls to a stop in a large circular driveway, and I gawk at the mansion. I've never been here before, and I don't think the others have either. Sadie's never invited us. I'm not sure if it's because her parents wouldn't like it, or if it's just because she's reluctant to flaunt her wealth, even to us, her closest friends. Everything looks *so* posh: the sprawling grounds that have to be tended by a gardener, or an entire crew of gardeners; the stately, elegant mansion that looks like it probably possesses its own name, something like Fox Hollow Manor or Cedar Hall; the tennis court I can just see peeking from behind the right side of the house.

Mom puts the car in park and turns to look at me. "Just... don't drink too much, okay? I know, I know"—she puts her hands in the air, shakes her head, and gives me a rueful smile—"I know it's a graduation party and there will be alcohol. And boys.

And I know you'll be drinking." She fixes her eyes on me, and I don't even try to protest or insist I would never. "But just not *too much*, okay?"

"I won't," I promise.

"And if you, er…" She breaks off eye contact with me and starts rummaging in her handbag, her face flushing pink.

I eye her curiously. What's she trying to say that's making her all embarrassed? What's she looking for in her bag? "I really have to go, Mom. I'm so late—"

She finally finds what she's looking for and yanks it out. Oh, no. It can't be—she shoves it in my hand—crap, it is. It's a box of condoms. My face burns as I grasp for something to say.

"Just always remember to be safe," she murmurs.

"Okay," I manage weakly.

"Anthony's going too, right?"

I nod.

"Good. I know he'll watch out for you. Say hi to him for me. And call me when you get there, okay?"

I nod again and open the door. I really have to hurry, or they're going to leave without me, and that would be *terrible*. "Bye, Mom. Thanks for the ride! I'll call when I arrive!"

"Have fun!" she calls out of the car window. "But not too much fun!"

She drives off, and I hurry to the front door and ring the doorbell. As I wait for someone to open it, I dig in my bag for my phone. It's 5:42 p.m. Anxiety bubbles up in my guts. They wouldn't have left without me already…would they? There's a text from Sadie sent at 5:25 p.m.:

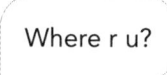
Where r u?

Before I can call her or ring the bell again, the door swings open. "You're here!" Sadie smiles at me. She's dressed casually in a white cropped tee, cream linen shorts, and white trainers. With her light brown hair tied up in a ponytail, she looks effortlessly chic. I'm the last to arrive, because Ant, Isla, Will, and Charlie are just behind her. Behind them, I catch a glimpse of a massive living area that must be the living room—decorated with expensive-looking furniture, family portraits, modern art, and what looks like a real Ming vase—with high ceilings and floor-to-ceiling windows leading out onto the back lawn.

Isla raises a perfectly shaped eyebrow. Her blond curls are meticulously blown out, and she's wearing a sparkly gold tank, black leggings, and a fitted black leather jacket. It's obvious she's dressed to impress whichever celeb owns the island. She looks amazing, like a celebrity herself. My heart sinks as I realize I'm envious. Why would Ant look at me, when he could look at someone like her? "What took you so long?" she says, her voice bored, annoyed, and amused at the same time. "We were about to leave without you."

"We were not." Sadie shakes her head a little and shoots Isla an exasperated look before turning back to me. "We wouldn't leave without you, Em. We were just going to wait for you outside. The helipad is outside anyway."

The thing I like about Sadie is how nice she is. She never puts on airs or acts like she's better than us. Also, sometimes I get the impression that she's embarrassed of her family's wealth. I've wanted to tell her that she shouldn't be, but that might make her even more embarrassed. She's also so generous all the time, like renting this place for all of us. If it weren't for her, I'd never get to do stuff like this. Even with my secret side hustle, I still can't afford to blow money like this. Not with my dad's medical bills.

"Why are you holding a box of rubbers?" says Isla, laughing.

Too late, I realize I'm still clutching it. "My mom," I mumble incoherently as I bend and stuff it into my bag, mortification burning my face again. As I straighten up, my gaze slides to Ant. Unlike the others, who are either laughing or grinning, he just looks distinctly uncomfortable, shifting his weight from one foot to the other as he avoids looking at me.

"Garrett will bring our bags," says Sadie. "Come on, the chopper's waiting for us."

Sadie steps out of the house, a faint whiff of some expensive-smelling perfume wafting into my nose as she breezes lightly past me. A middle-aged man, presumably Garrett (her butler?), who has been waiting patiently behind the group approaches and picks up Isla's bag, then mine, in addition to the one he's already shouldering. "Thanks, dude, but I've got mine," says Will to him, and

Ant and Charlie grab their own bags too, saving the poor man from having to carry six bags or make multiple trips.

We follow Sadie as she makes her way down a path, around to the back of the house, to where I finally see the helicopter on a helipad in the middle of a wide expanse of lawn. A fresh burst of anticipation surges through me, making my scalp and the tips of my fingers tingle.

This is it. An entire weekend with Ant, the final opportunity to get him to see me as more than a good friend. I know he cares for me. I just have to get him to see that we could be more. That we could be good together. No more chickening out now. This weekend, I'm going to stop being such a silly little mouse and finally tell him how I feel.

ANT

Sadie's butler and the pilot load our luggage into the hold. There are two seats in the front, one presumably for the pilot, two in the rear facing backward, and three in the rear facing forward. Sadie climbs aboard first and plonks herself in the seat beside the pilot's. "I don't get sick when I'm up front," she explains.

The rest of us follow her lead and climb aboard. Will on my left, Charlie on my right, and the two girls on the rear-facing seats opposite us. As I try not to think about what happened the last time we all got on a helicopter together, the pilot hands us headsets and instructs us on how to use them. *It's not the first time we've been in a helicopter, my dude,* I almost tell him, but it's better not to talk about it. Better not to think about it too. So I just keep my mouth shut and nod, like everyone else.

When we take off, I have the strangest, most horrible

premonition of disaster, and I have to clamp down the urge to fling myself out screaming.

I don't do that, of course, because that would be silly. But I'm probably not the only one who's having second thoughts because Isla's and Emily's faces are pale and grim. So I do what I usually do to lighten the mood: crack a dumb joke. "Hey Emily," I say loudly into the headset's microphone as I kick her foot. "What's the difference between a dirty bus stop and a lobster with breast implants?"

"I don't know, what?" Emily says dutifully.

"One's a crusty bus station…and the other's a busty crustacean."

Isla rolls her eyes and Will groans loudly, but Emily giggles, and I even get a chuckle out of Sadie. I turn to look at Charlie sitting beside me on my right, but from what I can see of his reflection in the window as he stares out of it, his expression just remains stony. Tough audience.

Seriously though, the guy needs to stop brooding so much. The trick is to just not think about stuff that gets you down. It's easy. You just gotta find things to distract yourself with. Like girls, for example.

"You girls are looking good this evening," I say.

Isla flips her hair as if to say, *Duh, I know*, but Emily smiles and flushes a bright pink. Shit. Maybe I shouldn't have said that. I have a sinking feeling she's going to try to tell me how she feels this weekend, and I don't want to break her heart, because she's like a sister to me. Although, she does look hot in that dress.

I have no idea how Will seems to guess where my thoughts are going because he taps away at his phone, then I get a real mature text from him:

> Looks like someone's going to get lucky this w/e

I tap out a reply.

> If u mean Em, u know I'm not interested in her that way

Luckily, the girls are too busy having a conversation about their outfits over the intercom (Sadie wants to know if Isla's pants are real leather, and Isla wants to know who Sadie is wearing and what season it's from, whatever that means) to notice that Will and I are texting each other. He texts me again:

> Why not? She's cute and she's so into u

It's too easy, where's the fun in that? I reply to shut him up about it, even though that's not why I'd never sleep with Emily.

Emily thinks I'm this guy with a bad boy exterior but a heart of gold, like those cheesy books she's always reading.

She's wrong. I don't have a heart of gold. I'm not a good person. I'm the kind who'll do anything to survive.

The ski trip made that very clear to me.

But Emily's a good person. She only did what the rest of us did because I made her. And she deserves someone better than me.

The problem is, if I tell her that, I know she won't accept it for an answer. I've been acting dumb for the past year, but that's not working either. So I guess the only solution is to break her heart. And I know just how to do it, how to break her heart so badly this weekend that she'll find some nice guy in college and forget all about me.

R u up for a bet? I text Will.

The ever-competitive Will straightens up as he reads my text, his eyes gleaming. What kind of bet?

The girls are still chatting, this time speculating excitedly about which celeb really owns the island and if we'll get to meet them.

Bet u won't be able to score with the girl I choose for u, I reply.

He smirks. I'm up for it if u r. What r we playing 4?

Hmm…how about five hundred bucks? If we both get our girls then it's a draw, I reply. He'll never succeed with the girl I'm thinking of for him, and I could do with some spare change. The money won't assuage the guilt and the knowledge that Emily will hate me, but it's for her own good.

Will nods his agreement, and I text him again: I choose Sadie for u

That wipes the smirk off his face. Even though Isla and him aren't together anymore, I know she still wants him. And Emily is too easy of a target. If she's heartbroken, she might fall into anyone's bed this weekend. Sadie, however, is a real challenge, and Will knows it. Even if he's supposedly the most popular boy in school, she's way out of his league. As far as I know, she's never been interested in anyone from school. Not even me, and I tried, really hard, because hey, there could be worse things than having a billionaire heiress for a girlfriend, right? She's out of all our leagues. Rumor has it that she once hooked up with the famous singer of some band and some European prince.

Will is scowling now. Ok. Then I choose Isla for u

I knew it. I've hit on her before, couple of years back before she and Will got together. For a few weeks, I tried all the tricks that usually work so well: paid her lots of attention, complimented her hair and her outfits, saved her seats in the cafeteria. She sneered down her nose at me for all my efforts. He's counting on her to blow me off again. I nod to say, *Game on.*

Will texts me again: Let's get Charlie to play too. Some distraction will be good for him

I sigh as I glance over at Charlie. Maybe we should. Maybe this will be just what he needs to get him back to his old self. To forget his girlfriend. What happened to her.

What we did to her.

U text him. He's still pissed at me coz he thinks I tattled on him to coach, adds Will.

I roll my eyes and text Charlie: Up for a game? And fill him in on all the details.

Charlie looks up at me from his phone. The expression on his face says all. He thinks that Will and I are the stupidest, shallowest idiots ever. Which, to be fair, maybe we are. That's stupid, no thx, he replies and goes back to staring out the window.

Oh well, we tried. He can keep moping if he wants. I can't blame him for not wanting any part of this, but for a moment I wonder why he's even coming along this weekend if he hates having fun so much.

I show Will Charlie's reply and shrug. *We tried.*

Will shrugs too. Maybe he really was the one who ratted Charlie out to their coach and got him kicked off the soccer team. But that's not my business. I have my own stuff to worry about.

Like how I'm going to get into Isla's pants and win the bet. A plan starts to form in my head. It's a good plan. I'm going to win five hundred bucks and get Emily to forget about me at the same time. It'll be satisfying too, after the way Isla rejected me that time. I'll dump her afterward. Or maybe I'll just ghost her.

This weekend is going to be so fun.

CHARLIE

I pull my flask out of my pocket and take a swig. The cheap vodka that I swiped this morning from my dad's stash burns my throat as it goes down. It's a good feeling. Better than the usual numbness I feel.

I don't have to look at them to know they're eyeing me. I know they're all wondering the same thing: *What is Charlie doing here?*

Yeah, I guess I'm curious about this island supposedly owned by some celeb. But I'm not curious enough to want to spend an entire weekend with them to do this. The stupid game Ant and Will just tried to rope me into joining proves definitively that I'm going to hate every minute of every second hanging out with them.

So why did I come?

Because there's unfinished business between us. When this opportunity came up, I saw my chance immediately.

Because tonight we'll be alone, just the six of us, for the first time since the incident. And there will be a reckoning.

Because unlike them, I haven't forgotten, or moved on.

This weekend, I'm going to make them pay for what they did.

—Why were they there?

—I heard it was some kind of party. A graduation party.

—Where did you hear that?

—One of them said it, on her TikTok.

—Oh, right. Because the owner made the island available for rent, right? I saw that. Rich kids, then?

—One of them was. They flew there in her family's private helicopter. That's how the bodies were discovered, you know. By the pilot, when he went back to get them.

—God. Poor guy. I saw the leaked photos of the living room. Before they got scrubbed off social media. All that blood.

—Yeah. Those poor kids.

ISLA

Good thing I wrangled our ride; this is definitely the best way to travel. We wouldn't get this stunning bird's-eye view coming by boat. Not only that, but all the *logistics* involved otherwise. Without a car of my own, I'd have had to carpool, since I don't have the money to splurge on an Uber for the hour-long drive down, and then *another* hour by speedboat. It made me feel exhausted just thinking about it.

Okay, if there'd been no chopper option, I'd have done it. I mean, as if I'd ever miss the chance to spend the weekend partying on *Taylor Swift's private island*. Who knows, we might even get to *meet her*. I mean, it's totally plausible that she might be here to meet us, right? Considering how much we're paying to rent it. The amount still boggles my mind, and once again, a small surge of resentment curdles my stomach and sends a sour taste in my mouth at how this kind of extravagance is just spare change to Sadie. It's unfair that some people are just born into a life of wealth and comfort, unlike the rest of us who have to actually *earn* it. Or like in the case of my mom, slog thanklessly away at her job but get passed up for promotion every single time because she's such a pushover. The memory of our last conversation worms itself up into my mind despite myself...

"I can't believe they gave the promotion to that sniveling bootlicker instead of you," I tell my mom. My eyes sting with tears at the injustice of it. The promotion would have meant a significant pay raise, and we wouldn't have to think about money all the time anymore. "You did all the work for that project, and he just took the credit for it. And you let him."

Mom just sighs and looks defeated, like she always does. "It wasn't up to me."

But she didn't have to take this lying down. She should have fought harder for it. Put that asshole in his place. Not let everyone walk all over her all the time. It's what I would have done. I want to tell her all this, but the look on her face stops me, so I just storm back to my room and slam the door.

I force the memory away, make myself unclench my fists. Life isn't fair, and that awful knowledge corrodes a hole in my chest. I suppose I have to thank my mom for letting me learn this valuable life lesson early on. To know that I have to fight and grab what's mine if I don't want to end up being stepped on by everyone else, like her.

But if I let myself go down this mental spiral again, it'll just ruin the rest of my day, so I shove it back down the dark hole it crawled out of and refocus on all the fun that's to come.

I focus on the view, which is breathtakingly spectacular. The sea is a shimmery turquoise expanse as far as the eye can see, the setting sun glinting off it like millions of tiny diamonds. As the sun sets over the horizon, painting the sky a riot of orange, red, and pink, the sea darkens gradually until it's almost black. "Christie Island," announces the pilot over the headset, and we all crane our necks to catch our first glimpse of the luxury private island. My breath catches in my throat when I make it out in the distance.

There's still enough light left for us to get a good look at the island as our helicopter approaches. It's very small, elongated, shaped almost like a kidney bean, and bordered all around by an absolutely exquisite-looking powdery-white sand beach, just like the photos on the internet. There's a wooden structure on the beach that must be the pier, jutting out into the sea at the long end. A gigantic glass mansion and huge infinity pool are right smack in the middle of the island, surrounded by lush manicured grass and trees. There's no other building on the island. I whip out my phone and take a few photos. When I post this on social media, everyone is going to die from envy. The thought sends a wave of deep satisfaction rolling over me.

But when I open up Instagram, the gray error message No Internet Connection pops up. *Ugh.* I stare dismally at the zero bars at the top of the screen. There must be internet on the island…

right? Otherwise, how will I be able to post pics on social media all weekend and make everyone I know jealous? If you don't post how much fun you're having, are you even really having fun at all?

"What are those things on the roof?" I ask. "Solar panels?"

"Yeah," says Ant. "It's how the house has electricity. And you see that small structure at the back of the house? That's the water tank. It collects rainwater. The filtration system purifies the water so it's safe for consumption."

"How do you know all this?" asks Emily, wide-eyed, as if he's spouting ancient wisdom or something, instead of things he probably just looked up on the internet.

"I googled the house and the island and read up on it while waiting for you to arrive," he replies, and I have to stifle a snort.

"Well, I'm glad there's internet," says Sadie.

"How do you know?" asks Emily.

"That dish on the roof. That's a satellite dish."

"That means there'll be TV too, right? Good, considering the exorbitant price we paid to rent the place," I say. Sadie turns to side-eye me. I roll my eyes. Fine, that *she* paid.

The pilot lands the chopper on the mansion's manicured lawn and switches off the engine, then gets down and helps Sadie out first. When he opens our door, I scramble out, eager to see if Taylor Swift is going to emerge from the mansion and welcome us.

That doesn't happen, and I feel my first twinge of disappointment. Okay, fine, I guess that was too much to expect.

The pilot—I notice now that he looks a little like a young

George Clooney—unloads our luggage from the small hold. When that's done, he turns to Sadie. "Miss Lombard, Elle told me she's arranged speedboats for Sunday to bring everyone back to New Bedford. But should I come with the helicopter for you?"

"Yes, please. Around five would be good. Would that be possible? Unless Daddy is using it…"

Daddy? How cringe. Is she six or something? Oh my god, this brings back a memory from freshman year, the very first day of school. I'd arrived around the same time as Sadie, just in time to witness the one and only time her dad was there to drop her off at school. She emerged from an inconspicuous black Mercedes S 500. Her dad, who was in the back seat with her, gave her a kiss and called her *Princess*. I stifle a snort at the memory.

Young George Clooney nods. "Sir hasn't said anything about using it on Sunday. I'll let him know you want it and be here at five."

It's comforting to know my ride back to Boston is secured, since I assume we'll be going back with her too.

He climbs back aboard, and we give the chopper a wide berth as he takes off. When it's far enough so our hair isn't being whipped around anymore, I look around again. We're still alone on the lawn. Nobody has come to greet us. Are we supposed to lug our luggage up to the house by ourselves?

Sadie must be thinking the same thing, because she frowns and says, "I thought there'd be a valet. I'll call Elle and ask." She starts digging in her bag for her phone.

I glare at Ant. "Didn't you say it comes fully staffed with a housekeeper, a valet, and a private chef?"

"It did say so," says Ant. "And a fully stocked bar."

Sadie is staring dismally at her phone. "I'm not getting any service here." She shoves it into her back pocket in disgust. "Well, I guess it's not surprising considering how far out from shore we are. But there'll be Wi-Fi in the house."

Will picks up his carryall. "Maybe the valet is in the bathroom or something? We'd better get inside. It looks like it's going to rain."

I glance up. He's right; there's a low mass of storm clouds gathering in the horizon. Even as we watch, the wind picks up, and I shiver as the temperature seems to dip suddenly.

"Come on, it's not like we have a lot of luggage." Will picks up Sadie's Chanel weekender bag. "I can get yours, Sadie."

What? Why is he helping *her*? I'm so dumbfounded, I can only stare at the back of his blond head as he heads toward the mansion, my face hot.

Yeah, we may have broken up, but I was sure he was starting to regret it, the way he'd been eyeing me recently. In fact, I thought we might get back together this weekend. I even packed my new bikini, which I knew would drive him wild. So what the hell is *this*?

I don't have the time to brood on it, because Ant now picks up *my* bag along with his own and winks at me. "I can get yours. Come on."

Oh, ew. If Ant thinks he has a chance with me, he has another thing coming. His body count is reportedly in the double figures. I'm not interested in someone who hits on anything with two legs and wears a skirt. What on *earth* is happening? I shake my head, then shrug and let him take my bag. If he wants to play valet, go ahead.

The land slopes slightly up, with the house perched at the top. We pass the pool on our way up, an infinity pool with the water flowing off one side continuously, and there's even a diving board on the deep end. I've only ever seen pools like this in magazines and social media. I feel glam just walking past it, imagining myself lounging poolside. The guys are going to love showing off on the diving board. Maybe we'll be lucky and it won't rain so we can start the party by the pool tonight.

The house is even bigger and more gorgeous up close. It's not as big as Sadie's mansion, but this aesthetic suits me more. There are three stories and it's supermodern, all sharp, stark edges, glass, and steel. I *love* it. It looks totally like one of those ten-million-dollar celebrity mansions that I was just gawking at on TikTok. The full glass windows aren't only all along the ground floor, but also on the upper levels, which means all of us will get to wake up with a million-dollar sea view. Not too shabby at all. Although how does anyone change? Or have sex? It's all kind of…voyeuristic.

I join Will and Sadie at the front door. Ant stops just beside me, standing a bit too close. My suspicion that he's going to try to hit on me this weekend increases. I push my irritation down and say, "Why are you two just standing there? Don't tell me the door is locked."

Sadie is frowning. "I rang the bell, but no one's coming."

How odd, and annoying. I hope this isn't a precursor of the kind of service we're going to get for our stay. Mentally, I deduct a star for the rating I'm going to leave this place on Google. I look inside the house, but there doesn't seem to be anyone around that I can see, and the large glass windows mean we can see practically everything inside. As Emily and Charlie trudge up to us, lugging their duffel bags, Will puts his right hand on the door handle and tries it. The door swings slowly open.

"Oh. It isn't locked," he says.

"We can see that, Captain Obvious," says Ant.

It's the kind of dumb remark from Ant that Emily would usually giggle at, but this time, she doesn't. Her face is pink, her expression stony. If I had to guess, she probably isn't too happy Ant carried my bag up, the same way I wasn't thrilled about Will getting Sadie's. Maybe she was hoping to lose her virginity to Ant this weekend (because she's definitely still a virgin).

Maybe I'm reading too much into this. Maybe Will was just acting chivalrous because Sadie's funding our weekend. Or maybe…maybe he's just trying to make me jealous.

Yes, that must be it. Because what's Sadie got over me? Sure, she's rich, but—and I say this completely objectively—I'm *way* hotter than her. He must be trying to make me jealous so I'd forgive him for breaking up with me and fall back into his arms.

Well, two can play at that game.

But there's time for all that later. Right now, we have a celebrity mansion to explore. Also the skies are about to burst open, the first few drops of rain splat fatly on my arm and cheek, and everyone's just standing around gaping like dumb goldfish. I push past Sadie and Will and step through the front door.

The interior of the house is just like the exterior: sleek and modern. There isn't a hallway; the entire ground floor is open-plan except for one door at the far end, which I'm guessing leads to a bathroom. The expanse of space is breathtaking, and with all this glass, it must get lots of light during the day. It's minimally decorated: a potted bamboo plant here, a large piece of art dominating a wall there. In the living area at the end are an enormous designer-looking leather sofa set and a large marble coffee table, and on the other side near the front door is the kitchen, also open-plan. In the middle is a long dining table of what looks to be one massive solid piece of wood with steel legs, with twelve velvet upholstered dining chairs in an assortment of pop colors. I still don't see any housekeeper, but the place must have been cleaned very recently because there isn't a speck of dust anywhere.

"Hello?" I call out. "Is anyone here? There's supposed to be a valet? And a housekeeper? And a chef? Hello?" My voice reverberates throughout the house.

But there's no reply, and nobody comes.

WILL

"This isn't cool. We just got here, and already the staff are slacking off," whines Isla, her voice sharp and high-pitched, the way it gets when she gets annoyed. It grates on me...but she's right. Not only is it not cool, it's also *weird*.

"Is there a welcome note?" says Sadie, peering around. "Does anyone see a note somewhere with Wi-Fi instructions? I wanna call Elle, get hold of somebody."

We split up to search this ground level. I find two sets of keys for the front door on the coffee table in the living area, but there's no welcome note.

Sadie has her phone out again and is jabbing at the screen. "There *must* be Wi-Fi. There's a satellite dish on the roof and a TV on the wall, so there *must* be satellite. No one's picking up a Wi-Fi network? Really?"

I check my phone. "I'm not picking up a Wi-Fi network either," I announce. The others check their phones too and shake their heads.

"The valet is probably supposed to give us all this info," Ant says. "But they're not here; none of them are."

"We can see that," snaps Isla.

Silence stretches out between us, settling thick and uncomfortable in the room. Are we really all alone here on this island? With no means of communication? My chest starts to feel tight. Cut off from the outside world. Like that time we…

"Maybe they're arriving tomorrow morning," says Emily hesitantly.

Sadie frowns. "Elle should have let them know we were coming tonight."

I'm starting to see what might have happened. "Yeah, but it was so last-minute. They probably weren't able to get hired help here immediately." Yes, that makes sense. There's no need to panic. I start to feel a little silly at my initial reaction and force a smile on my face.

Sadie's frown clears, and her shoulders relax. "Yeah, you're probably right."

Still, I'm uneasy. I don't like the way there's no Wi-Fi or cell service. I wander over to the kitchen and fling open cabinet doors. What I see calms me down. Thank god, the cabinets and pantry are fully stocked with food. The sight dispels the small stirrings of anxiety. "There's lots of food," I say with relief. "There's enough here to feed an army. Or maybe an entire graduating class of teenagers." *It's going to be fine*, I think. *We aren't going to go hungry.* "And the bar's fully stocked too!"

Everyone else visibly relaxes at my reassurance that there's food. Understandable, considering the trauma we went through that time. Except Charlie, who hasn't said anything yet so far and just looks as bored as ever.

He joins me now in the kitchen and zeros in on a bottle of Belvedere vodka. I watch as he opens the bottle expertly, as if he's done it a hundred times before, and takes a swig directly from it. Which is so unhygienic. Unless he has no intention of sharing the bottle.

"Want a shot?" He lifts the bottle up.

"Uh. Maybe later," I say.

"Okay, so the staff aren't here yet," says Ant. "It just means we have more privacy tonight. Look around, you guys. This place is amazing. I wonder how big the beds are."

That's what I like about Ant. He always sees the bright side of things. He bounds up the stairs two steps at a time, and I run after him because I'll be damned if I let him get first dibs on the best room.

There are six bedrooms and three bathrooms on the second level, and four bedrooms and two bathrooms on the top level. All the bedroom doors have keyed locks, almost like the mansion could be a hotel, to rent out the rooms individually if the owner wanted to. Some rooms are bigger than others, but all are huge with what looks like California king-size beds and floor-to-ceiling glass walls giving the same spectacular sea view.

I know it's supposed to be some modern architectural thing—and I get the purpose of it is to capitalize on the stunning views—but all this glass makes me uncomfortable. It gives me the sensation that there are eyes watching me all the time. Anybody outside the house would be able to see where we are, what we're doing. Lucky we're secluded on an island. I wouldn't want to live in a glass house like this where I wouldn't have any privacy.

There are two rooms on the second level with their own adjoining private bathrooms. Ant drops his duffel bag on the bed in one of them. "Claiming this one," he announces.

Isla shoots him a dirty look. "Oh no. You don't get to claim one of the only three bedrooms with their own bathroom like that."

"Well, I don't mind sharing the room, if you want," says Ant.

Isla rolls her eyes and snorts. "With *you?* Yeah, that's not happening."

"Now, now, children, calm down. Maybe we can draw straws or something," I say.

Sadie clears her throat. "You all do what you want, but I'm taking the room upstairs with the bathroom," she announces before she leaves us to go up to the third level with her bag.

Okay, fair enough. I guess she's entitled to whatever room she wants, since she *did* pay for all of us.

"That leaves two bedrooms on this level with their own bathrooms. Who wants them?" I say.

"I don't care. I'll just take one of the other rooms," drawls Charlie as he takes another swig of vodka. He really brought it up with him. At the rate he's going, he's going to be shit-faced before dinner. I'm about to say something to that effect when he takes off with his bag and his vodka to go upstairs too.

That leaves Isla, Ant, Emily, and me. "Are we really going to draw for the rooms?" says Emily.

"Wait here," I say.

Downstairs, back to the kitchen, I open one of the boxes of spaghetti I saw in one of the cabinets earlier on, take out four sticks, and head back upstairs.

"Pasta sticks?" says Isla.

"Two long sticks, two short. Whoever picks one of the long sticks gets a room with a bathroom," I say as I snap two of the sticks shorter, then hold the ends in my fist so we can't see which ones are longer.

"I'll go first," says Isla. She draws one out. It's a long one. "Yes! This room is mine. Get your filthy bag off my bed," she says to Ant.

Ant drops his bag on the floor. "Fine. My turn." He picks a short stick and groans. "Doesn't matter. Maybe someone will take pity on me and let me bunk with them later," he says as he casts a hopeful look Isla's way, which she ignores.

I suppress my smirk, because he's never going to win the bet, then hold the two remaining sticks out to Emily. She draws one out; it's a short stick.

"Looks like I get the other one," I say as I hold out the remaining stick for them to see that I didn't cheat.

"Whatever. I don't care," says Emily in a monotone. But she looks like she's holding back tears as she spins around and leaves the room. *Wow, she must have really wanted her own bathroom*, I start to think, but then the real reason she's so upset dawns on me. She's noticed the way Ant is hitting on Isla. This weekend is going to be hard on her.

"This is just for tonight, right? We're going to rethink sleeping arrangements before tomorrow night when the rest of the seniors are here anyway, right?" says Ant.

"Yep." I bring my bag to the remaining coveted bedroom and unpack my stuff.

When I'm done it's five to eight, and I'm starving. I head back downstairs. Maybe the staff have finally arrived, and the chef can make us dinner.

X X

Sadie, Isla, and Charlie are already milling around in the kitchen, looking as hungry as I feel.

"Still no sign of the staff?" I ask.

Sadie shakes her head. "I guess they really are only arriving tomorrow, and Elle can't get through to my phone to let me know."

"At least there's food," mutters Isla. "But if the chef isn't here, who's going to cook for us?"

Good question. Aside from the occasional sandwich assembly, I've never done much cooking, nor has Isla, and if I had to guess, I'd say Sadie's probably never cooked anything in her life either.

"Also, it's not like we can have pizza delivered…can we?" says Isla.

"Don't think there's anybody who'll deliver here," says Charlie with a straight face, but his voice drips with derision.

Isla flushes pink, and her lips press together in a thin line.

As we eye one another, I can feel the rising tension in the room. The past may be the past, but it's never as far behind as we like, is it? Other teens may be fine surviving off alcohol and snacks for an entire weekend…but we're not like other teens.

We don't like being hungry.

"I'll cook," says Charlie, straightening up.

"You will?" says Isla doubtfully.

"Yeah. I cook at home all the time. Let's see… Pasta okay for everyone?" says Charlie.

"Charlie, thank you," says Sadie. "Tell me what to do, and I'll help."

Sadie seems happy, but like Isla, I feel doubtful. Charlie's already slurring his words. Do we really want him in the kitchen around hot stoves and very sharp knives? "I'll help too," I say, so I can keep an eye on him.

"Great, you three have it all under control then," says Isla breezily as she flounces off to the living area.

Sadie may be the billionaire heiress, but I swear sometimes

Isla acts more like a diva than her. Now that I'm no longer with her I can see her flaws clearly. Once again, I'm relieved things are over between us. At least Sadie's less annoying.

As Charlie, Sadie, and I get to work preparing dinner, Ant comes downstairs, Emily trailing after him like a depressed lost puppy. But she stops and veers away when he goes to join Isla on the couch. He's already beginning his attack, the bastard.

"How about Bolognese?" says Charlie as he peers at the cans of sauce in a cabinet.

"Sounds good," I reply.

Charlie reaches for a can, but then he pauses. "Wait. Sadie, you're vegetarian, right?"

Crap, that's right. Sadie's been vegetarian ever since the incident. I should have remembered. Lost my chance to score some points there.

But she shakes her head. "It's alright. We can cook pasta Bolognese if you all feel like it. I'm not going to impose my dietary choices on all of you."

I swoop in. "No, no, it's no trouble at all. We'll just cook two pots of pasta. A pot of Bolognese, and a pot of…" I look in the cabinet too. "Tomato and basil! No trouble at all, and everyone can choose whichever they prefer."

Emily wanders over. "Oh, are you three cooking? Can I help?"

I wave her off. "Three of us are plenty. It's just pasta and ready-made sauce. We've got this under control. Go relax."

"Okay…" She shifts from one foot to another. "But, um, please remember that I'm allergic to dairy, so…"

I stare at her. I've forgotten that too.

"I remembered, Emily," chirps Sadie. "I instructed Elle to tell them to make sure they stocked the house with dairy-free food wherever possible. Hang on, let me double-check…" As she peers at the labels on the two jars of sauce, she mutters, "They'd better have gotten *this* right… Yes! See?" she holds up the two jars. "They're both dairy-free."

"Ahh, thanks, Sadie," says Emily before she wanders back to the living area.

Charlie puts two large pots of water to boil on the induction stove, and I sidle up to Sadie, who is opening all the spaghetti and sauces and putting them on the counter. "That's really thoughtful of you," I tell her.

"What, the dairy-free thing?" She shrugs. "It's nothing."

"No, I mean it. Isla would have never remembered something like that. She only thinks about herself."

Although Sadie doesn't reply, she blushes slightly, and I congratulate myself because I *definitely* scored some points there.

"What…the fuck?" says Emily. Emily, who never curses.

I look up. She's standing in front of the large painting hanging on the wall near the stairs, staring at it.

"What? What is it?" says Isla.

"Have you all seen this?" Emily's voice is tight, strangled.

We all stop what we're doing and go over to join her where she's still staring at the art on the wall.

I didn't really pay much attention to it earlier, but I take a good look at it now. As I absorb what I'm seeing, shock jolts through me; then icy tendrils of fear creep down my spine. It's a painting, or a print, of what looks like some people in a snowstorm.

Eight people, and two of them are crossed out with red *X*s.

SADIE

The art on the wall is a canvas print, and it's out of place, to say the least. The landscape in the picture is a grim, desolate, snow-covered wasteland; the figures in it huddled around a small fire under a makeshift tent as a blizzard rages all around them. Even though it's actually quite warm in the house, looking at such a wretched scene makes me feel so cold, I shiver involuntarily. The art is depressing, hideous, completely incongruous with the rest of the mansion. It doesn't even look good, or at least expensive. Definitely not the usual kind of thing you'd see decorating a house as nice as this.

Worst of all, looking at it dredges up memories of the thing that happened the previous winter. The nightmare that none of us want to remember or think about. The memory closes in on me now, no matter how I try to keep it away…

The snow is coming down much harder now, the flurries so thick in the air that it's a complete whiteout. I can't tell where the snow-covered landscape meets the sky because everything is a dirty white-gray. The wind is picking up too—moaning and howling all around us, whipping my hair into my eyes, biting the exposed skin on my face—making me wish I stayed home instead of letting them talk me into doing this. It was Will and Ant's idea to do heli-skiing. Why did I agree? And pay for the entire thing?

No one—not our guide, not even the local weather forecaster—predicted this storm. It seemingly came out of nowhere, with no warning whatsoever. Which is bad luck, but what makes it worse is we're not even on the path our guide, Lucas—who is now looking at the map in his gloved hands—originally planned for us.

"This is your fault. Your stupid idea," Isla shouts, pointing at Tom and Will, but her voice is teeny, drowned out by the roaring storm.

I can't help but agree with her. It was their idea for our guide to take us on a different route after the helicopter dropped us off, just because they wanted something different. *Before the storm hit, of course.*

Lucas folds his map away and zips it in one of the pockets of his snow pants. "Okay," he shouts to make himself heard. "I know visibility is a bit bad, but there's no need to panic. It's this way." He gestures with one gloved hand. "Follow me closely. I don't want to lose any one of you."

He starts off, and we all follow closely behind. Except for Tom, who zigzags all over the place. He never did like to follow instructions. I slow down, turn to look at him as he crests one gentle slope, which leads him farther away from us than seems to be prudent, considering Lucas's instructions for us to stick close to him. I shout at Tom, but he can't hear me over the wind of course. Luckily, after a while he turns and, to my relief, starts heading back toward us again.

But then he drops out of view, as if swallowed up by the snow.

No. I gasp and shove away the memory. I'm sweating and I feel sick, sick and cold, so cold it's like I can never be warm again.

Ant grimaces as he stares at the painting. "What is it?"

"It's a painting of the Donner Party," says Emily.

The Donner Party. The infamous, tragic American pioneers who got stranded in the snow for an entire winter, and…

"I've…I've seen this before," Emily continues. "In art class. This is part of the Granger collection, a historical archive." Her face is pale, her eyes starting to glisten.

I shiver again—or maybe it's more of a *shudder*—and look at the two red *X*s. "Why are two of them crossed out like that?"

"They got canceled," mutters Ant.

Always with the quips and terrible jokes, our Ant. He never disappoints.

Will lifts a hand, rubs one of the *X*s with his index finger. The red smudges off slightly on his finger. "Looks like it was done with a marker, and not too long ago."

"What? Why would someone do that?" My voice is a little too shrill, almost hysterical. I'm breathing too quickly, and I try to regulate my breathing.

"A snowstorm. Eight people," Will continues slowly. "Two crossed out. Just like…"

His voice trails off, but he doesn't have to finish. It's easy to understand what he means. *Just like us.*

Because once, there were eight of us, but now, there are only six. Two of us didn't make it. Unwanted images flash in my head, a horror montage, and my heart starts pounding in my chest. The deluge of memories makes me start to feel sick, like I can't breathe, like I want to throw up.

Isla wheels around and stares at us, her startled eyes sliding accusingly from Ant's face to Will's, to mine, finally coming to rest on Charlie's face. "Is this some kind of a joke?" she shrieks.

"Seriously, which one of you did this? It's not funny," I say as I dig with trembling fingers in my pocket for my bottle of Valium.

But it's not in my pocket. Did I leave it in my room? I don't understand. I always keep it with me. Panic surges in my belly. I *need* it. *Where is it?*

"It was you, wasn't it?" says Isla, rounding on Ant again. "You and your stupid pranks. It's not funny!"

Ant shakes his head vehemently. "Hey, look… I like a good prank as much as the next person. But like you say, this isn't funny."

"But…if it wasn't you…" Emily's voice trails off.

She doesn't have to finish her sentence. *Then who?*

"Someone else is here," I blurt out. I don't know why I said that, and I regret saying it as soon as I do.

"Someone drew this when we were all upstairs," says Will, as if he read my mind.

Immediately, instinctively, we all huddle together closer as we spin around, looking for an intruder. Emily presses up against me, and I can feel her trembling.

Not all of us have huddled up together though. Charlie stands apart from us, still studying the picture. "Whoever did it knows what happened. What we did," he says in a low voice. Seeing the picture must have jolted him sober, because he's not slurring anymore. I glance at him. He has a strange, unreadable expression on his face, and one hand behind his back.

"We didn't do anything." Isla glances around us quickly, as if afraid the person who vandalized the picture might have overheard him.

"Relax, Barbie. Look around. Do you see anyone else? It's just us. There's no need to keep up the act," says Charlie.

I don't understand. Why is he antagonizing her like this?

Isla's face is turning a bright red. "*Shut up*. You think this is *funny*? It *was* you, wasn't it?"

He shrugs. "Wasn't me." But his mouth quirks up a little at the right side, as if he *does* think it's funny.

"Maybe the last group who rented the place defaced this, and the owner and their staff didn't notice." Emily's voice is low, shaky.

"Yeah. Maybe it's just a coincidence," says Ant, but he doesn't sound convinced.

"Maybe," says Will. He doesn't look convinced either.

A brittle silence settles as we all fall quiet, try to figure out what the hell this is. It's like a shadow has fallen over the group. Something undefinable, something menacing. The fear emanating from everyone is palpable. Everyone is obviously thinking the same thing: *Is this meant for us? Was this a prank, or did someone do this on purpose? Does someone know? Is that someone here? Is this a threat?*

Until a sudden growl pierces the silence, making me jump.

Will smiles sheepishly. "Sorry, that was my stomach."

"Look," I say. "It's half past eight. We should eat. We can think some more about this after dinner."

I don't have to say it twice; Will nods slowly, and then Ant and Emily nod too.

None of us like to skip meals.

CHARLIE

I can feel Sadie's eyes on me as I pour the sauces into the pots of spaghetti and mix them in. She's been watching me since the discovery of that picture. Maybe she suspects I'm the one who did it. I mean, I can't blame her. If I were her, I'd suspect me too.

This weekend is turning out better than I could have ever expected. I have to admit I enjoyed the way the picture jolted them all out of their smug complacency. I enjoyed watching the fear on their faces. I wish Vera were here to see them when we discovered the picture and those crossed-out figures. She would have enjoyed it too.

No, actually, she wouldn't. She never took delight in these kinds of things. She wasn't cruel. Does this mean I'm cruel now? I suppose it does.

Vera wasn't like them. She was always sensitive. Emotionally fragile. It was her shitty parents, that much was clear. Her father had left, abandoned the family when she was a baby, before she could even remember him. After that, her mother had a revolving number of boyfriends, most lasting a few months before they left again (*Good riddance*, Vera always said). The longest one lasted two years, from when she was twelve to fourteen. She never told me outright—or why—but she was afraid of him—I could tell by the way her eyes widened, and by the way she clammed up immediately on the rare occasions that he accidentally came up in conversation.

So yeah, Vera was an anxious, nervous person, haunted by demons she kept tightly to herself. But when we were alone together, she relaxed her defenses, let down her guard. When she did, her smiles were incandescent, brighter than all the stars in the sky combined. For some reason she decided she could trust me, decided that I was worthy of it. She let me in her life, and she lit up mine in return.

She was the love of my life. The one I was going to spend my life with. The one I was going to grow old with.

I wanted to find work in a restaurant after high school, go to culinary arts school part-time, eventually become a chef. I enjoyed cooking, and it was a better, safer choice than trying to be a pro soccer player. Vera was going to go on to college, work toward becoming a vet. Human beings made her nervous, jumpy, but she came alive around animals. But first we'd take a year off after graduation, go backpacking in Europe together. The idea frightened her at first, but she knew I had a wanderlust that I wanted to satisfy before doing anything else, before settling down into the rest of our forever lives. Seeing me so excited about the idea, she eventually decided she wanted it too.

Remembering her makes my chest feel tight, like there's some kind of medieval torture device clamped around it and someone is twisting the screw to make it tighter. She didn't even want to go to that stupid ski trip to British Columbia. Like our Europe backpacking plan, she only went because I wanted to go, because I thought it sounded fun. She wouldn't have been there if it weren't for me. It's my fault that she's dead.

I should have listened to her. She was right about not trusting the rest of them.

I'll never forget the way they turned on Vera, like a pack of hyenas. *A danger to all of us*, Isla stated as she pointed her finger at my ex-girlfriend, and the rest of them jumped on that. What a fucking lie. Vera wasn't a danger to anyone. They all knew that. It was just the excuse they needed in order to do what they really wanted. To turn on the weakest links.

I've been trying to figure out what to do but couldn't come up with anything. Until now. When they started organizing this, I realized exactly what I could do. The plan started forming in my head almost immediately.

It's disgusting, the way they can think about partying and sex as if nothing ever happened. As if consequences are something only other people less privileged than them have to deal with.

Someone needs to teach them a lesson. Someone needs to make them pay.

This weekend, they'll all get what's coming to them. Especially Isla, who started it; Will, who carried it out; and Ant, who held me back.

Shit. I zoned out there for a bit. Have to be careful. Sadie is still watching me. I need to be careful she doesn't catch on to what I'm trying to do and ruin my plans.

I hold out a spoon with some sauce on it. "Do you think it needs more salt?"

She takes the spoon, looks doubtfully at it, as if I might be trying to poison her. Then, reluctantly, she brings it to her lips and tastes, gives me a small smile. "I think it's good."

"Dinner's ready," I announce loudly as I grab a pot and bring it over to the dining table.

"The stupid TV doesn't even work," says Ant.

I glance up to see him slam the remote on the coffee table. The giant flat-screen TV on the wall has the blue screen of death.

"There should be satellite TV, just like there should be Wi-Fi. But it's just not working," he keeps grumbling. He looks around, then strides to a sleek cabinet set in the wall in the corner of the living area, opens it. "Hey! I think I found the box for the TV or Wi-Fi!"

Everyone rushes over, and I join them too. "Does anyone know how to work this?" Ant asks. We all shake our heads. He presses the button on the mysterious box, waits. "Nothing's happening. It must be broken or something," he grumbles.

"What about the TVs in our rooms? Has anyone tried to see if they work?" says Emily.

"No idea," says Ant.

"We'll figure it out after eating," says Isla. "I need food now."

Will grabs the other pot, and Ant and Isla set the table while Sadie heads back upstairs, mumbling that she lost something.

I can sense the mood has changed. They're all on edge now, nervous and suspicious after the discovery of the picture and the lack of Wi-Fi. Which is weird, I admit. I need to calm them down or distract them with something so they let down their guard. Or get them drunk... I head back to the kitchen and open the wine fridge, which I noticed earlier on stored a dozen bottles of champagne. Grabbing two bottles of Dom Pérignon, I hold them up with a flourish. "How about some champagne to go with the spaghetti?"

Will snorts. "Champagne with spaghetti? Really? Can't wait until after dinner to hit the booze, Charlie?"

But Isla's face lights up. "Champagne with dinner. Boujee. I'm up for it. Ooh, and it's the good stuff too, isn't it? Dom Pérignon."

I knew she'd like that. Isla likes anything that makes her feel like she's better than everyone else.

Ant grins. "Dom Pérignon? That shit's *expensive*. Charlie's got the right idea; we should have them before the rest get here."

Good. A bit of alcohol will soon put everyone at ease. I'll get them talking soon enough. And I need them to talk if I want my plan to work.

If I pull this off, they will be *obliterated*.

—Why didn't they call for help?

—I heard they couldn't. It was so far out, they had no reception out there. They were completely cut off from civilization.

—What? You mean that luxury island had no satellite? That's hard to believe.

—No, no, it did. But apparently someone tampered with it.

—Tampered with it? How?

—I don't know. The police aren't releasing any details yet. But that's what I heard people saying on social media.

—Maybe it's just speculation.

—Whatever the reason, no one called for help.

EMILY

Ant is flirting with Isla.

At first, I thought I was imagining it. When he carried her bag up to the house, the initial shock of it felt like a slap. They went up, leaving me behind, nobody even noticing that I remained frozen there like a statue. Breathing a little too fast, blinking away the tears stinging my eyes.

I managed to convince myself I was being too sensitive. That it meant nothing, that he just grabbed her bag because it was the nearest one other than his own.

But as the evening went on, it became too obvious for me to ignore or deny. That comment to Isla about sharing rooms. The way when Isla sat down beside Sadie, he took the seat immediately on her other side. Sitting opposite him now, I have a front-row seat to seeing him fawning over her. Topping off her champagne glass for her. All his attention is focused on her.

She's flirting back now, laughing at a really terrible joke he just made ("A macaroni, a penne, and a spaghetti were drinking wine in a bar one evening. They saw a noodle sitting by himself and invited him to join them…because he looked cannelloni").

He's hit on other girls before, but I think what makes this worse is that this time I have a front-row seat to it. And that it's Isla. And I hate how that's making me feel: angry at him, and at her too.

"I forgot that you're allergic to dairy," says Isla, turning suddenly to me, making me jump.

I nod stiffly, my face hot. It feels like she's caught me doing something naughty, like she could feel the bad vibes emanating from me and is calling me out on it.

"I've never asked, but I've always wondered how serious your allergy is," she continues. "If you don't mind me asking? Like, if you drink some milk, you'd break out in rashes or something?"

"Hers is a little more serious than that," murmurs Ant, as if he cares.

"What? Like, she'd die?" says Isla incredulously.

"It's why she's always careful with what she eats," says Sadie. She glances at me. Perhaps she notices my discomfort, because she says, "Lay off her, Isla."

I'm grateful, but why does it have to be Sadie? Ant avoids my eyes, and hurt wraps itself around my chest, constricts it so it's hard to breathe.

Isla frowns and opens her mouth to retort something, but

Sadie continues, "Anyway, nothing like that is going to happen. I made sure there's lots of dairy-free options, and we're all going to be careful. Right?"

Everyone nods. Then Isla lifts up the small dish of grated cheese that Charlie put out for those who want to add it to their pasta—just the sight of it makes me anxious—and says, "Anyone want more cheese?"

She thinks she's so funny. I sneak another glance at Ant, but he's still steadfastly not looking at me, and the pain in my chest intensifies until it feels like my heart is cracking open.

"Um," says Sadie. She hesitates before continuing. "Has anyone seen a small white pill bottle lying around?"

"What kind of pills?" says Isla.

"It's just... I can't find my Valium," mumbles Sadie as she goes a bit pink in the face.

"Is that what you were looking for when you went back upstairs?" says Will.

Sadie gives a small nod. Her hair falls in front of her face, hiding her downcast eyes, but she can't hide the tremble in her voice. "I've looked everywhere, and I still can't find it. Did one of you take it?"

Everybody shrugs or shakes their heads.

"Where did you leave it?" I ask.

"It was in my pocket." Her blush intensifies, as if she's embarrassed. "I...I usually keep it close by."

"Maybe it fell out when you were getting in the helicopter," says Isla. "Or when you were getting out. Anyway"—she makes a dismissive motion with her right hand, as if to say this is boring—"what I want to know is who drew on that picture." She looks at Charlie, then Ant, her eyes narrowing. "Come on. Which one of you did it?"

"I told you, it wasn't me," says Ant, throwing his fork down on his plate irritably.

Charlie takes a slow, deliberate sip of his champagne, then puts the glass down coolly. "I would never do something like that."

I eye Ant. Ant is flushing a little. Could be the champagne, or could be he was the one who drew on the picture and realized after doing it how dumb it is, and is too embarrassed to admit it now?

As for Charlie, he'd be one of the last people to make jokes about Vera dying. Ant, maybe, but not him. If he did it, it wouldn't be a joke, but a reminder. Yeah, that would make sense. And we'd deserve it.

Don't think about it. Knowing who did it, isn't worth the memories it's dredging up.

Will chimes in. "The staff will most likely be here tomorrow and show us how to connect to the Wi-Fi. In the meantime, there's enough food stocked to last us for weeks, and nothing to worry about."

With that, the conversation moves on. Isla is doing most of the talking as Charlie refills everyone's glasses, going on and on about how excited she is about Yale and how great college is going to be and how bright her future is.

She always has to be the center of attention. Ant doesn't take his eyes off her as he eats.

"Yale really loved your application essay, huh?" I blurt out, shocking even myself. It's the one jab I know will definitely get under her skin. Maybe the glass of champagne I've had is making me feel bolder than usual.

The effect is instantaneous, like I've dropped a bomb on her. Isla's face pales and her mouth snaps shut, and for a moment, satisfaction bubbles in me like, well, champagne.

The feeling doesn't last long though. Isla's lids lower, and she gazes through her lashes at me—a curious, calculating look that sends nervous regret shooting down my limbs—before she turns to Ant and whispers something in his ear, eliciting an earsplitting grin from him. Then she resumes talking about Yale, as if I never said anything.

I should have known better than to have said that. The thing about Isla is she can be vicious with people who she thinks might hurt her in any way. She might get together with Ant just to get back at me for saying that.

Even though I've lost my appetite, I fork the pasta into my mouth as I stare out of the window and try not to cry. The storm clouds have fully arrived, and it's like the skies have split open with the downpour. It's a real, proper thunderstorm. Huge, fat raindrops lash against all the glass walls, and whenever lightning flashes, it's almost as bright as day outside for a second, and I can see the trees outside thrashing their limbs around, each one performing a violent, solitary dance.

"Guess we're not having a pool party after all," says Charlie softly on my left, almost only to me, before he tosses back another glass of champagne.

He has the right idea. What better way to drown out Isla's and Ant's flirting than with champagne? I hold out my glass to Charlie. He looks at me, understanding dawning on his face, and tops it up. "Cheers," he says, and we clink glasses.

The golden bubbly liquid fizzles in my mouth and throat going down. Champagne probably isn't meant to be gulped down this way, but who cares? I hold out my glass again, and Charlie refills it one more time.

"What about you, Sadie?" says Will. "Are you really going to defy your dad and go to Tisch instead of joining him at his firm?"

Oh, that's right. Sadie applied and got accepted to Tisch at NYU. It was a bit surprising because although she did theater, she never seemed that passionate about acting. She was never even onstage in any year-end production. She just helped with the makeup, costumes, props, and backdrops. My theory is she applied to go to Tisch just to rebel against her dad's plans, which were for her to major in business management and join the family business. "Your dad must be so mad," I say. "Are you really going?"

Sadie shrugs. "Yeah, I'm going. He's a bit mad, but he'll get over it. Lucky for me, he's got Noah."

"What if little Noah doesn't want to join the family business either?" says Ant.

"So far, he's up for it. But if he changes his mind…" The right corner of Sadie's mouth crooks upward in a wry smile. "Then I guess my dad will just have to get over that too."

They're still talking, but their voices seem to fade in and out. I'm on my second—no, *third*—glass now and my tummy and head are all bubbly from the champagne, but I don't feel better. I'm starting to feel worse, actually. Not only sick in my heart, but now I'm also starting to feel sick to my gut. The uneaten spaghetti on my plate is an unappealing mass of fat white worms, the tomato sauce starting to congeal, like blood spilled on an icy stone floor…

Without warning, bile rises up my throat. I dash to the bathroom. Luckily, I make it in time and throw up into the toilet, and only a little puke splashes on the tiled floor.

Knocks on the door; then Ant's voice calls from outside, "Em? Are you okay?"

"Yeah. Fine." *Leave me alone.*

After a while, the nausea subsides, and I clean up the puke. It's beyond mortifying that I puked like this, before we even really started the party. I rinse my mouth, then splash water on my face.

When I come out, they're already clearing the dirty dishes away. Ant and Isla are loading the dishwasher. I join in to help.

Ant is staring at me. Maybe because I'm dumping the cutlery in the dishwasher a little harder than necessary. "Were you sick in the bathroom?" he says. "Sure you don't want to go lie down instead?"

"I'm not drunk. The food just disagreed with me," I reply without looking at him.

He shrugs and saunters away to the bathroom, not bothering anymore with me. I'm trying not to cry when a hand clamps down on my arm, its nails digging into my flesh.

"What the hell did you think you were doing with that admissions essay comment?" hisses Isla, her breath hot in my ear.

"Nothing." I try to yank my arm away, but her grip on me just tightens.

"We had a deal," she continues through clenched teeth. "Better keep your mouth shut, or I'll shut it for you."

"Hey," says Sadie, who has brought a stack of cutlery over. Her look shifts from Isla, to me, and back to Isla again. "Is everything okay?"

Isla lets go of my arm. "Yeah, everything's great. Isn't it, Emily?"

"Yeah. Just peachy." I rub at the spot on my arm where she grabbed me, hard enough to leave little crescent marks where her nails dug into my skin.

She shoots me another warning look before tossing her blond curls over her shoulder and stalking away.

Sadie frowns. "Is everything really okay?"

"Yeah." I turn away, because even though my little outburst might have slipped out of me earlier out of frustration, I don't actually want to get Isla in trouble. Not to mention, I can't afford to break the deal I have with her.

When the dishes are done and I join the others at the counter, I see that Charlie has set out dozens of bottles of rum, tequila, vodka, and various sodas. It's surprising how he's taking charge of all this—first the food, now the drinks. He's been so listless the past year and a half, as if he couldn't care less about anything, but ever since we arrived on the island, he seems to have really come alive. He seems driven, even. Maybe the sea air is helping him feel better.

I wish it made me feel better too.

If I'd known it was going to go like this, I wouldn't have come.

I sneak a look at Ant, catch him still looking at me worriedly, and my heart stutters.

Maybe I'm just being overly sensitive.

I should tell him how I feel. It's what I came here to do. What's the worst that could happen, right? Even if he rejects me then, it's not like it'll be any worse than what's happening right now. Besides, maybe he's just flirting with her because he doesn't know how I feel about him. Maybe if he knew, he'd act differently.

I make up my mind. I planned to tell him how I feel this weekend, and I'll do it.

After a few more drinks.

Will grabs the bottle of tequila. "How about some shots?"

Shots should do. Liquid courage, right? "I'm in," I say, even as Isla arches an eyebrow, and Sadie shoots me a dubious look. "Honestly, I'm feeling better," I insist. And I am, after puking. Or maybe it's just because I've made up my mind.

"Hell yeah," says Ant. He locates the shot glasses in a cabinet and lines six of them up on the counter.

"Found the limes and salt!" says Isla.

Will fills the shot glasses with tequila, and Sadie slices up the limes into wedges.

"What's the salt for?" I ask.

"Wait, you haven't had tequila shots before?" says Isla incredulously. "You put some on your hand like this. Then you lick, shoot, and suck." She licks the salt off her hand, downs the shot of tequila, slams the empty glass on the counter, grabs a wedge of lime and sucks it.

One by one, the others down their shots. "Woo! Hits the spot!" says Ant. They're all grinning, relaxed, all of them already slightly drunk from the champagne, like me.

I pick up a glass and sniff at the tequila. The smell of it stings my nose. I don't want to tell them I haven't tried tequila before. Or vodka. Or that the hardest thing I've ever had before the champagne were some Bacardi Breezers.

"You don't have to do a shot if you don't want to," says Ant.

"Especially if you might get sick again," adds Isla.

It feels almost like they're daring me to, and I don't want to be the odd one out. I hold out my hand, and she shakes salt on it. I lick, then gulp down the tequila. It burns my throat going down, and I cough. Oh god, the taste. I grab the lime that Charlie passes me and suck on it, and that makes it better.

"Wooo! Go, Emily!" Ant pounds my back, as if I'm a guy, just some buddy.

"Another round!" says Isla.

Will refills the shot glasses with tequila, then holds one out in a toast. "To the best party weekend ever!"

"To graduating and getting out of our parents' control," says Sadie.

"To us," says Isla. "May we live forever."

"To friends and lovers," says Ant, throwing a look at Isla. My heart sinks, and the shot of tequila I took threatens to make a reappearance.

"To Vera and Tom," says Charlie.

My heart stops, and Isla's mouth drops open. We're all silent as Charlie knocks back his shot without bothering with the salt or the lime. I feel cold all over, and my stomach hurts, as if tendrils of ice are forming in my tummy and spreading out to the rest of my body.

"Dude," says Ant.

"What the hell," says Will.

"Oh, did I go and ruin the mood?" says Charlie. "Sorry."

"This is so unnecessary, Charlie," says Isla before her lips press together into a thin line.

Sadie is quiet, pale-faced. She says nothing and just stares at the floor.

"I just feel like we should be able to talk about them. And not pretend all the time that nothing happened," says Charlie, stone-faced.

"I'm so sorry, Charlie," I hear my voice saying in a whisper. My heart is doing strange things in my chest, beating too fast, fluttering like a bird's wings, and I feel sick. "About what happened."

Charlie turns to face me. "You mean *killing Vera*? You can say her name, you know. You can say their names."

"Hey!" Ant takes a step forward. "Emily didn't do anything."

Charlie's gaze, suddenly furious, turns on Ant. "Yeah, okay. She just watched you all do it, and then—"

"Whoa, whoa!" Will pushes himself between the two of them. "Charlie, you need to chill, man. Maybe you should go lie down. You've already had too much to drink—"

"Don't touch me," says Charlie.

"No, he's right. We should say their names," I say. My face is tight, tingling, burning. Something wet plops on my collarbone, and I become aware that I'm crying. "And I'm just as responsible as everyone for them dying. And I also…I also—"

"Only because I forced you to! You were almost catatonic!" shouts Ant.

"Don't interrupt her," says Charlie softly, a strange expression on his face, his eyes trained on me. "Let her get it off her chest."

I open my mouth, but this time, no words come out. I gulp like a fish. I try to take a breath, but it feels like my throat is closing. Tightening. Swelling.

"Em?" says Ant.

I try again to breathe, but I can't.

"Emily, what's wrong?" says Sadie.

"Her skin looks weird," says Isla. "Is that a rash?"

I point at my throat, clutch at Sadie's arm, because I finally get what's happening. Why I'm feeling off. *My pen. I need my pen.*

Understanding dawns in Sadie's eyes. "Oh my god, it's an allergic reaction. She can't breathe."

"She has an EpiPen," says Ant as he looks around frantically. "Did you bring it? In your bag? In your room?"

I nod frantically and gesture upstairs.

Ant runs toward the stairs. Black dots are starting to form in my vision. I clutch Sadie's arm harder with one hand, claw at my face and throat with the other. "Hurry!" she shouts after him.

"Jesus," says Charlie. From what I can still see of him—my vision is narrowing as my eyes are starting to swell shut—he looks horrified. "Is there anything we can do? There must be something we can do," he babbles as he whips out his phone and taps at it. "Fuck! I can't even search the internet!"

"I don't understand. Did she eat some of the cheese?" says Will.

My eyes shut completely; I can't open them anymore.

"Oh my god, her entire face is swelling up," says Isla.

My lungs are screaming for air. I collapse to the floor, still clinging onto Sadie's arm. She sinks onto the floor with me. "Ant!" she screams.

In the dark, stars explode behind my eyes. So much shrieking and shouting around me. My heels kick against the floor. I am afraid. I don't want to die.

I never told him, I think.

ANT

I run up to the second level, praying that Emily chose one of the rooms here. I didn't even bother to find out which floor she's on, let alone which room she took. Why didn't I care to know? "Hurry!" someone screams as I try to guess which must be her room.

Stay calm, I order myself. *But be fast!* Okay, I know it's one of the rooms without a bathroom. But the first room I come across is unoccupied. I throw open the door of another—unoccupied again; there are too many fucking rooms!—then another. Thank god, this third one is hers; her bag is at the foot of the bed.

I dash over to it and yank at the zipper. But I'm slow and clumsy—my hands are shaking so badly, and slippery with sweat—and when I finally manage to get it open, I don't see anything resembling an EpiPen. Swearing, I start rifling through her stuff.

I know what hers looks like—and how to use it—because I've

seen her use it once. It was the second week of freshman year. We were in the cafeteria, and Emily had just finished eating her packed lunch. She—or rather her mom—always packed all her lunches for school, since her allergy is so severe and she already had a few allergic reactions when she was younger because too many restaurants were careless about what was in their food, and they'd learned their lesson.

That time, though, Emily was still hungry after eating her packed sesame chicken noodles, probably because that morning in gym the teacher had made us do this dumb running test where we had to run as many laps as we could around a track in twelve minutes. It's funny how all these details are forever seared into my brain now.

The food selection in the cafeteria that day was surprisingly good. I'd grabbed the nachos and chocolate ice cream. Emily was staring at my ice cream, so I told her it was dairy-free. Sometimes the cafeteria came through with options like that. She took a spoonful.

It was clearly labeled dairy-free. I didn't make that up or anything. It was supposed to be dairy-free, but it wasn't. Within minutes, Emily started having trouble breathing and broke out in a rash. But she was familiar with the symptoms, understood what was happening, knew what to do. I watched as she got one of the EpiPens that she always carried with her out of her bag and jabbed it into her thigh. Then, she calmly asked me to call for an ambulance.

"Ant!" someone screams, and I grab the bag and upend the entire contents onto the bed. My heartbeat thunders in my throat and in my head, *thump thump thump,* as I sift through them. There are too many things. Shoes, a pouch that turns out to be carrying an astounding assortment of makeup, and so, so many clothes. Why are there so many clothes? It's taking forever to sift through everything. I can't find the pen, and I feel so sick I might just vomit too.

It's not here. I look again and again, even emptying the makeup pouch to make sure, but the pen isn't here. Surely Emily can't be dying. She's told me before how bad her allergy is—*It's bad,* she said the third time we ate together, *just a tiny amount can trigger anaphylaxis. That means everything swells up and I can't breathe—* but surely no one can *die* from this. *Where is the fucking pen?*

Maybe there's another compartment in her bag. The sudden thought strikes me with the force of lightning. I grab the bag, yank it open wider and peer inside; sure enough, there's a zipper along the interior. *You stupid idiot, it should have occurred to you earlier,* my brain shouts. I yank at the zipper, but it catches on the fabric and gets stuck. Panting, I keep tugging until I finally manage to work the damn fabric out of the zipper and unzip it all the way. Reaching in, I grab something bulky; it's her wallet. I throw it on the bed and reach in again, grope around. This time my hand closes around something slim. In fact, there are even two of them. Of course. I remember her telling me now: *One isn't enough. I need another fifteen minutes later if medical help doesn't arrive in time.* I pull them out, and relief bursts in my chest because they're EpiPens.

I run downstairs, almost tripping on the steps. "I've got it! I've got it—"

Charlie and Sadie are kneeling on the floor. Sadie turns to me, her lower lip trembling, her cheeks glistening wet. She moves aside so I can see Emily, who is lying on the floor.

Emily is completely still. Her face is swollen, unrecognizable, dark purple, monstrous; a ghastly caricature of herself.

Her mother's face floats before my eyes. *I really appreciate the way you always keep an eye out for Emily, Ant,* she once said to me, ruffling my hair, back when I was young enough not to feel embarrassed by that.

It's not too late. It can't be too late. I shove Sadie aside, yank off the pen's cap, and plunge the needle into Emily's thigh until I hear the click. Terrifyingly, Emily doesn't flinch. She doesn't move at all. I hold it for ten seconds the way she told me how to use it. I'm doing everything right, so she has to be okay.

"Ant," says Sadie softly.

I ignore her. "You're going to be okay, Em. Everything is going to be fine."

"She's not breathing anymore," says Will. "She stopped breathing a minute ago."

"Why didn't anyone do CPR?" I put my fists on Emily's chest and push hard and rhythmically, *one two three four*, then open her mouth and blow air into it, like the way I've seen people do on TV, even though I have no idea if what I'm doing is correct. And again: *one two three four*. Blow. *One two three four*. Blow. "Someone should have done CPR!" I shout at them again even though I already know the answer. No one attempted CPR because like me, no one knows how to do it. Why have I never learned?

"I tried," said Charlie.

I shove him. "You should have tried harder!"

"Ant, stop. Charlie tried," said Sadie.

I ignore them and go back to my useless attempts at reviving Emily.

"I can't believe she's dead," says Isla.

"No. No," I say even as I stop trying, because I know she's right.

Emily is beyond resuscitation.

Emily is dead.

ISLA

Emily's face is hideous. Swollen, a dark purple, barely recognizable, like something out of a nightmare. I don't want to keep looking at her, but I can't seem to tear my eyes away, the same way you can't tear your eyes away from a car crash. Luckily, her eyes are swollen shut too, so she's not staring at us. I don't think I could bear it if she was staring at us.

God. I can't believe she's dead. Talk about a horrible and *stupid* way to die.

Although if her allergy is so bad, I guess it's a wonder she even made it this long?

Jesus. She was my friend. I did like her, even if she surprised me with that admissions test comment just now. So why am I having irrelevant thoughts like this? I must be in shock.

Or maybe it's because I've seen too many deaths already, and this isn't even the worst thing to have happened to us.

There's a soft hiccup. I finally manage to look away from Emily to see Sadie is crying.

"I don't understand," she says. "The food was all dairy-free. Both the spaghetti and the sauces. I checked the labels!"

But what about the obvious thing? "There was the grated cheese."

Ant jerks at that and stands up. It's like my words have jolted him into action. He points at Charlie. "You were the one who grated the cheese and put it on the table."

"What?" Charlie shakes his head and raises his palms. "Yeah... but...that was for the rest of us. Emily knew better than to add that to her spaghetti."

Ant takes two steps and grabs Charlie's T-shirt at the neck with both fists. "You fucking *moron*. Some of the cheese must have fallen into her plate. It's your fault she's dead. *It's your fault.*"

Charlie doesn't do anything to defend himself except to keep shaking his head. "No! That cheese never went anywhere near her plate. I'm telling you, I was next to her, I kept an eye on it."

"You killed her with that stupid cheese!" shouts Ant, gripping Charlie's shirt even harder and now looking like he's about to start throwing punches.

"Maybe she was so upset with you flirting with Isla that she ate some of the cheese on purpose," spat Charlie.

Ant's swarthy face pales until it has a sickly yellow undertone. "Shut up! You piece of shit!"

"Stop! Stop!" Sadie wedges herself between the two of them, such a stupid thing to do because she could get herself hurt if they really do start throwing punches. "Will, help!"

Will grabs Ant's arms by his elbows and pulls him back, but Ant tries to twist out of his grip as he shouts, "Let go of me! He killed Emily! I'm gonna kill him!"

"We don't know that," says Will, surprisingly calmly.

He's trying to impress her, the realization bursts into my head. *Even now.* The way he jumped at once to action when Sadie asked for his help. The way he's acting so calm, so reasonable, the unflappable leader. It's how he acted with me at the beginning too, when he was trying to win me over. When he always took my side, backed me up.

And now he's dropped me, for whatever reason I still don't understand, and is trying for Sadie. Our *mutual friend*. I hate how much this stings, like he plunged his hand into my chest and has my heart in his fist. I hate that he still has the ability to make me feel this way. I should be the one who has blithely moved on. I scowl at him, but he doesn't meet my eyes.

Fuck him. Emily is dead; honestly who cares about Will? Finally, the numbness from the initial shock begins to dissipate, and the horror of it seeps slowly in. I sink heavily onto one end of the couch.

"Does champagne contain dairy?" says Will suddenly, breaking the heavy silence.

That's so ludicrous that I frown at him.

"Lots of things can contain traces of dairy, you know," he says, taking in my expression.

I shake my head. "Champagne is made from *grapes*. *How* can it contain dairy?"

"Sometimes foods can contain dairy because of the way it's made. They add stuff during the processing. We can't know for sure that it doesn't contain dairy unless it specifically states that it's dairy-free. Don't you know that?"

"Well, if you know so much, why didn't you check the label to see if it was dairy-free?"

"I didn't think of it," he mutters. "But it's not like anybody else did either. Not even Emily."

"It's not usually the kind of thing that would occur to anyone to check," says Charlie softly.

Sadie's face has gone pale. "We should have checked the alcohol too."

Ant plops on his ass on the floor beside Emily's body—Jesus, that *face*—and, like Sadie, begins to cry.

"Could there possibly be anything else that she ate or drank that might have contained dairy?" says Will, still so unnervingly calm. Some might say, cold-blooded.

Sadie sniffs, wipes her eyes and her nose with the back of her hand. Even though she looks as shaken as I feel, she replies, "She had the spaghetti with the canned sauce—I checked those, so we know they definitely don't. And she had the champagne and that shot of tequila." She goes over to the trash and rummages through it, retrieves a bottle, peers at it. "The Dom Pérignon doesn't state that it's dairy-free." She peers at the label on the bottle of tequila. "And neither does the Patron Silver."

"We should, like, cover her up or something," I whisper, because the sight of that horrible swollen purple face is starting to really freak me out, sear itself into my brain. If I keep looking at it, I'm going to start seeing it in my sleep. This is not how I want to remember her.

But nobody moves.

"Actually," says Will, "we're not going to leave her to just lie here, are we? We can't call the police, so we'll have to wait until the boats arrive tomorrow to let other people know what's happened. They'll take the body back to shore."

The body. A hysterical gurgle rises from my throat, and I clamp it down.

"Can we put her somewhere else in the meantime? Maybe somewhere cold?" continues Will.

The boats. My god, fifteen other people are arriving tomorrow, thinking they're going to have the party weekend of their life. At the thought of us having to break the news to them, the hysterical laugh I've been forcing down breaks free and escapes my throat.

"I'm going back on one of those boats tomorrow," says Sadie. "I don't care if I get seasick. I don't want to stay here any longer."

"I think we can all agree the party is canceled," Will agrees grimly. "In the meantime, we shouldn't leave her body here in the living room. It's warm in here."

"Isn't it a really bad idea to move dead bodies?" says Charlie.

But I get what Will means, and from the look on the rest of their faces, they're starting to understand too. *It's warm in here.* Meaning, the body is going to start stinking soon if we leave it here.

"We could put her in her room and turn up the air conditioning there," I suggest. "That'll slow down the…the…you know."

Ant blanches, but everyone slowly nods in agreement.

Ant and Will lift Emily by her shoulders and legs and, with a lot of huffing, get her up the stairs and onto the bed in her room. As Ant pulls the quilt up to cover her completely—finally covering up her face, thank god—I turn the air-conditioning in the room on and adjust it to the lowest possible temperature. Then I turn back to look at the lump on the bed under the quilt that was my friend. I still can't quite believe it's Emily, and that she's dead.

"Emily," says Sadie, starting to cry again.

"We should put a towel under the door so the cool air stays in," says Will.

Sadie wipes her tear-streaked face and nods. "I'll get a towel from one of the bathrooms."

Ant sits on one side of the bed and places a hand on the quilt, over the body. He remains like this, as still as a statue, not moving even when Sadie returns with the towel.

"Come on, Ant," says Will.

"Leave us alone," says Ant.

Sadie shifts from one foot to the other, wringing her hands.

Will and I exchange looks again, and I shrug. I mean, I understand if he needs more time with her. "We'll be downstairs if you need us," I say. "Don't forget to wedge the towel under the door when you leave."

I step out, the others behind me, leaving Ant in the room with the body.

"I need a drink," Will says heavily as he closes the door behind us.

"Me too," I say.

"You know what." Sadie sniffs and wipes her face. "I'm going to go to bed."

As I watch her trudge off heavily, a horrid little thought inserts itself into my brain. *At least my secret is safe now.* It makes me sick, and I shove the thought away quickly.

Downstairs in the kitchen, Charlie, who didn't come upstairs with us, is starting back on the tequila.

"Hey. Leave some for us," I say.

"There's lots of alcohol left, don't worry," he mumbles.

I join him at the counter and mix myself a big cup of vodka with orange juice. As I do, I realize my hands are shaking uncontrollably. I take a big gulp. "What a night, huh? We just arrived, and already someone is dead."

The right side of Charlie's mouth quirks up, and he laughs humorlessly. "Very on brand for us. *Ring around the rosie, a pocket full of posies. Ashes, ashes, we all fall down,*" he sings tunelessly.

What the hell? It's super creepy.

"Everyone else is leaving tomorrow with the boats too, right?" I say.

A funny look crosses Charlie's face, but his gaze remains fixated on the bottle of tequila in front of him. He doesn't look up at me or reply.

"What the *fuck*?" says Will, who was just behind me when we were coming down the stairs, but for some reason he stopped in front of the big canvas print and is staring at it.

"What?" I say.

"You all better come see this." His voice is strange. Strangled.

When I go over to join him, I see immediately what he's looking at.

A new big red *X* has appeared, crossing out a third figure in the picture.

SADIE

It's a relief to be in my room. All I want is to be alone right now, to have the privacy to process what's happened. To be able to cry as much as I want.

I lock the bedroom door and wipe away the tears blurring my eyes.

Emily is dead. She was so excited about this weekend, and now she's dead, barely hours after we arrived.

When we're alone together, we always end up dying.

I climb in the large bed, crawl under the quilt cover, and curl up into a ball, even though I doubt I'm going to get any sleep tonight. Even under the quilt, I'm still cold. I reach automatically for my bottle of Valium, before I remember. I can't even pop a pill to prop me up through this anymore. Regret barrels through me. I shouldn't have come here, shouldn't have done this.

I shut my eyes tightly. But as soon as I do the memories start to stir again, the ones that always come at night. I can usually dull them with Valium, these ghosts that won't stop haunting me. But without my pills, I'm powerless to prevent them from taking over...

"Tom!" I scream. "Stop! Stop! Something's happened to Tom!" I shout at the rest of them, trying to shout louder than the howling wind drowning out my voice.

Thank god our guide hears my shout and skids to a stop. "What?" Lucas yells back. The others stop and turn back to look at me too.

I ski down nearer to him. "Tom was over there, but he's disappeared!" I gesture to where I last saw Tom before he vanished so suddenly.

They all turn to look. So do I, squinting as the snow beats down on us, blinding us, and the wind screams in our ears. Tom must have fallen, and we can't even see him through all the snow.

We wait and wait, but he doesn't appear.

"Stay here," Lucas shouts. He starts climbing up the slope sideways, laboriously. The slope is steep here, and it takes him forever to climb up to where I pointed, a distance that takes probably only ten seconds to ski down. Standing still for so long, I get colder and colder. The wind bites through my ski jacket and pants, and soon I can't feel my hands and feet anymore. I start to shiver uncontrollably. I have never seen a snowstorm like this before, ever. The snowfall is so relentless, the wind blowing it into our nostrils so hard that I almost feel like I'm choking on it.

Lucas has stopped climbing, even though there's still no sign of Tom. Lucas is bending down. What is he doing?

Finally, he straightens up. He seems to be shouting something now, but it's impossible to hear him over the shrieking of the wind when he's all the way over there. What's clear though, is that something is wrong, because we still don't see Tom. Maybe he's twisted an ankle, needs more help than Lucas can provide. I start to climb up, and after a while, Charlie, Will, and Ant do too. So do Emily and Vera, but Ant and Charlie shout at them to stay put and wait.

The climb is hard and tiring, but at least it warms me up again. Lucas looks like he's on the phone. When I finally reach him, he's put his phone away and is crouched over, staring at something on the snow. No, not on the snow. In *the snow. There's a black crack stretching several feet, a black crack in the snow. An icy fist seizes my heart. I sink on my knees and peer in. It's so dark inside at first that I can't see anything, but gradually, I start to make out the vague outline of a person lying at the bottom of the crevasse.*

"He said he thinks his leg is broken," *shouts Lucas, as Charlie, Will, and Ant also reach us.*

"Fuck," *says Charlie, perfectly summing up everyone's feelings, because if Tom has a broken leg, we'll all have to wait here until a helicopter comes to get him. In this blizzard.*

Tom moans, the sound reverberating through the crevasse up to us.

"You called for a rescue team?" *I ask Lucas.*

I can't see his eyes, but the way his mouth tightens into a grim line gives me a sinking feeling in my gut.

"I tried, but I'm not getting any cell service," he shouts back. "What about you guys?"

I dig out my phone from my jacket pocket. I have to remove my glove to swipe up and unlock the screen, and my hand goes numb again immediately, it's so damn cold. Lucas shows us the number for the emergency rescue team on his screen. I have zero bars, but I try calling anyway. Silence…until the call goes dead. I shake my head. Will, Charlie, and Ant all try too, but nobody has any service.

This is bad, this is so bad. What are we going to do?

A loud *rat-tat-tat* shocks me out of the memory's grip, jolts me upright. The last icy tendrils of that blizzard slowly unfurl their clasp around my heart. *Why do I have to relive this?* I think bitterly. If I could wipe it all from my memory, I would. As I wipe away the tears on my cheeks, the sound comes again. *Rat-tat-tat.* Someone is knocking on the door.

"Sadie," Isla's voice calls from the other side. "Are you awake?"

What does she want? "I'm coming." Even though I really don't want to, I get out of bed and unlock and open the door.

Isla's face is pale, bloodless, her eyes so wide they look like they're going to fall out of her head. The look of her sets my heart racing. "What is it?" I say.

"Someone crossed out a third figure in the picture."

"What?" is the only reply I manage to muster.

"Just come."

Downstairs, everyone, including Ant, is gathered around the canvas print on the wall.

There's a new red *X* crossing out a third figure.

"Someone just did this," says Isla.

"I don't understand," I say. I look at the rest of them. They're all wearing identical grim expressions on their faces.

"Eight figures, three crossed out," growls Ant.

"It's obvious now, isn't it?" says Will. "The people in this picture are supposed to represent us."

WILL

Sadie's eyes are two large orbs in her pale face, as she takes in my words. "You mean..."

I point at the *X*s. "The first two figures crossed out represent Tom and Vera..."

Sadie begins to shake her head as horror dawns in her face.

"And this new one stands for Emily," finishes Isla.

"Who did this?" cries Sadie.

"Well..." I fold my arms across my chest. "That's the question, isn't it?"

"It's fucking sick," growls Ant, staring at Charlie.

Sadie's head whips to look at Charlie. "You did this? Why?"

Charlie, who is standing a little farther away from the group, his face pale, crosses his arms defensively in front of his chest. "You all just *love* accusing me."

"We're accusing you because it's obvious you did it," spits Ant.

"I didn't do anything. I told you, it wasn't me," Charlie says slowly. He sobered up a little over dinner, but now he's beginning to slur his words again. The distinctive smell of tequila wafts off him.

"You were the only one who stayed here while the rest of us went upstairs," Isla points out.

"I was in the kitchen. I never went anywhere near this picture."

"Bullshit," says Ant.

"Well then, who did it, if it wasn't you?" I ask. "If it wasn't you then you must have seen who, since you were down here the entire time."

Charlie shakes his head. "I didn't see anyone. I was really shaken, okay? I never thought... I was just working on getting drunk. I was downing tequila behind the island. This area wasn't even in my line of vision at all."

"He's lying. Nobody believes this," says Ant. "Charlie was the only one who could have done this!"

"That's not true," says Charlie. "*Will* could have done it."

His words send a jolt of shock through me, and I feel my face grow hot. "What? Why would I—"

"I dunno. But you could have done it," he repeats. He speaks slowly, like he's trying to think and enunciate clearly through his alcoholic fog. "You were trailing behind Isla when the two of you came down, then you stopped in front of the picture. Neither of us were looking at you to see what you were doing there. You could have drawn that *X* just before calling our attention to it."

The initial shock I felt transforms to indignation, but all I can do is stutter incoherently as they all swivel to look at me. I can see their expressions change from thoughtful to doubtful, and then suspicious. "Hang on," I finally regain enough composure to say. "Are we sure this new *X* was drawn after Emily died? Did anyone look at the picture before that? Anytime during dinner? I didn't."

One by one, they shake their heads.

"So it could have been drawn any time after we noticed the first two *X*s," I point out.

"But that would mean…it could have been any one of us," says Isla slowly. "We all went to use the bathroom at some point, which meant walking past the picture."

We exchange looks as her words sink slowly in. *It could have been any one of us.* But why would any one of us do this?

"Or…it could have been someone else," says Sadie. Even though it isn't cold, she's shivering, and she wraps her arms around herself. "When we were all busy cooking and setting the table and stuff, and we just didn't notice."

"Wait, what?" says Isla. "You think there might be someone else in the house?"

Sadie's suggestion is unsettling. We haven't seen anyone. Could there really be someone else here? Someone who knows what we did, and is toying with us? Did we even lock the door? I stride over to the front door and try the handle. The door swings open. "The door wasn't even locked," I tell them. "Anyone could have come in when we were all upstairs checking out the bedrooms."

"If they weren't already inside to begin with," whispers Sadie, her eyes wide.

I turn the latch on the door, make sure it's locked now. "Maybe we should search the house. Just to make sure there isn't anyone else in here."

Isla and Sadie nod quickly in agreement.

"I still think it's Charlie," says Ant darkly, but then he shrugs. "Fine, let's do it."

"Wait," says Sadie. "Do we go as a group? Do we split up? I don't think we should split up."

"I agree," says Isla quickly. "We've all seen what happens in horror movies when people split up."

Yup. They get picked off one by one. "Fine," I say. "We stay together."

We check the entire ground level first. It takes almost no time at all because the only closed room is the bathroom. As we search, I take stock of any possible entries or exits. The glass walls are just that—walls that can't be opened. There is no back door; the only entry or exit is the main entrance door.

The bathroom is empty and still stinks a little of puke.

Poor Emily.

I can't get sad about Emily right now. There might be someone else in the house. I have to *focus*. Okay, so there's a small window in the bathroom that can be opened, but only partially. Impossible for anyone to squeeze through.

Everyone looks to me as I lead the way up the stairs. I'm used to it, used to most people following my lead. It's a role I assume naturally, which is why I've always been the de facto leader of the group. See, most people are like sheep: frightened whenever something doesn't go exactly to plan; wanting a strong leader to follow, to tell them what to do.

I don't like what's going on with this picture thing. I don't want to show it—and I certainly wouldn't admit it to anyone—but it's truly gotten to me. Because while Emily's death could have been nothing more than a horrible freak accident, the figures being crossed out with those red *X*s… That's something else entirely. That's *deliberate*. Some asshole is trying to mess with us.

Furthermore, it means whoever is crossing out the figures in the picture *knows what happened.* What we did. Or at least, enough to do this. The thought leaves me cold. Whoever it is, I can't show them how much it's freaking me out.

Or could it really be one of us?

It's a conclusion I don't want to come to…but who else would know? Well okay, there's the Canadian rescue team who found us, and the cops who initially got involved. Sadie's dad, and their lawyer and PR firm. Maybe some of the others told their family members, even though they weren't supposed to. (I certainly didn't; my parents got the story we all agreed on sticking to.) But none of those people are here, and why would they do this anyway? It can't be some random person we don't know. Sadie's PR firm managed to keep the entire thing clean out of the press. Not even the rest of our classmates knew what really happened.

Yeah. The more I think about it, the more I'm sure it has to be one of us. The simplest explanation is usually the best one. Not sure where I heard that before, but it makes sense. One of us is trying to mess with the rest. And I'm pretty sure I know who, even if he keeps denying it.

But I'll go along with this act for now. We gather on the landing of the second floor. Isla and Sadie sticking closely beside me, their faces pale, frightened eyes darting around us. Charlie with a small frown on his face. Ant glowering at Charlie.

All sheep except for one, who thinks he's a big bad wolf. Well, I'm going to sniff this wolf out.

"Someone should stay here by the stairs to make sure that nobody comes up or down them," says Charlie.

Sadie's eyes widen. "We said we wouldn't split up."

"No, Charlie is right," I say slowly, even though I wish I was the one who thought of it first and not him. "Someone has to stand guard. Otherwise, someone could be hiding upstairs on the third level and make their way down while we're checking out the rooms on this floor."

"I…I guess that makes sense…" says Sadie. "But I don't want to be the one."

"Neither do I," says Isla.

Charlie shrugs. "I can stand guard."

I eye him. Why is he so eager to volunteer to stand guard? To split from the group?

"Are you sober enough to do that though?" says Isla.

Charlie snorts and waves us away. I bite my tongue and play along, because I can't think of a reason to argue.

"I don't trust him," Ant mutters as we check my room and bathroom quickly, making sure to check under the bed and in the closet.

"I know," I say grimly. "He had the best opportunity to draw on that picture."

"The cheese too, that was entirely his idea," continues Ant. "He grated it. He was sitting beside Emily; he could have easily snuck some onto her plate."

"But why would Charlie want to kill Emily?" Sadie whispers back, obvious distress on her face. "That has to be an accident."

"Come on. Isn't it obvious? He holds a grudge against all of us, for what happened," says Isla. "You know I'm right."

Sadie's mouth snaps shuts.

I mull over Isla's words as we search the other rooms and bathrooms on this level, keeping an eye on Charlie each time we come out of a room. But if I'm hoping to catch him trying to do something, I'm disappointed. He's in the same position every time I check on him—just leaning against the wall by the top of the stairs, his arms crossed in front of his chest, looking bored.

Still, Isla and Ant are right. No matter what Charlie says, it's clear that he had both the opportunity and the motive. And it's clear he hasn't been mentally or emotionally well for a while. Is he even really tipsy right now? Or is it just an act?

Still, it's hard to wrap my head around it, the idea that he murdered Emily in cold blood. Could he really have done that? He did seem upset just now too. I thought he liked her. Or at least, hated her the least. Could he really be that good of an actor?

Finally, as we're checking Emily's room—the room is so uncomfortably cold, and I try my best not to let my gaze rest on the still, unmoving lump under the quilt cover—Sadie says reluctantly in a whisper, "Did anyone else notice what he was doing earlier on?"

I turn to look at her. "When? Doing what?"

"When we first discovered the defaced picture."

What? "What do you mean?"

"It was like…he was trying to goad us to talk about…about what happened, or something." Sadie shakes her head. "Never mind. Maybe I was just imagining it. Let's just finish checking the rest of the house."

It's a bit of a slog to check all six bedrooms and three bathrooms on this level, but finally we're done and head back to the landing.

"Find anybody?" slurs Charlie.

I shake my head.

"Pity, I was hoping you might have found the chef, or at least the housekeeper. Anyway, nobody tried to sneak past me."

"Let's check the third level," I say.

"Serious question," says Charlie as we file up the stairs. "What happens if we really do find someone hiding in the house? Is there a game plan? Do we tackle them? Tie them up? Torture them until they confess that they drew on the picture?"

"You're awfully glib about all this," spits Ant. "Considering Emily just died."

"Why are you taking it so hard? It's not like she was your girlfriend," says Charlie, his face suddenly darkening. "I was the one who lost a girlfriend, remember?"

They look like they're about to start throwing punches again. What's the point of flinging accusations around? No one's going to admit to anything. We have to catch them, find proof. And Charlie's room is coming up soon. Cursing inwardly, I step quickly between them. "Look, let's just finish checking this level, okay? And then after that, you can all go to bed, or go try to drink yourselves unconscious, or work out your issues in a death match, whatever, I don't care."

Charlie and Ant mutter curses under their breaths, then reluctantly draw apart.

I haven't been up on this level yet. It's a bit smaller than the second floor. The first room we enter has Sadie's bag on the floor by the wardrobe. We check the room and bathroom quickly—she's already hung her clothes neatly in the closet—then move on to the next room, which hasn't been taken by anyone. Nobody hiding there either, nor in the guest bathroom.

The last bedroom on this level is Charlie's. His bag is unzipped, his clothes spilling messily out of it onto the floor. I start by looking under his bed, the way I did for all the other rooms.

I'm about to stand back up when something under the bed, in the corner right by the edge, catches my eye. Something red.

Like someone dropped it and it rolled a little under the bed. I reach for it.

I can barely believe it. It's a red marker.

This is it, the smoking gun. We have our wolf.

CHARLIE

Will gets back on his feet and holds something up. His mouth is pressed together in a grim line as he stares at me. "A red pen," he announces. Sadie gasps and Isla narrows her eyes at me.

A red pen. The words don't make any sense. It doesn't help that my brain is fuzzy from all the alcohol I've been guzzling, especially after the shock of Emily dying. Then it begins to sink in. A red pen, like what's being used to cross out the figures in the picture. And…he's holding it up like that because…because he found it in my room? But—

"I knew it, I fucking knew it," says Ant through clenched teeth. "It was you." He swings, and his fist catches my jaw before I can see it coming. There's a *crunch*, strangely painless at first, but the pain follows a second later. I stagger and fall on the floor. He's on me in an instant, pinning me down. "You're the one who crossed out those figures in the picture. What the hell are you trying to do?" he roars.

"I didn't do anything. That pen isn't mine." I can barely move my jaw, which hurts like hell, so the words come out thick and barely coherent.

"Bullshit! You killed Emily, you…you…"

"I'm telling you that isn't mine! I have no idea why it's in my room!" *Why* is it? How did Will find it? Understanding dawns slowly in my fuddled state. *I'm being set up. Someone is setting me up.*

"I'm going to kill you!"

Ant's hands close around my neck and begin squeezing. His face is red, his eyes burning with so much hate he looks almost demonic. My attempts to push him away or pull his hands off my neck are futile; his grip just gets tighter. The same hands that murdered Tom. I'm about to die the same way, murdered by the same person. The irony is not lost on me.

I try to shout at him to let go but I can't get any sound out. The girls are screaming, horrified shrieks, and so are my lungs, screaming for air, and black spots are starting to appear in my vision and blot out his face. I'm going to die just like Emily, just like Tom…

Relief, as his hands suddenly release my neck. I suck in air in large gulps, pain searing my throat where he squeezed. The black spots in my vision remain. Did Ant really just try to kill me?

Of course, it wouldn't be his first time. Murdering someone.

"Let go of me!" Ant tries to shake off the others who must have pulled him off me. "This asshole killed Emily!"

"He said the pen isn't his," says Sadie, who looks as stunned as I feel.

Ant glares at her. "Well, he's lying. You can't believe—"

"We should at least hear him out," says Sadie.

"Hmm." Isla's voice is cold as she side-eyes me. "Yeah, let's hear him out. And *then* we can decide what to do with him."

I laugh sourly. The sound is strange and hoarse, coming from my bruised throat.

"What's so funny?" says Isla.

"You just love doling out death by committee," I rasp.

Her eyes narrow. "Who said anything about death? If you're the one who killed Emily, we'll just hand you over to the police. Better start talking, by the way. You have one minute to convince us it wasn't you."

Hand me over to the police. Isla didn't even blink as she dished me that bullshit, as if I'd believe it. They'd never simply hand me over to the police, who'd just let me go since I didn't do anything. They'd be too afraid that I'd keep coming after them.

I glance at Will, who hasn't said anything. He just keeps staring at me as if he finds me disgusting.

I pull myself up slowly, try to clear my head. "I told you, that pen isn't mine. I've never seen it before in my life. I have no idea what it's doing in this room."

They all stare at me; Sadie thoughtfully, Ant glaring daggers of hate, Will and Isla doubtfully. "Why should we believe that?" says Will. "I found it under your bed. Are you calling me a liar?"

"I don't know why you found it under this bed. As for whether you're a liar... I don't know, Will. Why don't *you* tell *me*?"

Now it's Will who looks like he's going to charge me.

"Wait," shouts Sadie. "Everybody, think about it. Isn't it too obvious, a red marker just turning up like this? Why would the person who crossed out those figures just leave it lying around conveniently for anyone to find?"

Silence as we take in her words. "Yeah," I say. "Someone planted it there. Someone's trying to *frame* me."

"Who could have come in your room?" says Isla, the note of disbelief in her voice as plain as the doubt on her face.

"I didn't lock the door, so it could have been anyone. It could have been Ant or Sadie, when they stayed upstairs just now."

Ant says *What?* but I ignore him and continue.

"Or it could even have been you or Will earlier on, before you came down for dinner, since I was the first one to come back downstairs."

"That's ridiculous," says Will. "If I did that, how could I have crossed out the third figure in the picture afterward?"

"Easily, if there's more than one red marker," says Sadie thoughtfully.

Will's mouth snaps shut, but his face turns redder.

I'm starting to feel grateful to Sadie for being the only reasonable one who hasn't jumped on me...but she isn't done talking. She's frowning. "If it wasn't you, why were you being sketchy earlier on?"

"Sketchy?"

"Like you kept trying to get us to talk about…that time."

I try to look confused. "I have no idea what you mean."

She comes up to me, reaches into the back pocket of my jeans and pulls out my phone before I can stop her.

"Hey! What are you—" Shit. Who knew she could move so fast? Okay, maybe it's just me who's slow. I shouldn't have drunk so much. I try to grab it back, but Will and Ant move to block me. "Give that back."

"When we first discovered the crossed-out figures in the picture," she says patiently. "You were acting weird." She taps at my phone. "What's your PIN?"

I shake my head, but Ant twists my arm hard behind my back. "What's your PIN, bro?"

I just laugh at him, but Sadie holds my phone at my face so it recognizes me and unlocks. Ignoring my curses, she begins to search through my phone.

It doesn't take long before she finds what she's looking for. She taps at the screen, and a voice recording starts playing:

Whoever did it knows what happened. What we did. My voice, loud and clear in the now quiet room.

We didn't do anything. Isla, lying.

Relax, Barbie. Look around. Do you see anyone else? It's just us. There's no need to keep up the act. Mine again, goading, persuasive. Trying to get them to talk.

Shut up. You think this is funny? *It* was *you, wasn't it?*

"What the hell?" says Will. "You were recording us?"

"Why?" says Sadie.

They all stare at me, their eyes full of confusion, mixed with a good dose of suspicion.

"Why?" I laugh again. "*Why? You killed my girlfriend.* Okay, fine, you're right. I *do* hold a grudge against all of you."

The look on their faces makes me want to laugh again. Isla begins to shake her head, but I point at her, and she freezes.

"You convinced everyone that Vera had lost it. That she was mentally unstable and a danger to the rest of us." The words curdle in my mouth; sour, poisonous. I spit them out.

"She was," Isla insists. "She was hysterical and starting to hurt herself. Who's to say she wouldn't have hurt one of us next?"

"*Shut up!* Vera wouldn't have hurt a fly. You picked on her because she was the weakest link."

Sadie begins to cry as Isla continues to shake her head, her blond curls bouncing stupidly around her face.

I jab at Isla's face. "You murdered her."

"I didn't touch her!" she has the audacity to say.

"You got your boyfriend and Ant to do it."

"It was an accident!" cries Isla at the same time as Will says, "We were just trying to get her to stop freaking out!"

"You're murderers." I wish I had my phone right now and was recording all this. What a pity Sadie caught me recording them earlier.

"As if you didn't join in later on, when it was Tom," says Will with a sneer.

Ah, there it is. When the shiny, perfect, *I'm-such-a-good-guy* mask drops, we get to see the real Will underneath: the guy who would do anything to be on top. Who will always put himself first at the expense of everyone else, just like his girlfriend. Sorry, ex-girlfriend. They really should have stayed together, they're so perfect for each other.

"Is that why you came? To take revenge on us?" says Isla.

"Why Emily?" shouts Ant, taking a step toward me and looking as if he'd like to strangle me again. "She didn't do anything. She refused to…to join in at first until I made her. *Why kill her?*"

"I told you, I didn't. I just wanted to record all of you confessing to what we did, and then blast it on social media," I snap.

My words hang in the air. A long, stunned silence. "That's it? That was your plan?" says Sadie uncertainly.

The idea popped into my head fully formed when I realized it would be just the six of us, alone. With their tongues loosened by alcohol, I could finally get them to confess to what really happened, record it, blast it out, give it to the police. I fantasized about it the entire afternoon. Even if the police still don't get them for murder, it would have destroyed them completely. Vengeance for Vera. It would have been so perfect.

"You snake." Isla strikes the flat of her right palm squarely across my left cheek. Then she spins around to face the others. "*He wants to hurt us.* We can't let him get away with this."

Ant grabs me by the elbow, as if I'd run away if he wasn't here to stop me, and says through clenched teeth, "I still don't buy that he didn't kill Emily."

"What if he murders us in our sleep?" says Isla.

Well. It didn't occur to me before, but now that she mentions it, that doesn't seem like such a bad idea at all.

Isla points at me. "Look! Look at the way he smiled when I said that! We need to do something about him!"

Will's gaze shifts between them and me. There's a dark look in his eyes, one I've seen before. He licks his lips nervously.

Something grows in my belly. Something I haven't felt in so long that it takes me a few seconds to recognize what it is: fear. Well, how about that? And here I thought I didn't care any more if I lived or died.

"We can't let him hurt us," says Will slowly, as if pronouncing a sentence, and the fear in me magnifies exponentially. "We—"

"Maybe we can just…keep him locked in his room?" Sadie cuts in quickly. "Until the boats come tomorrow."

Will frowns at first. His gaze shifts to Sadie and he tilts his head. *You sure you want to take the risk?* he seems to be asking her. When Sadie starts to frown too, he shrugs. "Okay. I guess we can do that. Good thing these bedroom doors can lock."

What? I shake my head. "You can't be serious. What if I need to take a piss or something?"

"I guess you should have thought about that before you pulled all that shit," snaps Isla.

"You can piss in that bottle," Ants points his chin at the

half-full bottle of vodka that I brought up with me, which I put on the bedside table.

"You can't lock me in here."

"You should be thankful we've decided to do only that," says Isla coldly.

That shuts me up.

Will grabs my door key from the bedside table, and they leave without another word, slamming the door behind them. I can hear them conversing in hushed whispers outside, then the rattling of the key in the door lets me know that they've locked me in.

I sit for a moment, stunned by the turn of events. I've forgotten just how dangerous they can be when separated from the rest of society. When they no longer feel like they're bound by the same rules.

I need to get out. Any one of them might change their minds at any moment about just keeping me locked up in here, might get too paranoid about me and decide I'm a problem they need to take care of once and for all.

When it's been quiet outside for another few minutes, I press my ear against the door. There's no sound outside at all, so maybe they've all gone to bed. I try the door, but it's indeed locked. This is ridiculous. Surely there must be a second key for this door. I look everywhere, but can't find another one.

Lightning flashes, and in that brief split second, the storm raging outside is on full display. The windows. It's the second floor, but even so, maybe I can tie the bedsheets together and make a rope or something, like people do in the movies. I inspect the floor-to-ceiling glass windows that make up the entire wall that faces the ocean…to discover that they don't open. I'm an animal trapped in a glass exhibit, like in one of those lousier zoos. Immediately, I start to feel like I can't breathe. I pace the room. If the windows don't even open, how the hell do people get fresh air in the rooms?

Oh, okay, there's an air vent in the ceiling. Fine. I check it out, but even if I could reach it, which I can't, it's way too small for anyone to squeeze through.

Sighing, I fling myself on the bed and stare at the ceiling. The memory of Ant's hands around my neck makes me shudder. If Sadie hadn't intervened, I don't doubt that the rest of them would have decided to handle me differently.

The way Will looked at me just now. How would he have chosen to eliminate me as a threat permanently? Hold my head underwater and claim I drowned while going for a swim? Push me off a cliff and say I fell? So many ways to kill someone and get away with murder, when there's no one watching. And murder is something that, as they've already proven, isn't beyond this group.

At least I have the rest of this bottle of vodka here. I guess there's nothing to do but drink it. Half a bottle is too much, but some will help me sleep. I take a big swig and swallow. The vodka burns its way down my throat and esophagus, makes its fiery path down to my stomach, a familiar and welcome friend.

I haven't been able to go to sleep without the aid of alcohol ever since Vera died.

I tried telling the police what really happened, but they wouldn't believe me. They closed the case files with Vera's death declared an accident, and Tom's as caused by sepsis. Such a shame I didn't manage to get a recording just now of them admitting to what really happened.

They're not going to get away with it, I promise Vera in my head as I take another swig. *I'll think of something else. I won't stop until I get them. Until they get what they deserve.*

Vera. When I close my eyes, I can see her: her long glossy hair that curled at the ends, a brown so deep it was almost black. Her white skin. Those large, haunted eyes. The way she laughed when I teased her about looking like a fairy-tale illustration of Snow White.

I promised her I'd take care of her, and I failed. I broke my promise. What good is a person who doesn't keep their promises?

If she came back as a ghost to haunt me, I wouldn't mind. At least I'd see her again.

I wish she would.

X X X

By the time my head is pleasantly foggy again, I've drunk a good part of the remaining vodka. My bladder is also full, so I relieve myself into the same bottle. I put the bottle in one corner of the room. I'm sure to have one hell of a hangover, and I wouldn't want to forget in the morning and drink my own pee.

Stumbling back to bed, I collapse on top of the bedspread and close my eyes. Oh, okay. I must be really drunk, because the room starts spinning around me.

I can't believe Emily is dead. Poor Em. She wasn't so bad. She and Sadie. Mostly harmless. Bad taste in boys though.

So weird to die like that. So horrible.

A sound outside the door. Footsteps?

Must have imagined them.

Rattling. My imagination? No. Faint, but there. Didn't imagine it. Door opening. Someone here. To let me out? I open my eyes, turn my head.

—Did you hear about the picture on the wall?

—Picture on the wall?

—Oh my god. So apparently there was this strange picture on the wall. Some painting. Really creepy.

—How was it creepy?

—Well, first of all, it was of the Donner Party. Some of them, anyway. You know, the pioneers who got stuck in snow and then…well, you know what they did.

—In that luxury celebrity house?

—Weird, right? But that's not even the creepiest part.

—Tell me.

—The figures in the picture were all crossed out with Xs, in red.

—What, like, with a red pen?

—A red marker. Well, some of them, at least.

—What? What do you mean?

—I heard that some were crossed out in blood.

—Jesus. That's so sick.

—Right?

—Were the figures in the picture supposed to be the six teens?

—That's the thing. There were eight people in the picture. Eight figures crossed out in red. But there were only six of them in that house.

ANT

"*No!*" I jerk awake, shouting.

A dream, it was just a dream. A nightmare. I shake my head. With the heavy quilt cover up to my neck, I'm drenched in sweat. I'm just in my boxers, but the sheets are so soaked it's like lying in a wet puddle.

Just a nightmare. I laugh out loud, wince at how shaky that laugh is. Because Emily can't be dead. I must have gone to bed shortly after dinner and dreamed it all. I sit up and swing my legs over the bed. If I get up and go downstairs, she'll be there already, preparing breakfast, being careful with what she eats as usual. She'd laugh at me. *Hey, why do you look so glum?*

Nothing, I'd tell her. *Just a stupid dream, that's all.*

Because it can't be real. It's not possible. There's no way we survived that other shit only for her to die like this.

Just a dream, I tell myself again, but I can't seem to make myself stand up.

The first time I met her, we were ten, and my family had just moved into the apartment across the hall from hers. My dad had gotten a promotion, but it meant we had to move from San Jose to Boston, and I was determined to hate everything about it, determined not to make any new friends, determined to be so miserable that my parents finally understood I would never be happy here and move us back. It was easy to convince myself I hated Boston; the shitty weather, the boring food, that *accent*.

The third day after we moved in, someone rang our doorbell. The petite woman with straight black hair cut in a chin-length bob introduced herself, explained that she lived just down the hall and wanted to welcome us to the building. She came with her daughter and a homemade chiffon cake.

My mom invited her in, cut the cake into slices. *I'm not eating that*, I said snottily. *It's green.*

My mom made it with real pandan, Emily said shyly as our moms laughed as if I'd said something funny.

Made with real panda??

Pandan. It's a leaf. It's delicious.

I don't know what the hell that is. It looks gross, I insisted.

It's yummy. You're being stupid, Emily said. Her mother chided her for calling me stupid, but she just stared at me, her eyes issuing a silent challenge. I crammed my slice into my mouth, and damn it, it really was delicious, all fragrant and fluffy. Emily smiled then, and I couldn't help it, I grinned back at her, my mouth still full of cake.

After that, even though we didn't go to the same school, we spent most of our afternoons together. I was an only child, and Emily's sister was too old and cool to play with her baby sister. We often rode to the park one block away on our bicycles, our moms making us promise to keep an eye on each other. And that's what we did. We looked out for each other.

I should have kept my eye on her last night. What am I going to tell Mrs. Chang when I see her?

We only just arrived last night. *Great start to the party weekend!*

I stare out the window. The storm has finally stopped, but the sea is still dark and choppy, the waves crashing angrily on the shore, the trees still bent under the wind. The horizon, however, is clear, the sun already high in the sky. I check my phone: 9:53 a.m. Are the others still sleeping, or am I the last to get up?

I have a sudden terrible urge to go to Emily's room to check if she's still there.

As I unlock my door, I consider going into Charlie's room before anyone can stop me. If it weren't for Sadie last night, he'd be dead by now. He's lucky I haven't killed him. In fact, I still might. He deserves to rot in hell.

After locking him in last night, we gathered back in the living room downstairs. I was too upset to sleep, and we needed to figure out what the hell was happening. Everybody looked pale, exhausted, and shell-shocked.

"You all can't really believe that he didn't have anything to do with Emily's death?" I demanded.

Will ran a hand through his hair. "I mean, either it was an accident, or someone murdered her."

"We already know he wants to hurt us," said Isla grimly.

Sadie, however, shook her head. "We have no proof it was him. The only thing we can do is tell the police what happened and let them investigate."

And so, he got to spend the night in his comfortable bed in his comfortable room, even as Emily's body lay cold and stiffening. He won't admit he killed Em, but I don't believe it was just an accident, even if the others do.

I wonder if he really did pee in the vodka bottle. Maybe he didn't; maybe he got so drunk he peed all over himself in bed. I luxuriate in that thought for a moment as I stand outside Emily's room, needing to go inside and dreading it at the same time. As I put my hand on the door handle, I notice the rolled-up towel sealing the bottom of the door.

The towel is the thing that finally breaks me out of my fantasy that she might not be dead after all—brings me crashing firmly back to reality—makes me yank my hand away from her door handle with a gasp. It wasn't a nightmare. My best friend—how odd that I finally realize that only when she's gone—is dead. She really did die last night.

My nerves break, and I stumble away from her door.

X X X X

After using the bathroom, I go downstairs to find Will and Sadie in the kitchen. Will is sitting on a high stool at the counter, tapping morosely at his phone, and Sadie is pulling various things out of the fridge and cabinets and putting them on the counter.

"Hey," says Will as I sink onto a stool beside him.

"Got any reception on that thing?"

"Nope, still nothing," he informs me.

I was afraid that they might try and talk about Emily, but thank god, they don't. They just stay silent, like me. Which is good, because I'm barely managing to keep it together. If we have to talk about Em, I might start crying.

"What are you making?" I ask Sadie.

"A Bloody Mary. I have a headache." She opens a carton of tomato juice. "I'm making Will one too. Want one?"

I've never tried one before, but… "Sure, why not?"

I watch as she pours tomato juice into three glasses, then adds a good amount of vodka into each of them, followed by dashes of some weird-looking sauces I've never heard of, salt, pepper, and lime juice.

"That's a Bloody Mary? More like a bloody disgusting," I say.

"It's the best thing for a hangover that I know of," she shoots back. "Cheers."

Sadie and Will down theirs. I take a sip of mine and gag.

"Not a big fan?" says Sadie, laughing a little.

"It tastes as foul as it looks. Where'd you learn to make it?"

"From watching our chef. My mom has him make it for her often enough."

I take another sip. It's still bad, but maybe a little less bad than the first sip. "The others still sleeping?"

"I guess."

We sink back into silence.

"Someone should check on Charlie," says Sadie quietly. "He might need to use the bathroom or something."

The very sound of his name sends rage curling through my limbs. "He'll shout for us if he needs to."

Sadie sighs. "Do you really think he had something to do with Emily's death?"

Fuck, there we go. I do *not* want to talk about this. I do *not* want to think about how her killer might be just sleeping off a hangover upstairs. Already, I feel the urge again to go up there and beat the shit out of him before he can protest his innocence.

Will tilts his head to one side. "If not him, then who?"

He sounds genuinely interested in the answer, as if he's open to considering other possibilities, which infuriates me further. Is he still trying to score with Sadie? Because I'm *not* interested in our dumb little bet anymore. "It was definitely him," I snap. "He drew on the picture; who else could it be? I don't buy that being-framed story for one second. And he outright *admitted* he wanted to destroy us."

Sadie shakes her head. "But he said he just wanted to—"

"He must have been so frustrated when he didn't manage to record us confessing that he took it out on Emily during dinner."

"Hmm," says Will after a while. "Maybe. Anyway, I'll be glad when I don't have to be anywhere near him anymore."

The stairs creak as Isla makes her way down to us. "Still no sign of the chef or housekeeper?" Her brows are drawn together as she slides onto a stool beside me.

Where *is* the staff? "Yeah, they should be here by now." The uneasiness I felt yesterday when we first arrived and didn't find anyone here creeps back into my guts, slithers around inside.

The others shift uncomfortably from foot to foot, and we all fall quiet. They're all weirded out too.

"Whatever. The boats are arriving soon, and I'm leaving as soon as they're here," mutters Sadie.

"I have such a headache." Isla rubs at her forehead; then her eyes brighten. "Oh, are those Bloody Marys? Could you make me one as well?"

"Sure." Sadie makes another one and sets it in front of Isla, who downs the entire thing almost in one go too. Her hand trembles slightly as she puts the glass back down, betraying how shaken she must also be feeling.

For the first time that I can remember, I don't really have an appetite. But, I guess to distract myself more than anything else, I head to the kitchen to see if there's anything to eat.

There's fancier stuff like pancake mixes and eggs and bacon

in the fridge, but I'm in no mood to cook, and neither is anyone else. There's an assortment of cereal in one pantry, so cereal it is. I grab a box, and a carton of milk from the fridge. This seems to suit the others as well because they all grab bowls and spoons and help themselves to the cereal too.

"Have you all already packed your bags?" says Will through a mouthful of cereal and milk.

"Yeah," says Sadie.

"Yup," says Isla.

"I didn't even unpack," I say.

"Guess the game is off then," murmurs Will.

Sadie frowns. "What game?"

"Nothing," Will and I say in unison, and Sadie and Isla exchange glances. I feel my face turn hot. Will can be such an ass, sometimes it truly shocks me. Like okay, it was my idea at first, but that was before Emily died. It's hard to imagine that just yesterday I was in the mood for stupid shit like that. The way I treated Emily last night. Guilt stabs at my guts, and I lose whatever appetite I had and fling my spoon down and ask, "What time are the boats arriving?"

"Um…" Sadie checks her phone. "My dad's PA said she arranged for the speedboats to depart New Bedford at ten, so they should be here in half an hour or so, thank god. I wish I could call her. Just to make sure they're coming, and on time."

"There's that box we found last night," I say.

"You think it's for the satellite?"

"No idea, but I'll see if I can fix it." I go back to the black box in the cabinet and try pressing the button again. It's the main button on the front of the box, so it has to be the power button. But again, nothing seems to happen. I pick up the remote for the TV and switch the TV on. It's still just a blank blue screen.

Isla comes up next to me, eyes fixed on her phone. "Still no Wi-Fi," she tells me. "Sadie needs to get a refund for this place, honestly. No staff, no TV or Wi-Fi. It's like the freaking Middle Ages here."

Cut off from civilization… And even though there's plenty of food, someone still died.

I suppress a shudder, focus on the box. When I grab it in the cabinet from its shelf, the reason why it's not working finally becomes clear. "You guys. I know why it's not working," I tell them grimly, and flip the box around so they can all see the cables sticking out at the back. "It looks like the cables have been cut."

ISLA

Ant is right. The cables have been cleanly cut through with wire cutters or something. A shock of terror jolts through me.

"What? Let me see," says Will. He and Sadie come over to join us. When they see it too, they freeze, blood draining out of their faces.

Will frowns. "There was no satellite right from the beginning. These cables were cut before we arrived." He looks around at each of us. "Which means it couldn't have been Charlie who cut these cables."

"Someone cut these cables to isolate us," I whisper, and shudder. I feel cold, shaky. "*Someone is out to get us.*"

"I knew something was wrong." Sadie's voice is high-pitched, on the verge of hysteria. "I knew it since we arrived yesterday and nobody was here."

"Let's all calm down. Maybe the last people to rent this place did this because they were pissed off by something. Like maybe they were pissed off by the nonexistent staff service," says Ant, even though uncertainty clouds his features. "This might not have anything to do with the painting being defaced, or Emily's death. I still think that was all Charlie."

I want to scream at him. "This can't be a coincidence! I'm telling you, someone is out to get us. And it's looking like it isn't Charlie!"

"Look. This should be fixable," says Will. His face is pale, but his jaw is set in a determined line. "We just have to rewire the cables back together."

I eye him skeptically. "Oh, and you know how to do that?"

"As a matter of fact, I do. I've seen an electrician do it before." He pushes Ant aside and searches the wall at the back of the cabinet with his fingers for a while. Then he shakes his head. "Weird. I can't find the ends of the cut cables. I might need to break the wall to pull them out." He knocks on it with his knuckles. "It's just plaster. All we need is a hammer or something."

"Wait," says Sadie. "That's destroying property. I'm the one renting this place. They're going to come after me for any damages."

"It's an emergency, isn't it?" I point out the obvious. "Someone is dead, and *something is wrong.*"

"Yeah, you're right." Sadie nods. "Break the wall, Will."

It doesn't seem likely that there'd be a hammer in any of the bedrooms or bathrooms upstairs, so that leaves just this area. We look on every shelf and drawer and cabinet, but there aren't any hammers or screwdrivers or any tools at all to be found.

"Can't we just use like a rolling pin or something to break the wall?" I ask. "You said it's just plaster."

"Oh! I think I saw a rolling pin in one of the drawers in the kitchen," says Sadie.

Sadie is back in a flash with the rolling pin. Armed with it, Will breaks the plaster at the back of the cabinet piece by piece until he's made a hole almost the size of the entire cabinet. But there aren't any cables to be seen. "I don't understand," he growls. "Where are the cables? They should be here."

Ant shakes his head grimly. "Whoever cut the cables must have yanked them out completely too."

We fall silent, trying to wrap our heads around this.

"You all," says Sadie. She's frowning as she checks the time on her phone. "The boats are going to be here soon. We need to get down to the pier. And I really think we should check on Charlie."

Ant rolls his eyes. "He's probably still sleeping it off after that bottle of vodka last night."

"In any case, I'm going to make sure he's awake and see if he needs anything before we head down to the pier," says Sadie. "Uh. Who has the key to his room?"

Will reaches into the pocket of his shorts and hands it to Sadie.

"I'll go with you," says Ant. "It's not safe for you to face him alone."

"I don't think he'd attack me, Ant," says Sadie. Still, she doesn't protest further as Ant follows her to the stairs.

I check the time on my phone. Fifteen minutes until the boats arrive and we're out of here.

"What is it?" says Ant.

I look up to see Sadie frozen in her tracks, in front of the canvas picture.

Sadie doesn't answer. A creeping sensation crawls over my skin as Will and I hurry over to see what she's looking at too, even though I already know—can already guess—even before I see it.

On the horrid picture of the Donner Party, a new, fourth red *X* has been drawn, crossing out yet another person in the picture.

"What the fuck," mutters Ant.

A horrible feeling of déjà vu settles over me. For a moment, the memory of Emily standing exactly where we're standing now comes back to me so strongly that it almost feels like her ghost is here with us.

"You can't tell me that Charlie drew this one too," whispers Sadie.

Ant shakes his head. "He must have managed to leave his room somehow. Gimme the key."

Sadie hands it to him, and he starts bounding up the stairs two steps at a time.

But even as the rest of us run up after him, I know that doesn't make sense. A fourth person has been crossed out, leaving four still standing. "If the four of us are here," I tell them shakily as we gather outside Charlie's room, "then the person who died must be…"

"No." Sadie's right hand flies to her mouth, and she shakes her head. Her eyes are shiny already with fresh tears.

"Maybe no one has died," says Will. "Maybe it's a warning? Of something that hasn't happened yet?"

His words sink in, making me feel even worse. "Like…that one of us is going to be next?"

But there's no need to speculate any further, because Ant has unlocked the door. He turns the handle and pushes it open.

For a moment, nobody moves. Nobody dares to step inside.

"Charlie?" Sadie calls in a shaky voice.

There is no answer.

"Oh, for fuck's sake, he's just still sleeping," says Ant as he marches in.

Charlie is lying in bed on his stomach. The room stinks horribly. What is that smell?

"Time to get up, dude," says Will loudly in a *he-can't-be-dead* voice. He grabs Charlie by the shoulder and shakes him roughly. "Boats will be here soon. Charlie? Oh, hell." Will lets go.

I see it the same time he does. The reason why it stinks so badly in here. Charlie's face is resting in a dried-up puddle of vomit on the bed.

"Oh my god." Sadie clamps a hand to her mouth and shakes her head. She looks like she's going to hurl too.

"Is he dead?" I whisper.

Ant steps forward, grabs Charlie's shoulder, the same one that Will just let go of, and shakes desperately. "Come on, dude! Wake up!"

Even though Ant is jostling him so hard, Charlie's head barely moves—he's as stiff as a mannequin—and he still doesn't wake. It's then that it really sinks in fully. Charlie will never wake again.

"Stop it. He's dead, can't you all see?" says Sadie, and she bursts into tears.

SADIE

Bile rises up my throat, and for a horrible split second, I think I might be about to be sick all over poor Charlie's corpse, add my own puke to the mess on the bed. Luckily, my body unfreezes, and I dash out of the room, make it into the nearest bathroom in time to be sick into the toilet bowl.

That stench in his room. They way they kept shaking him, as if they couldn't believe he wasn't just pranking them or something. The way his head flopped around, slapping into his dried puke.

I hurl again and again, until there's absolutely nothing left in my stomach, and still I continue to dry retch, the room seeming to swirl around me as I do.

Poor Charlie. Like Emily, he wasn't a bad person, not really. Not like the rest of us.

When I'm certain I'm not going to be sick anymore, I flush

the toilet. As I'm rinsing my mouth at the sink, someone comes to stand in the doorway. I turn to see Isla.

She hovers, swaying a little, looking shell-shocked. "We've turned down the temperature in his room too."

"I just can't believe it," I tell her.

She nods.

Will and Ant are waiting in the hallway just outside.

"Listen," Will says. "This is terrible, and I'm not trying to be callous or anything. But we can't miss the boats. Anyone who wants to get off this island needs to be at the pier, like, right now, or they're going to leave without us."

✗ ✗ ✗ ✗

We hurry down to the wooden pier with our bags. "We should have never set foot on this island," mutters Isla as she plonks her bag on the pier. She straightens up and looks around. "I don't see any boats. We can't have missed them; there's nobody here."

I pace the pier, staring into the distance. Although the storm from last night has broken, the sea is still restless, tumultuous, angry looking; the dark water broken by white foam and froth like that of some rabid animal; the sun hidden behind menacing black clouds.

There is no sign of any boats.

Will kicks a pebble into the water. "What is everyone going to think when they arrive and find out that two people are dead? We haven't even been here a full day."

Two of our friends are dead, and there might be someone after the rest of us, but the thing he's most concerned about is how this is going to make him look. He's side-eyeing me now, probably hoping my family's PR team will keep all of this hushed up again, like they did the last time.

But I don't have the mental or emotional capacity to care about what he's thinking or how he feels right now. "I just can't believe it." I wrap my arms around myself, but I'm still shivering violently, haven't stopped since we discovered Charlie. Poor Charlie, on that bed. "It looks like he died in his sleep, doesn't it?" I bite my lip. "Alcohol poisoning? We shouldn't have locked him in. If we hadn't locked him in, he wouldn't have drunk the entire bottle."

"He did drink a hell of a lot last night," mumbles Ant, frowning. "I've heard of incidents like this. Of people getting too drunk and then choking on their own vomit. But..."

"But the whole thing stinks." Isla sounds like she's going to burst into tears. "Another accident? And that new X on the painting? The cut cables?" She shakes her head. "We all know Charlie had a problem with alcohol. And yeah, I might buy the story that he drank himself to death, if all the other things hadn't happened. You can't tell me both their deaths were accidents, one after the other like that. Someone is out to get us." She looks around us, her arms wrapped tightly around herself. "Can't you all feel it? It's like we're being watched right now. *We need to get off this island.*"

Ant checks his phone, his brows furrowed anxiously. "They're late."

We stare at the distinctly boatless horizon, and at each other.

"It's only ten fifty-five," says Will, forced cheerfulness in his voice. "The forty-five minutes is just an estimation, right? And besides, who knows what time they actually left New Bedford?"

"Right. They could have been delayed," says Isla desperately.

Will lowers himself and sits down on the pier. Ant and Isla sit too, but I start pacing again.

"Could you stop pacing?" says Isla, her voice wobbly.

"Sorry," I say. I stop walking and direct my nervous energy to nibbling at my right thumb's nail bed instead.

Will says suddenly, "We need to talk about everything that's happened. Figure out what's going on."

"Do we have to? I mean, we're going to be out of here soon." Isla's eyes dart once again to the horizon.

"No, let's do it," I say. "It's not like we have anything else to do while waiting."

"Somebody cut the cables for the satellite, so we wouldn't be able to communicate with the outside world or call for help," says Will grimly. "*Before* we arrived."

"So it couldn't have been one of us, like we said," I say.

"Someone crossed out two people in that painting. Then Emily dies, and one more person got crossed out."

Isla shakes her head. "Her death could have been an accident, but I thought it was suspicious from the start."

"I never believed it was an accident. I told you all that someone killed her," says Ant. "I told all of you!"

"You thought it was Charlie. But it couldn't have been, could it?" I say.

"No, even though we found that red pen in his room," says Will grimly. "Because he died next, and another figure got crossed out."

"There must be someone else on the island. Someone who's out to get us. But *who?*" Isla's voice is high, almost hysterical.

My eyes meet Will's. "It has to all be related. The cut cables, the deaths, the crossed-out figures. It has to be the same person behind all of it."

We fall quiet as we look at each other, so the only sound is the lapping of the waves and an occasional squawk from some faraway, solitary seagull.

"I think I see them!" says Ant, scrambling up to his feet, making me jump.

"Where?" I say.

He points into the distance. I squint in that direction, but I don't see anything.

"I don't see anything," says Will.

After a little while, Ant droops. "I guess it was just the light glinting off the water. What time is it?"

Will checks his phone and frowns. "Eleven thirty."

"They'll be here," I say, nibbling at my nail bed again, trying to tamp down the hot ball of worry blooming in my gut.

"They'd better," says Isla, hugging herself. "They'd better."

"We need to focus on getting off this island. Then we can try to figure out who the hell is doing this," Will says decidedly.

I can sense everyone's mood growing darker and more anxious, if that's even possible, with each passing minute that the boats don't show. Will is lying on his back, staring up at the sky, his hands behind his head, his brows knitted together furiously as if he's in deep thought. Isla keeps checking her phone, as if she can manifest some cell service into existence. And Ant just stares morosely into the distance, trying to catch sight of those boats he was so convinced earlier that he'd seen. I sit down too, after Isla snaps at me again to stop pacing.

With nothing to do but wait, my mind keeps slipping back in time, back to the memories—reexamining them, probing them, picking at them like at a wound that isn't healing. I can't help it. Now that we're alone together again, it's hard not to think about what happened the last time we were alone together too…

"How the hell did he get all the way over here and fall in there?" says Ant.

"Why didn't you stick close to Lucas like he told us?" shouts Will into the crevasse.

"I…I…" stammers Tom.

"He didn't actually drift that far away," I say, feeling the need to come to his defense. He's already injured. He doesn't need them shouting at him too. "It's just really bad luck."

"Okay, but what the hell do we do now?" shouts Ant back.

We stare at each other, but nobody has any idea what to do, not even our guide.

"Is someone coming?" Even over the howling of the relentless wind,

I can hear the pain, fear, and panic in Tom's faint voice as it drifts out to us.

"We need to get him out," I say.

Lucas frowns. "That's not a good idea. If his leg is really broken, moving him will probably make his injury worse."

"But he's going to freeze to death down there," says Charlie.

"Actually, he's out of the wind, so he's probably less cold than us," says Ant. "But I'm going to turn into a Popsicle soon if we keep standing here."

"Right," says Lucas. He appears to have come to a decision. "We can't stay out here, this storm is just going to get worse. And you're right, we risk hypothermia the longer we stay." He gets his map out and checks it again. "Okay. There's a shelter not too far away. It's over there"—he turns and gestures into the distance; luckily, he's gesturing to the side, not up the mountain—"maybe around five hundred yards or so. We need to get him out of there, move him to the shelter. Once we're out of the storm, we can try calling for help again. Maybe there'll be cell service there."

That sounds like a good plan. Hope surges inside me, and I nod quickly.

"I don't see it," says Will.

"I know you can't see it right now with such lousy visibility, but it's there, trust me," says Lucas.

"Okay, but how do we get Tom out?" I ask. The crevasse looks like it might be around eight feet deep.

"Tom, can you stand?" shouts Lucas. "On the leg that isn't injured?"

Tom tries, but then he cries out in pain. "I can't move."

I can see why. One of his legs is twisted and trapped under the ski of the other one. The angle of it is grotesquely wrong, and I feel sick even looking at it. Tom must be in terrible pain, because I have no doubt that his leg must be horribly broken. It's a wonder he's even maintaining consciousness.

I feel like crying as our situation sinks fully in. I know we shouldn't be moving him, but Lucas's idea to take shelter is the only option we have. It's clear to everyone that if we stay out here, in this blizzard, in this extreme cold, all of us will be dead in a matter of hours.

Well, there is one more option, which is the rest of us ski down and just leave Tom here. But I know Lucas would never do that. I wouldn't either…or the others…I hope.

Will clears his throat. "Maybe we should head down. We can get help for Tom when we're back in town."

"What?" *says Tom, panic evident in his voice.* "Wait, you guys, don't leave me here."

"It's probably the smartest thing to do," *says Ant.*

"We can't just leave him here," *I say.* "Look at this storm. He'll be buried under all the snow. He'll freeze to death."

Lucas thinks about it. "We have to get Tom out of there," *says Lucas. He bends, starts detaching his shoes from his skis.* "Okay. I'm going to go down there," *he shouts at us.* "I'll get him on his feet. Then you guys can pull him out first, then me."

Yes, another good plan. Our guide is so calm, so smart. Thank god we have him.

Lucas removes his gloves and his ski shoes, which makes sense. His feet are going to be so cold, but ski shoes are much too big, clumsy, and dangerous for what he's about to do. Will and Charlie remove their gloves too and help hold on to Lucas as he steps in. They lower him carefully down to the bottom.

So far so good.

Then comes the hard part. Tom's scream is hard to listen to as Lucas tries to remove his feet from the hopelessly tangled mess of ski shoes and skis.

Finally, he succeeds in freeing Tom's legs. "You okay?" he shouts at Tom.

Tom doesn't reply. His face is so pale he looks like he's about to pass out, but he nods.

Lucas helps Tom to get up. When Tom is standing on his good leg, Will and Charlie reach in for him. They pull him out. It's not easy; his face scrapes along the rock as he's hauled up, and he makes little cries of pain the entire time. I'm shocked by how quickly our ski trip has turned into a nightmare, like that movie where that trapped hiker had to cut off his own arm.

Finally, miraculously, they manage to pull him all the way out and drop him on his back on the snow. Will and Charlie are exhausted from the effort, I can tell.

"Good work, guys. Okay, I'm ready to come out now. My feet are freezing," *says Lucas.*

"I can't do it," *says Will.* "My arms are burning, and I can't feel my hands. You do it, Ant."

Ant removes his gloves, gets down, and reaches in like Charlie does. They grab Lucas's hands and start pulling.

Lucas is halfway out when his hand slips from Charlie's. He dangles from one arm, clinging onto Ant for one split second; then Ant drops him too.

"Shit! I'm so sorry!" shouts Charlie.

There's no reply. I scramble back to the edge and look down. Lucas is sprawled at the bottom, his eyes closed. Blood gushes out from a gash on his forehead near the hairline; he must have banged his head on a sharp edge of a rock in the crevasse when they dropped him.

"Lucas? Are you okay?" shouts Will.

But Lucas doesn't reply. He doesn't budge.

"Why aren't they here?" says Isla, her voice snatching me back into the present. "I just want to get off this island." She's starting to cry.

I feel like crying too. Then again, that's how I usually feel all the time anyway.

"Maybe they're delayed because of the weather conditions." Will runs a hand nervously through his hair. "I mean it's calmed down now, but the sea was pretty choppy earlier on because of last night's storm."

"Yeah. Maybe," says Ant.

As we wait, my mind keeps going over everything that's happened ever since we arrived yesterday evening.

The way Emily died in my arms.

The way we found Charlie.

But before all that, the conversation between Emily and Isla that I stumbled onto. The way Isla was grabbing onto Emily's arm. *Keep your mouth shut, or I'll shut it for you*, was what I think I heard Isla tell her before I asked if everything was okay. That was a *threat*. What the hell was that about?

Screw it, I have to know.

"What did you mean last night, Isla," the words burst out of me, "when you told Emily, *Keep your mouth shut, or I'll shut it for you?*"

WILL

What? I look at Sadie, then back at Isla. Why the hell was Isla threatening Emily?

I'm not the only one who's surprised. Ant jerks, as if electrocuted, and whips his face around to look at the girls too.

Isla's eyes dart from Sadie, to me, to Ant. "I have no idea what you're talking about," she says, stone-faced.

Sadie stands up. "I heard you. After dinner, when the two of you were loading the dishwasher."

"You must have heard wrong." Isla stands up too, her eyes fixed on Sadie, a cold warning blazing in them, as if daring Sadie to contradict her.

But Sadie doesn't cower away this time like she usually does when confronted by Isla. "I don't think I did. You seemed angry. Stop pretending you weren't. You said, *Keep your mouth shut, or I'll shut it for you.* And Emily died minutes later, her throat literally shut so tight she couldn't breathe anymore."

I get up too, and so does Ant. I'm just trying to make sense of this, what Sadie is saying, but Ant is staring at Isla, his fists clenched tightly into balls. "Why did you tell Emily to keep her mouth shut? *Keep her mouth shut about what?*"

"Oh my god!" explodes Isla. "Will you all just… Calm down! It's none of your business! I didn't do anything to Emily, okay?"

She's lying, or hiding something. When she lies there are little tells. She'll look away from you, shift her gaze into the distance, for example, like the way she's doing now. Her right foot will start tapping the ground, like the way it's doing now, *tap tap tap*. She's probably not even aware she does these things. I cross my arms. "If you didn't do anything to her, then tell us why you were threatening her."

Isla's gaze shifts quickly between the three of us again. She looks like an animal trapped, calculating the best means of escape. But she must realize we're not going to let this drop, because she finally heaves an annoyed puff of air and rolls her eyes. "Oh, for crying out loud. It has literally nothing to do with any of you. And *she* threatened me *first* last night."

"What are you talking about?" I say.

"Emily threatened you? How?" says Sadie, looking as confused as I feel.

"Just spit it out," says Ant.

Isla crosses her arms and clenches her jaw. "I told you, it's none of your business."

What did Emily say to Isla? Emily hadn't spoken much, if at all, the entire evening. Except at dinner…something about Isla's Yale application essay…? I try furiously to recall her exact words… and then they come back to me. *Yale really loved your application essay, huh?* was what Emily said.

Why would Isla consider that a threat?

Unless…unless…

"Oh my god. Did you cheat on your application essay to Yale?" I ask.

Isla's reaction to my question is instantaneous. She blinks rapidly, and her face flushes a deep pink. Wow, I was right. *Bingo.*

"That's ridiculous." Isla has arranged her face into scornful derision, but she's not fooling anyone now.

I can't help but laugh. "Oh man. You totally did."

"Did you get Emily to write your essay for you?" asks Ant softly.

Isla uncrosses her arms and stamps her right foot. "Oh my god, you're all so annoying. Okay, fine. So what if I did? She was happy to do it."

Now that it's out, it makes perfect sense. Isla has always been a straight-A student, but so was Emily. Emily spent a lot of time studying, working for it. Isla, on the other hand, never seemed to have to study that much. So, she got Emily to do her application essay.

"That's why you sit next to Emily in all your classes together," says Sadie slowly, shaking her head. "How long have you been cheating off her?"

"Do you have to sound so judgy? She was happy to do it," Isla repeated sullenly. "It was a mutually beneficial agreement."

"Jesus. Is that how she got the money to help pay her dad's medical bills? Because you were paying her?" Ant shakes his head.

"Listen," says Isla, jutting out her jaw. "She wanted this. She charged me a lot for her help. I'm not rich like Sadie. I gave her three hundred a month, almost all of what I earn from babysitting and dog walking. She benefited from our arrangement. But this is all none of your business. And if you breathe a word of this to anyone else, I'll—"

"You'll what, Isla?" says Ant. His entire body is tense, quivering like an arrow notched in a bow. He looks like he's on the verge of exploding and taking down everyone with him. "Shut us up forever, like you did Emily?"

Isla throws her head back and laughs. "Are you seriously accusing me of murdering Emily?"

"Did you?" says Ant softly.

The problem, as we all know, is that she's perfectly capable of murder.

Like the rest of us, I guess.

Man, it's really not looking too good for Isla, the way it went down. Of all the stuff that Emily could have threatened Isla about, she chose to threaten her about Yale—the one thing in Isla's life that she holds important, that she wants most of all—and the next thing you know, *boom*, Emily drops dead.

Isla's face is bright red, her blond curls bouncing around on her shoulders as she shakes her head furiously. "I told you, I didn't do anything to Emily."

"She threatened to spill your secret—threatened your admission into Yale—and then she died," growls Ant. "I'm really, really finding it hard to believe you right now, Isla."

I put a hand on Ant's shoulder, but he shrugs it off.

He's always had a temper, but would he really attack a girl?

If the girl in question murdered Emily—then I think, yes, he would.

Isla must realize the same thing because she takes a step back away from him. "I thought we already worked it out that there's someone else here who's behind all this. Not one of us. The person who cut the cables."

"I don't know. Maybe somebody else cut the cables for some reason. And then you saw your chance to get rid of someone who's a threat to you. Maybe the two things aren't related," says Ant.

Isla takes a deep breath and raises her hands palms up. "Look, how could I have killed her? I wasn't even sitting anywhere near her during dinner! How could I have—"

"You got out the salt," says Sadie.

"What?" says Isla.

"For the tequila shots. You got out the salt."

"Yeah? And then what? Are you accusing me of spiking the salt with grated cheese?" A high-pitched laugh bursts out of Isla. "That's ridiculous. In that case…" She points at me. "You were the one pouring out the shots; you could have spiked the tequila with cheese." Her finger swivels to point at Ant. "You were the one setting up the shot glasses; you could have put it in then. And you." She points at Sadie. "You could have put it on the lime wedges."

"Yes, but none of the rest of us had a motive," I point out. "Unlike you."

She turns to look at me. Hurt flashes on her face for a moment, and the light in her eyes seem to go out. *You too? I thought you were on my side*, her eyes seem to say.

I feel a small twinge of guilt…and doubt.

"I think the sun is frying your brains," she finally sputters. "What about Charlie then? How could I have killed *him*?"

Silence, and then Sadie says in a low voice, "How *did* Charlie die? We don't even know for sure."

"Well, I guess we should have looked more closely," says Isla.

She's right; we should have when we found him. Now all we can do is speculate. But we had no time just now; we had to rush down here or miss the boats. The boats that don't ever seem to be coming…and all we can do right now is keep waiting.

X X X X

The boats are still not here.

I check the time on my phone again: 1:34 p.m. We've been waiting here for almost three hours. I'm hot, I'm thirsty, and I need to piss.

Ant shifts from foot to foot, looking uncomfortable, then

strides to stand on the edge of the pier with his back facing us. "Sorry, I have to relieve myself. Look away, ladies."

Sadie and Isla turn away from him quickly as Ant unzips his shorts and starts peeing over the side of the pier into the sea.

"Me too." I face the other side and relieve myself too. *Finally.* I thought I was going to burst.

After we zip up, the girls turn back around.

"I need to go too," says Isla, her face pink, frustration written clearly on it.

Sadie sighs. "Me too. And I'm so thirsty. This is ridiculous. We've been waiting for *three hours*."

I know what everyone's really thinking though. What no one is saying. What no one wants to hear. "We can't stand here all day," I say slowly. "I think it's clear by now that the boats aren't coming."

Isla shakes her head. "We can't know that for sure. Didn't you say just now that the delay must have been due to the rough sea after the storm?"

Sadie nods. "Yeah, we don't know for sure that any of this isn't just bad luck. The boats could arrive at any moment, and I don't want to run the risk of missing them."

"Maybe you can all wait here while I head back to the house for a while," says Isla. "I just need to use the bathroom very quickly. And get some water. I'll bring water back for you all. The door isn't locked, right?"

"No. I left the keys on the kitchen counter," I tell her.

"All alone?" says Ant incredulously. "Everyone knows from

watching horror movies that you don't separate from the group. That's how you get yourself killed."

Isla blanches at his words.

"I'll go with you," says Sadie. "I need to use the bathroom too."

Isla nods, and the girls hurry off.

Ant kicks another pebble on the pier into the sea, then eyes me. "You really don't think the boats are coming, huh?"

"I mean, there's always hope. A huge delay due to the bad weather earlier on. Some other kind of problem. But they were supposed to be here three hours ago, bro. *Three hours.*"

He sighs. "Yeah, I don't think they're coming either." He looks up at the sky. "So where does that leave us?"

Good question. With no way off the island, no means of communication, two dead bodies in the only house…and an unknown killer who possibly wants us all dead. *We're still in danger.* The thought sends icy fingers down my back. "You've got a point with the horror movie thing. Maybe the four of us should stick together."

"Yeah. We should head back to the house too. I think I'm starting to get heatstroke from waiting here. We should look at Charlie more closely anyway. See if we can figure out what he died from."

But what if they finally come while we're back up at the house? They won't know to wait for us. They'll just drop off the others and leave. *Without Emily and Charlie.*

An idea strikes me. "Maybe we can leave a note here or something for the boats in case they come."

We tear a blank page from the book I brought with me—that I thought I might finally get around to reading—and with a pen scrounged up from Ant's bag, I scrawl on it:

> We want a ride back on the boats
> DO NOT LEAVE WITHOUT US
> We're in the house, please come get us
>
> Sadie, Will, Isla & Ant

We gather four small rocks and use them to pin the paper down at the end of the pier's walkway, so anyone arriving will see it as soon as they step onto the pier.

I square my shoulders. "Alright. Let's go join the girls and look at Charlie again."

ANT

The mansion comes gradually into sight—a glass and metal beast hunkered on the hill, cold, patient, watching, waiting—as we climb back up the sloping ground to it.

It's funny how glad I was to see it the first time when we first arrived yesterday, back when I still thought it was going to be the setting for a fun, debauchery-filled weekend. Because it's lost all its appeal now. Now, all I can see when I look at it is Emily lying dead on the cold tile floor inside.

"Imagine if the staff is finally here, waiting for us when we go in," I say.

Will shudders. "Not funny."

It's not a particularly funny joke, no. Imagine if some creepy valet suddenly popped up and whispered *surprise*.

Man, I gotta stop watching all those horror movies.

Isla and Sadie are in the kitchen, getting bottles of water out from a pantry.

"Have the boats finally come?" Sadie says excitedly.

"No," says Will.

Isla frowns. "Then why are you here? We need you to keep an eye out for the boats. I told you I'd get water for everyone."

"If we waited out there any longer, we'd get heatstroke," I say.

Understanding dawns on Sadie's face. "You don't think the boats are coming, do you?"

Will and I shake our heads. "But we left a note on the pier telling them to come get us here because we want to leave, in case they do."

"Okay. I guess that works," says Sadie dejectedly.

"Also, I think we should look more closely at Charlie and try to work out what happened," says Will. "Have you two gone upstairs?"

Isla shakes her head. "No. We used the bathroom, and then you guys came as we were getting water."

There are two opened half-full bottles of water on the counter, which must be Isla's and Sadie's. I grab a new bottle and chug almost all the water inside, and so does Will. God, that feels so much better. I was so *thirsty*.

"Well, should we head up?" says Will.

"No time like the present," says Isla thinly.

We trudge upstairs to Charlie's room. It's hard to enter when you know there's a dead body inside waiting for you. The others hesitate outside the door too.

"The hell with this," mutters Will as he reaches for the door handle.

He barges in, as if his bravado can dispel the eeriness. It's so cold in here—just like in Emily's room—that goose bumps spring up immediately on my flesh. That sour, rotting stench of vomit hits me again, and I gag. I pull up my T-shirt to cover my nose. The others do the same.

Reluctantly, we venture closer, crowding around the bed. Charlie's face is pallid and slack, the color of his skin gone an ashy gray like a zombie in a movie. To my relief, he's lying in the exact same position we left him. I mean, of course he is; I don't know why he wouldn't be, right?

I find that my anger at him is gone, and other emotions finally flood in. I swallow, but I can't get rid of the lump that's risen in my throat.

He used to be so fun, loved a good joke too. Before everything happened. Before Vera died, and he stopped hanging out with us. With a pang, I remember suddenly how he had my back freshman year, when I pranked our history teacher and almost got caught. If he hadn't come running and told me what he overheard about Mr. Finlay checking everyone's lockers, I wouldn't have been able to get rid of all the incriminating evidence in mine in time.

And I almost strangled him last night. Heat rises in my face, and I can't bear to look at him anymore, can't look at the bruises around his neck.

No, I'm not sure anymore that it was Charlie who killed Emily.

Not after the discovery of the cut cables, and especially not after what Sadie exposed about Isla threatening Emily just before she died. I side-eye Isla, who is pulling a face as she stares at Charlie.

Thinking about yesterday evening sends a torrent of guilt flooding through me again. I was so self-absorbed—fantasizing about what I'd do to Isla when I got into her bed—I didn't even pick up on that weird exchange between Emily and Isla last night.

How long was Isla using Emily? And now that she's valedictorian, now that she's gotten into Yale and we've all graduated, and she doesn't have any use for Emily anymore—now that Emily is a loose thread, a threat—Emily dies. How very convenient for Isla.

The more I think about it, the more guilty Isla looks. She really latched on to the fact that Emily was allergic to dairy in a big way last night, asking those probing questions. Seeing the grated cheese on the table, she might have come up with her murderous plan right there and then.

Red-hot rage simmers in me. Last night, I fantasized about her. Now, I'm fantasizing about her in a very different way. What I want to do now is wrap my hands around that slim white neck and squeeze the shit out of it.

I promise I'll find out who did this to you, Em, I swear silently. *And I won't let them get away with it.*

As if sensing my murderous thoughts, Isla glances uneasily at me, then shifts a little farther away from me.

"Should we flip him over?" says Sadie, yanking me back to the present.

Isla blanches. "I don't want to touch him."

"If it isn't alcohol poisoning, how would we know what the cause of death is? It's not like we're forensic experts or something," I point out.

Will gingerly pulls down the quilt covering Charlie. Charlie is curled up in a ball in the fetal position, looking strangely vulnerable, with his knees up to his chest and his hands wrapped around his legs. The lump in my throat returns, threatening to choke me. Even though Charlie's been so self-destructive for the past year and a half, it's still horrible he's come to this end. *God, it's so fucking hard to look at him.* I have to force myself not to look away.

"Well, there's no blood or any visible wounds. No sign of a fight," says Will, as if he's in CSI or something. "Other than the bruises on his neck, and that was just Ant," he adds, eyeing me.

"Could Ant have injured him worse than we thought?" says Isla. "Maybe damaged his windpipe or something? Bad enough so he died in the night?"

No. *No.* Guilt surges in me. Could I have? Could it really be my fault? "But what about the vomit?" I say desperately. "It looks like he got sick, then died because he choked on his vomit." *Why are all exorcists alcoholics? Because they can't handle their spirits.* Oh man, I'm beginning to lose it. I need to get out.

"It does look like he died because of alcohol poisoning, or he choked on his vomit," says Isla.

I nod quickly. "That happened to Jimi Hendrix. That's how he died, choking on his own vomit."

"Who's Jimi Hendrix?" says Isla. I open my mouth to reply, but she cuts me off with a wave of her hand. "Either way, I dunno. It doesn't look like anyone murdered him. He probably just drank himself to death. Please, can we leave now? It's awful in here," she whispers.

I don't blame her for wanting to get out. I can feel the stench of his vomit seeping into my hair and the pores of my skin. I desperately want a shower.

"Wait." Sadie points to the dried-up puddle of vomit. "What's that?"

I look more closely. She's right; there's something small and white. It looks half dissolved. "What is it?" I ask.

"It's…a…pill?" says Will.

Well, damn. "So not only did he become an alcoholic; he was on drugs too."

"Was he?" Sadie's brow creases. "I don't think I've ever seen him take anything other than booze."

I shake my head. "He was obviously more discreet with the drugs than with his booze. But this makes sense. It's why he died. Whatever drug he was taking plus the alcohol caused an overdose."

But Will is also frowning. "Wait. Sadie, didn't you say you misplaced your Valium?"

"Misplaced… Someone took it, more likely," she grumbles, eyeing us. And then she puts two and two together, and her eyes widen. "You think this is my Valium?"

"Well, does it look like it?" says Will.

She frowns and squints at it, although she's careful not to get too close to it, of course. "I...I can't tell. Not half digested like this. I mean...it's also white, so...it could be?"

"Okay. He could have stolen your Valium, took it to get even higher. And then he ODed accidentally," says Isla slowly. "Or this isn't your Valium at all, and he was murdered by the same person who killed Emily."

Sadie frowns. "You mean, like, that person forced him to down those pills and OD? But how? How did they get in his room? We locked the door, and Will had the key."

Will nods. "It was in my jeans pocket last night. And this morning I transferred it to my shorts pocket. But yeah, I had it all night."

"Did you lock *your* room?" says Isla.

Will's features twist in shock, and he goes pale. "I...I don't know. I mean I think so. But I'm not... I can't swear on it."

"Dude," I say. "You gotta keep your door locked. Someone must have gone in your room last night and taken the key."

"Then they could have killed me too. So why didn't they?" snaps Will.

"This all seems so..." Isla shakes her head. "Wouldn't it have been easier for the killer to just, I dunno, stab Charlie or something, than to force him to swallow enough pills and then wait for him to OD?"

She has a point. "Maybe we're just being paranoid," I say. "Maybe Charlie stole Sadie's pills and accidentally ODed by himself. Maybe nobody killed him after all. Em's death could have been an accident too."

"But what about that painting? And the cut cables?" says Sadie.

Silence falls in the room. It seems to be even colder than when we first entered, and my skin is crawling with goose bumps.

"Listen," says Isla quietly. "Can we continue this discussion outside? Please?"

Will and I pull the blanket up to cover Charlie completely. It just seems like the least we could do. Outside, though, my relief is short-lived, because I can still smell the puke hanging around me like some noxious cloud.

"I'm so hungry," says Isla. "We didn't have a chance to grab lunch."

"We should eat something," says Will. "I'm starving too."

My stomach rumbles, as if pitching in to agree. I know it may seem weird to be hungry and want to eat considering we were just in a room full of puke and a corpse, but what can I say? It's been hours since breakfast, and I don't like being hungry.

"Good idea," says Isla.

"Shouldn't we keep a lookout for the speedboats in case they arrive?" says Sadie.

Isla shrugs. "We've already left a note."

"Yeah. Maybe it isn't necessary," says Will, his voice flat.

"If the boats don't come today, it means the sixteen others aren't coming at all," whispers Isla.

Chills run down my spine. Why aren't the others coming? What's happening back there?

Just us, alone. And once again, we're dying one by one…

Sadie's lower lip trembles, but she squares her shoulders. "Well, thank god Jeremy's coming for us with the chopper tomorrow."

"Is he though?" mutters Will, and another chill runs down my spine.

Sadie's head jerks up to look at him. "What do you mean?" she asks, looking as alarmed as I feel.

"The boats were supposed to arrive with the others, and they aren't here," says Will slowly. "So why are you so sure the helicopter will be here tomorrow?"

Sadie shakes her head. "It was Elle who arranged for the boats—"

"Supposedly," mutters Isla.

"—and maybe she screwed up," continues Sadie, ignoring her, "or maybe it was the bad sea conditions, like we said. But Jeremy confirmed personally to me that he's coming, so he's coming. You all heard him yesterday. And unlike Elle, Jeremy has been our pilot for six years. So yeah, I trust him."

"Okay, fine," says Will. "So, even if the boats don't show up, all we have to do is just wait it out till tomorrow."

With two dead and decomposing—slowly, luckily, thanks to the air-conditioning—bodies in the house with us. And maybe with someone trying to kill us. Someone hiding in the shadows…

I shudder, shove the thought out of my mind, and try to sound upbeat. "So…who's gonna cook?"

"Can you guys take care of it?" Isla shakes her head, grimacing. "I really need to take a quick shower first. I just can't eat while smelling like puke."

"Actually, I wouldn't mind a shower first too," I say. "After being in that room. The smell does tend to cling to you."

Sadie brings a lock of her hair to her face, sniffs it, and wrinkles her nose.

Will sighs. "Fine. You all go take your showers. I'll see what I can whip up."

That surprises me. Since when can Will cook? Maybe he's feeling inspired after seeing Charlie cooking yesterday.

"Are you sure?" asks Sadie. "I could help…"

"Nah, it's okay. I can shower after eating."

"But…is it a good idea for you to be alone downstairs?" continues Sadie uncertainly.

"In the kitchen, with all those knives at my disposal?" Will snorts. "I'll be fine. I'll make sure the front door's locked."

"Thanks, Will," says Isla.

"Sadie's a vegetarian," says Will. "Anyone else have any other dietary restrictions I should know about? Any allergies?"

Everyone shakes their head.

"Alright, I'll take care of lunch. Just make sure you all lock your doors," adds Will before he heads downstairs. "Remember, we still haven't figured out who drew on the picture."

—Apparently, there were two other kids from that school who died a few years ago.

—How did they die?

—Trapped in an avalanche in British Columbia. And get this: they were trapped there with these six teens. The ones on the island.

—The two who died in the avalanche were there with these same kids?

—Yeah. They were a party of eight on that ski trip.

—So, this picture on the wall...you're saying these deaths are somehow related to the previous incident? Like two died and the rest escaped, but death came for them in the end? That's so Final Destination.

—Creepy, right?

ISLA

First that horrible ski trip, now this.

It's like Death is following us, picking us off one by one. *Who's going to be next?*

I shake my head, try to shake away all these morbid thoughts. Shake away the image of poor Charlie on that bed. It's no good; it doesn't help that I can still smell his vomit. I so can't wait to wash it off.

Did someone kill him, or was it really an accident? Our fault he died, because we locked him in his room?

No. I can't start doing this. We're all responsible for our own choices, and Charlie was the one who chose to drink that much *and* pop that Valium. Possibly. Jesus, talk about poor choices.

But…who drew on that painting?

Maybe it isn't as sinister as that. Maybe Emily and Charlie's deaths were accidents—they just seem so *accidental*—and someone took the opportunity to cross off more figures in the painting just to mess with our heads.

I desperately want to believe this. But the more I think about it, the more I don't know what to think. Also, it's hard to think when I'm so hungry. First steps first. I need to wash off the stench of this vomit. A hot shower will clear my head. Wash away the sight of Charlie on that bed.

Just the very sight of the bathroom soothes my sun-beaten head. It has one of those big fancy bathtubs like those luxury hotels, right next to the glass wall overlooking the sea. There are even bath bombs in rainbow sorbet colors lined up on a rectangular wooden tray, and an essential oil–scented, hand-poured soy wax candle that must have cost a fortune. Staring at them, I can almost forget all the horrible things that have happened since we arrived. Maybe I should take a bath instead. I do love bath bombs and candles, and these ones are so luxurious. I could never afford them at home. Maybe a good soak will help even more than a shower to clear my head.

As I turn on the faucet to start filling the bath, I can't help but remember the last time I was in one. It was at that hotel, and Will joined me in the tub. Something twists in my chest again. I came here hoping we might get back together, but I'm beginning to realize that it may not be what I want anymore. Not after the way he dumped me like that. Also, even more of my friends dying has put things sharply into perspective. There are more important things in life than pining over somebody who doesn't want me back. I need to have more self-respect. I can't be a doormat like my mother.

When the tub is almost full, I test the temperature of the water to make sure it's good—hot enough to soothe, but not scalding. There's a small box of matches beside the candle. I light it and pick out a bath bomb. Even just doing all this is making me feel less stressed already. I peel off my tank top…but as I start to pull down my skirt, I hesitate.

Whichever celeb owns this place must be an exhibitionist. With the entire wall made of glass like this, anyone looking in from the outside will be able to see me. And there aren't even curtains or shutters that I can draw to block out the outside while I undress and get in the tub.

What if there really is a crazed killer hiding on the island somewhere?

They could be watching me right this very moment.

I suppress a shiver as I peer outside. I don't see anyone, but maybe I should forget about taking a bath and just get in the shower. The shower is back in the corner, away from the glass wall, and the huge tub partially hides it from anyone who might be looking in.

But then, I start to get mad. This weekend was supposed to be so freaking amazing, but it's turned out to be so horrible, and now I'm too afraid to even take a bath? Screw this. I'm tougher than this. I refuse to be so freaked out that I can't even take a damn *bath*.

Defiantly, I strip off completely, lower myself into the steaming hot water, and drop the bath bomb in.

The fizzing, steaming water rises around my face. It smells heavenly. I close my eyes, hold my breath, and slowly sink lower and lower, until my head is completely submerged in this warm, amniotic pool, shutting out the awful world outside, where bad things just keep happening. And the one person who I thought would understand, would be by my side through it all, isn't even mine anymore.

I bob up and suck in a deep breath through my mouth, wipe away the bathwater (tears?) from my face. *Forget about him*, I tell myself fiercely. *He had everything, and he chose to throw it all away. That jerk doesn't deserve someone like me.* But the ache in my chest continues, lingers. I can't believe that he treated me like this, when I've been nothing but the perfect girlfriend to him.

Stop thinking about him!

And don't think about what's happened.

Like the Valium.

And how Charlie's death might be partially my fault.

Thank god nobody else saw me scoop up Sadie's little bottle of pills when it fell out of her pocket when we were climbing up to the house. As if it wasn't bad enough that Sadie basically accused me just now, on the pier, of killing Emily. If she knew I was the one who took her Valium, she would have screamed bloody murder, and I wouldn't even have had the chance to defend myself.

I only took it as a joke. I was going to return it to her eventually.

And, well, fine, I wanted to try some. It was supposed to be a party weekend, right? Is it so wrong to want to get a little high?

I only tried one. When we were all unpacking in our rooms before dinner, I popped one, and whew! Coupled with the champagne, it got me high, alright. I blame it for making me flirt back with Ant over dinner.

But when I got back to my room later that night, it was gone from the bedside drawer where I could have sworn I left it.

So Charlie was the one who took it. He must have seen me pocket it and swiped it from my room after I went back downstairs. I didn't lock my door. He went downstairs after me, so he could have totally snuck into my room and stolen it.

He must have taken more than one last night, and with all that vodka he was guzzling...no wonder he ODed. And yes, his actions were his own choices. So why is there still this little voice inside that keeps saying, *If you hadn't left Sadie's pills so carelessly in your room, Charlie wouldn't have been able to swipe them and die?*

But, no. *No.* He died horribly, but his death wasn't my fault. Just like how Emily's horrible death wasn't my fault either. And I hate to think it, but honestly, with such a ridiculously serious allergy, it was also probably just a matter of time before she accidentally consumed some dairy and died anyway.

Did I remember to lock the door just now? Yes, I'm pretty sure I did.

I sink lower into the bath again, but this time stop when my face is just above the surface. The warm water glides over my skin, and I close my eyes. *Think calm thoughts. Think relaxing thoughts.*

Don't think about the two dead bodies in the house.

No, stop!

It's not like I can do anything to help them, so I push them out of my mind and focus my thoughts on going home tomorrow. And after that, on how bright my future is going to be when I start college. *Yale.* Thinking about Yale always makes me happy, makes little bubbles of happiness in my tummy, like these bubbles in the bath. I fought so hard for it, harder than anyone could ever know, and I deserve this happiness. Unlike my mother, I will get what I deserve.

A shadow falls over my closed eyelids.

I open my eyes, blink stupidly at the person standing over me.

I must have forgotten to lock the door, I manage to think before all thoughts are shoved out of my head.

SADIE

It isn't a good idea to separate from the group. Like Ant said, everyone knows from watching horror movies that when someone heads off alone, it's a sure sign they're getting themselves killed next. I almost repeated it, standing there in the hallway just now—but I didn't want them to laugh at me for being silly, so I held my tongue when Will insisted he'd be fine downstairs. Besides, Isla and Ant were right; the slight but unmistakable stench of vomit lingers on my hair and clothes, and I want to take a shower too.

Now, back in my room, I lock my door—making sure to check that it's locked before heading over to the glass wall to check the pier.

It's definitely too far to make out the note they say they left on the pier walkway. But from here, on the third floor, I should be able to see if anyone arrives, and there's no one. No boats.

In the bathroom—I'm so glad that I insisted on having my own private bathroom—I strip off quickly and jump in the shower. The water is hot—heated by solar panels, I remember Ant saying.

It strikes me suddenly that he seems to know an awful lot about this house and this island. That he did a lot of research. Why? *Does he know more than he's letting on?* I wonder, before I push away the thought. God, I'm becoming paranoid.

The hot water feels good beating down on me, like a warm, cleansing rain.

If only it could also wash away everything that's happened.

When I close my eyes, Emily's and Charlie's faces join Vera's and Tom's faces in my head, new ghosts to haunt me. They float in the dark behind my eyes, swirl like snowflakes in a terrible storm. The storm that rose out of nowhere…

Emily, Isla, and Vera have climbed up to join us.

"What's going on?" cries Vera. "Is Tom okay?"

"I'm okay," says Tom where he's sitting on the snow, his weak voice barely audible above the angry wailing of the wind.

"Where's Lucas?" shouts Isla.

Nobody answers her. None of us have the words. The girls take us in, process the way we're grouped around something. They come nearer, notice the crevasse. Look in and see Lucas. "Oh my god," says Isla. "What happened?"

"Charlie dropped him," says Ant.

"You dropped our guide?" says Isla. "Jesus, Charlie!"

Charlie looks like he might cry. "It wasn't like I did it on purpose!"

"Is he...is he dead?" says Emily.

"I don't think so. We need to get him out," I say, an echo of the words I just said a few minutes ago. "Someone needs to go down there and check if he's okay. Quickly."

"I'll go," says Charlie. He removes his gloves again and his ski shoes. Will and Ant don't say anything, don't have any objection to that.

They help Charlie, who gets down there without any mishap. I hold my breath as he bends over Lucas, checks his breathing. He checks for a long time. I watch as his shoulders slump, and he punches the ground. When he straightens and raises his face to us, I know even before he speaks. "He's not breathing."

Vera cries out incoherently, and I sink into the snow on my knees. Lucas is dead. How is this possible? How could this all have happened? We didn't really know him, but he seemed like a nice guy. And now he's dead. It's senseless, horrible.

But the emotion that grips me most is fear. We're stuck on a mountain in a foreign country, a blizzard raging around us, and our guide is dead. How are we going to make it out of here?

"Get me out of here," Charlie calls to Will and Ant. "And don't drop me."

"We won't," Will and Ant say together.

Before they pull Charlie out, he pauses as if a thought strikes him. He retrieves Tom's skis and ski shoes, and hands them up to Will and Ant first. Then they pull him out, luckily without a hitch this time.

"This is so fucked up," shouts Isla. "What are we going to do?"

"Lucas said there's a shelter over there, around five hundred yards away," says Will. "We should get out of the storm. We can figure out what to do later."

"We can't just leave his body here," says Emily, horrified.

Ant takes her by the shoulders. "We have to. The rescue team will come back for his body later."

"Okay, but how the hell are we going to get Tom there?" says Isla.

It's a good question. The shelter isn't uphill, so if it weren't for Tom, we could all glide there relatively effortlessly on our skis, use our ski poles to propel ourselves along. Obviously, Tom can't do that now.

"Someone will have to pull him," says Charlie.

"Pull him?" Isla laughs, the shrill sound mixing and mingling with the wind's shrieks. "How?"

"It's not that far. He can stand on his good leg," I say. "If he can balance on one ski, another person can pull him along with a pole."

Isla shakes her head skeptically, and Ant starts to say, "I don't think—" but Tom says, "I can try."

Everyone exchanges looks. Then Will says, "I suppose it has to be one of us guys again."

"I can pull him," I say.

Charlie shakes his head. "I'll pull him. You can stay beside him and hold on to him, make sure he doesn't fall over."

I nod.

"I'll help too," says Emily. "But wait. What if we drag Tom all the way there, and there isn't even a shelter?"

"Yeah. Maybe someone should go there first and make sure," says Ant.

"I'm the best skier. I'll go," says Will. *"Hang tight, I'll be right back."*

He clips his skis back on and heads off in the direction Lucas indicated. Emily and I get Tom's ski shoe on his good leg, and Charlie pitches in to help him up and clip on his ski. Emily and I stand on both sides of Tom, prop his arms around our shoulders. This close, I can see exactly how pale his face is. Despite the freezing wind, sweat beads his upper lip and forehead, making his hair cling to his face. He's breathing shallowly. Even though he's trying to put on a brave front, he must be in so much pain.

"Don't worry," I tell him. *"It's going to be okay."* Tom gives me a strained smile and squeezes my shoulder.

A minute goes by, and then another. Tom is shivering and so am I, my teeth chattering in my head. A frightening thought creeps in—What if Will doesn't return?—*but I push it away.*

I have no idea how long we stand here, waiting for Will. In this relentless subzero hell, the seconds crawl agonizingly by. More bad thoughts are growing in my head. I'm just thinking, Something is wrong, he should be back by now, something is very, very wrong, *when there! I see Will in the distance. His figure grows larger quickly as he glides back to us on the snow. He has a big grin on his face. My relief is so immense, my knees almost buckle.*

"It's there! I found it! Follow me!" *he shouts, before turning around and heading back.*

Isla, Ant, and Vera follow after him quickly. Charlie gets in front of Tom and holds out one of his poles. Tom grabs it with his right hand, keeping his left arm around my shoulder. Emily stays by Tom's right side, one hand under his right elbow to help keep him steady.

Slowly, the four of us begin to advance. Only five hundred yards to go. Five hundred yards, and we'll be safe.

Despite the hot water beating down on me, I shiver.

It's all too easy to forget, but I have to remember to be careful around the rest of them. Because sometimes I start to forget, and that's not safe. Not when I'm stranded alone with them on this island.

Remember what they did. Remember what they're capable of doing.

I towel dry and dress quickly, and head back down to the kitchen.

WILL

"Shouldn't we wait for the girls?" Ant eyes the food that I've placed on the counter hungrily—a loaf of whole grain bread, a packet of sliced ham, a packet of Swiss cheese, a jar of mayonnaise, a tomato and an avocado for Sadie, and cans of soda.

I reach for the bread and ham. "You can wait if you want, but I'm gonna start. I'm starving. I don't know about Sadie, but Isla always takes her own sweet time in the shower."

"Oh yeah, good point. Girls always take such a long time."

By the time Sadie joins us five minutes later, I've already wolfed down most of my ham and cheese sandwich. I stuff the last bit of my sandwich into my mouth, chew, and swallow. "I found all this, so, *ta-da*, everyone can make their own sandwich. I figured nobody's in the mood for alcohol right now. But if I'm wrong, everything's in the bar; help yourself."

"Oh, thanks. No, this is great."

As I assemble another ham and cheese sandwich with mayo, Sadie slices up the tomato and avocado to make her sandwich. She brings it to her mouth, then pauses.

She sneaks a glance at me, doubt clouding her features. *Is this sandwich safe to eat?* I can practically see her think. Honestly, Sadie is so transparent, I almost have to laugh.

And then, a more sober thought: *The paranoia is starting.* Just like in those last few weeks.

It's ridiculous, of course. Why would I want to kill her? Besides, this is a fresh tomato and a fresh avocado. How would I poison anyone with this even if I wanted to? If I wanted to poison all of them, I would have cooked something; that would have been much easier. I pointedly help myself to two more slices of bread, and her look of doubt changes into embarrassment and she takes a small bite, then grabs a can of soda. Unopened, so no way I could have spiked it with anything.

Besides, I'm strong, an athlete. I don't have to resort to poison to kill someone. No, poison would be a weaker person's method of choice. Or a girl's. Probably Isla's go-to if she ever wanted to kill somebody.

"Isla's still upstairs?" Sadie asks, as if reading my thoughts.

"Yep." Ant polishes off his ham and cheese sandwich too and starts to make another one. "Maybe she decided to take a bath instead."

Sadie is watching him eat too. She shudders slightly; then she starts to cough.

"Whoa, you okay?" I ask.

"Soda…went down…wrong way," she coughs out.

I get up and thwack her back with the palm of my hand to help. My blow knocks her almost face-first onto her plate on the counter.

Like I said, I don't have to resort to poison.

I finish my can of soda, crush it in my hand. *Crunch*. Unlike Sadie, I have a better theory on who's actually trying to kill us all. "You know, I've been thinking."

"'Bout what?" says Ant.

"We all agree that Emily's and Charlie's deaths weren't accidents, right?"

They nod.

"Which means the killer has to be right here on this island." My voice trails off as I look at Ant, then at Sadie. "The killer's been moving so fast, we haven't had time to think, only to react. But I think it's obvious that we were *lured* here." As my words hang in the air, I turn to face Ant. "Wasn't it your idea for us to come?"

Ant's face pales. He puts down his sandwich carefully. "What are you saying?"

"It was, wasn't it?" I say in a low voice, the words rushing out now. I've been puzzling it out, and this is what I keep coming back to. "You're the one who told us all about this island, let us know it was available for rent. If it weren't for you, none of us would even be here. It all started with you."

Sadie stares wide-eyed at Ant. "Will is right. You're the reason we're here in the first place. You persuaded us to come. And you researched this place."

"That's…that's ridiculous!" sputters Ant, scrambling from the stool up onto his feet. "Why on earth would I…? I have no reason to want any of this to happen. What about *you*?" Ant jabs a finger at me.

I frown. "What about me?"

"Charlie was pissed off with us because Vera died, but the other one who died *was your best friend*. And you don't seem too shaken up about Emily and Charlie." Ant's finger keeps jabbing at my chest. "You don't seem sad *at all*."

I stare at him. "Yeah. You know what? Maybe I'm not acting normal. I'm in shock. I'm still just trying to process it all, okay? Are you seriously accusing *me*? Why would I want Emily or Charlie dead?"

"Maybe…maybe you want revenge for Tom's death," he stutters. But I could see he realizes how silly that sounds even as the words leave his mouth. We made the decision together back then, and he knows I was fully on board. What revenge would I be taking for a decision that we made and carried out together?

But Ant's not done speaking. "And okay, fine, maybe I was the one who first suggested coming here. But I wasn't the one who organized everything." His face whips around to look at Sadie. "Maybe we should be asking why the staff that's supposed to be here isn't. And why haven't the others arrived like they were supposed to? Your assistant—"

"My *father's* assistant," she corrects stiffly.

"Whatever. She works for your family, and she was the one arranging all this. Where are the valet, chef, and housekeeper, Sadie? Why are we all alone here?"

"I...I don't—" Sadie takes a step back. "Elle said she arranged everything. You think I wouldn't be calling her right now to ask if I could? You think I like being trapped somewhere with no service?" she says indignantly, trembling a little. I can almost hear the words *especially with you* almost tumble out, but she bites her lower lip.

"Well, she's not doing her job very well," growls Ant.

"Technically, her job is to assist my dad, not me," Sadie mumbles.

Ant glares at her. "You know what?" He's going around the counter now, advancing slowly on her. "The more I look at it, the more I think you look the most suspicious of all. You're the reason why we came one day early. Did you get your assistant to make sure we'd be alone on this island?"

"*What?* I was planning to come alone first! *You all* were the ones who wrangled a ride in my chopper!" she cries, backing away. She stumbles and falls, landing on her butt on the cold tiled floor.

"Whoa, calm down, Ant." I put my hand on his arm, but he shakes it off, keeps advancing on Sadie until he looms over her, looking like he's going to kick her, which he very well might. Ant may crack jokes, but as we all know, he's very capable of violence. Just like me. And he wouldn't hold back just because she's a girl.

But then something clicks together in my head. "Wait," I say. "What's her name again?"

Sadie turns to look confusedly at me. "Who?"

"Your dad's PA."

"Elle." She shakes her head. "Why?"

"Elle," I mutter.

"What?" says Ant, throwing me a confused look too.

I ignore him. "This Elle. How well do you know her?" I ask Sadie.

"Um." She picks herself up from the floor—glaring at Ant as she steps sideways so that I'm between her and him—then furrows her brows. "Not very well. She's new. I think she started working for my dad two months ago? He had to get a new PA after the last one, Kristen, had a nervous breakdown." She rolls her eyes. "My dad's PAs never last long."

Warning bells are going off in my head now. "What does she look like? Have you met her?"

"Yeah, I have, a couple of times. Why?"

"Yeah, why?" says Ant.

"What does she look like?" I repeat.

"Uh…she has dark blond hair, shoulder length. Hazel eyes and freckles. I think she's about my height?"

"How much do you know about her?" I ask.

"Not much. We don't really chat." Sadie looks even more confused than ever now.

"My guy, why are you asking about her dad's PA?" says Ant.

"I'm asking," I say grimly, "because Tom had an older sister. Eleanor."

Ant and Sadie are both staring wide-eyed at me now.

"Think about it," I say. "Nobody else knows what happened in that shelter, other than us and our families." Well, and the rescue team and the Canadian authorities, but I highly doubt they're trying to kill us. "So if we're going off revenge as a motive, who better to want it than a family member of one of the people who died?"

"I know Tom had a sister, but I've never seen her before," murmurs Ant.

"Tom's sister also has dark blond hair, hazel eyes, and freckles?" asks Sadie.

"Well, when I saw her, she had brown hair, but yeah, hazel eyes and freckles like Tom," I say. And obviously, hair can easily be dyed.

"Holy shit," says Ant.

"Do you have a photo of this Elle?" I say.

"No. Why would I have a photo of my dad's PA? Do *you* have a photo of Tom's sister?"

"No." I think. "She's probably on social media…"

"But we can't check because we have no network," completes Sadie, shaking her head in frustration.

"Oh man," breathes Ant. "Are you saying Tom's sister got a job working for Sadie's dad in order to carry out some elaborate revenge scheme on the six of us?"

I nod grimly. "Think about it. It all makes sense. This Elle was the one who arranged everything, right? The rental, the transport. She could have easily gotten the staff out of the way by telling them we didn't want them. And she was the one who put the idea in Sadie's head to come here early on the helicopter." She has to be the one behind all this. Pulling the strings, setting all the pieces of the trap in place. Manipulating us all, like puppets.

"Oh my god." Sadie sinks onto a stool. She looks as shaken as I feel. "Oh my god. She was the one who arranged all the food. I told her about Emily's allergy when I instructed her to arrange for dairy-free food to be stocked. She could have purposely gotten alcohol that has dairy in it—added during the distilling process—like Will said."

Ant runs his hand through his hair. "Of all the theories that we've had so far, this one makes the most sense." He startles suddenly, his eyes growing wide. "Do you think she's on the island with us right now?"

"Like, hiding somewhere?" whispers Sadie, and shudders.

I'm starting to feel creeped out too. I'm almost never afraid of anything, but the possibility that there might be someone hiding here on the island with us—creeping around the house, hiding in the shadows, bent on vengeance, on destroying us—chills me to my bones. Sneaking into my room at night and taking the key to Charlie's room, then putting it back into my jeans pocket…

"Guys…" Sadie is gripping the counter so hard her knuckles are white. "Isla's been upstairs for a long time."

Oh, no. "Isla?" I shout.

There's no reply. *There's no reason to panic*, I tell myself. *If she were still in the shower or bath, she wouldn't be able to hear me.* No reason to panic at all… So why do I have this awful feeling that yet another terrible thing has happened?

The painting. I run over to it. Ant and Sadie must be thinking the same thing because they run for it too.

I spot it immediately. No. *No no no no.* The new red *X*, crossing out the fifth figure.

SADIE

I feel lightheaded. Things are starting to take on a surreal quality, as if nothing that's happening is real. As I stare at the figures huddled against the snowstorm in their makeshift shelter in the picture, the blizzard starts to become more real. I can hear the howl of the wind, feel the sting of ice and snow being flung into my eyes.

Every time we think we're safe, it turns out we're wrong…

I blink the snow out of my eyes. Gradually, hazily, finally, a tiny structure materializes in the distance, although at first I can't be sure if I'm actually seeing it or if I'm just imagining it. It flickers in and out of sight, hidden again and again by the flurries of snow being hurled around in the air. But as we get closer, it becomes clear that it has to be the shelter that Lucas told us about.

And not a moment too soon. Beside me, Tom bursts into tears of relief. From the way he's leaning on me, I can tell he's ready to collapse. "Thank god," says Emily. I'm exhausted too.

There's a separate smaller structure a few steps away that must be the outhouse, but the main shelter is made of big blocks of stone, with a small wooden door and one slit set high up in one wall, probably for ventilation. Once we're all inside, it takes both Will and Ant to pull the door shut behind us, straining against the force of the wind. The sounds of the snowstorm aren't completely shut out, just muted, but it makes a huge difference, just being out of the wind and not having it screaming and howling in our ears and being blinded by the snow. To my relief, even though it's not insulated, it's a lot less cold inside.

As Charlie collapses on the ground to catch his breath, Emily and I help Tom sit down and remove his ski. "You okay?" asks Will, and Tom nods.

"Still no service." Isla paces the stone floor, holding her phone up and away from her.

"It's probably the storm. We should be able to get some network again once it dies down," says Will.

"Okay but I only have sixty-two percent battery left," says Isla. "I don't understand. It was fully charged when we left this morning."

I know why. "It's the cold. Phone batteries lose power quickly when it's very cold." I check my own phone: it's only a little better at sixty-eight percent, and it was fully charged just before we set off too.

"We need to conserve our phone batteries," says Will.

We settle down to wait. But instead of dying down, the blizzard just keeps getting worse. The snow just keeps falling—endless, blinding, *suffocating*—even when the sun has gone down and we sit in complete darkness, not willing to use our phones even for light.

I must fall asleep at some point, because the next thing I know, a *loud* boom *shocks me awake, reverberating through my bones, rattling my teeth in my head.* We've been bombed, *I think in shocked wonder.* We've been hit.

"What was that?" cries Vera, her disembodied voice floating out of the dark. The darkness is complete, all-encompassing; utterly disorienting from the blinding white of the snow-filled day.

"Shh. It's okay," says Charlie.

But what *was* the sound? If it weren't for Vera crying out, I would have thought I imagined it. What could it have been?

We hold our breaths and listen. Something is different. What is it? It takes me a while to realize: I can't hear the wind anymore. It's now completely, utterly, silent. My heart lifts. "I think the blizzard has stopped," I say.

A rustling sound. "Will," says Isla, "what are you—"

"I'm going to check outside," says Will. Light beams, the suddenness of it blinding for a second; he's switched on his phone's flashlight and is standing. I look around me; the rest of us are lying or sitting on the stone floor, huddled in pairs or small groups for warmth. I'm sitting between Tom and Emily, Ant on Emily's other side. Vera clutches tightly to Charlie nearby.

Will strides over to the door and pushes at it, but it doesn't open. "Ant," he says.

Ant gets up. The two of them put their shoulders against the door *and push. They put all their weight into it, but it still doesn't open. "It's probably a bit stuck because of all the snow," says Ant.*

Charlie gets up to join them. The three of them push and grunt and curse and swear.

"They should have built this stupid thing to open inward," says Will.

"If it opened inward, it wouldn't stay shut in a storm," Tom points out in a strained voice.

"I don't understand why it's so stuck," says Will. "How much snow can there be?"

A horrible thought is dawning in my head, the realization of what the earlier boom *and impact might have been. I scramble to my feet, pull out my own phone. Forty-nine percent battery left now. Turning on the flashlight, I shine it at the slit set high in one wall, the one that's there to let the air circulate.*

My light reveals that it's almost completely blocked by snow.

"Oh my god," I whisper. "That loud sound. It must have been an avalanche. Look. We're buried in snow up to here."

"Isla," says Will, his voice jolting me back to here and now with a shock. I can't keep getting trapped in the past. I need to stay in the present. He spins and bounds up the stairs two steps at a time, Ant and me following closely on his heels.

Will pounds on Isla's door. "Isla?"

There's no reply. But when Will tries the handle, the door swings open before us.

He groans. "I told you all to lock your doors."

"I did. I locked mine," I whisper.

"So did I," says Ant.

Will draws himself up, visibly steels himself before stepping in. Isla's room is dead quiet. I pad in after him, peer anxiously around us, but she's not in the bedroom. The bathroom door, however, is ajar. "Isla?" I call out, but once again, there's no reply.

"She's dead, I know it." There's a panicked note in Ant's voice. "Whoever got Emily and Charlie has gotten her too."

"Shut up," says Will between clenched teeth as he pushes the bathroom door open. "Isla? We're coming in."

Will cries out. He's staring at the bathtub. No, he's staring at what's in the tub. When I walk closer, I see what he sees. The sight is horrific. Just like Emily's swollen, purple, oxygen-starved face. Just like Charlie's; gray, slack, lying in his own puke.

Isla is in the bath, and she is most definitely dead.

WILL

The thing that impressed me most about Isla—why I found myself falling for her almost right away, when I met her in our freshman year—was her determination.

She was attractive: tall and slim with a great figure and china-blue doll eyes, like a younger Margot Robbie. So I was surprised that her physical assets weren't what attracted me to her the most.

Isla was simply the most determined person I'd ever met—she knew what she wanted from life, and she seized it like a pit bull latching their teeth on to someone's balls. She told me once that the worst thing in the world was to be a doormat, and she never wanted to let anyone step on her. So, she never let anyone or anything stand in her way, not when she decided she wanted something. She was like a female version of me; falling for her was as easy and natural as falling for myself. I knew immediately that together, we would get whatever we set our hearts on, dominate the world.

We ruled that school. Our peers sought our opinions for everything, and our teachers loved us. It was clear to everyone that our futures were bright, that we were destined for greatness.

It was just too bad the ski trip went so wrong. Otherwise, I'd never have broken up with her. I tried really hard to make it work, I did. But every time I looked at her, it just reminded me of that horrendous month trapped in that shelter.

Even when we were trapped there—literally buried alive under all that snow—my faith that we'd survive, that we'd make it out okay, never faltered. It could not be the end, not for Isla and me. We were strong, the ones who'd always make it. The last ones standing in a zombie apocalypse, when everyone else was dead. It was a fact as infallible, as indisputable as the laws of physics. We'd burn everything down, sacrifice everyone else first. We were survivors.

That's why it's such a shock now to see Isla lying in the tub, her frightened, water-distorted face just under the surface, eyes bulging wide open, unable to believe in her final moments that she was finally bested forever.

It's also why, for the first time since we arrived, terror grips me, clenching its cold fist around my lungs so I can't breathe. For the first time, I feel vulnerable. Because if this person can take Isla down, then they can do the same to me. For the first time, I wonder if I'm going to make it out of here alive.

But then red-hot rage takes over, shooting down my spine, crackling down my limbs to my fingers and toes. I welcome the emotion. It reenergizes me, washes the horrible doubt away.

Enough of this bullshit. If Tom's sister—or whoever this person is—thinks they're going to get the best of me, they've got another thing coming. They may have gotten Isla too, but they're going to find that I'm a much different animal. No one ever gets the best of me. No one gets the jump on me.

I'd make sure they die first.

ANT

The sight of Isla in the water is truly horrible—the water eerily distorting her features as she stares up at us, like a scene from some horror movie. In fact, I'm pretty sure I've seen this exact scene in one; I just can't remember which movie right now. My mind is all jumbled thoughts and half screams. I barely even clock Isla's nakedness. As I stare at her, goose bumps break out on my arms.

Just an hour ago, she was still alive; sparkling, vivacious, brimming with hunger for everything life could give her. Now, she's just another corpse, dead like Emily, like Charlie.

There's no blood, no bruises. The tiled floor just around the tub is all wet. Her eyes are wide open, staring horribly, accusingly.

"Someone held her down until she was dead," whispers Sadie. "That's why there's water everywhere. Isla must have been thrashing around, fighting against being held down."

The imagery of it is so shocking, I feel my blood run cold. I've heard that drowning is a super painful way to die.

Then something occurs to me. Something so obvious, so horrible—*Why didn't it strike me right away?*—that it snatches the air right out of my lungs. "*The killer must still be in the house,*" I hiss urgently. "Will, you were downstairs the entire time, so they couldn't have left."

Sadie startles, looking aghast, and Will's head whips around frantically, as if to check that that person isn't hiding in the bathroom right this very moment.

My god. We're starring in our very own horror movie. Our own slasher flick.

"The bedroom?" whispers Sadie.

We head back quietly into the bedroom. My hands feel conspicuously empty. If only I had a weapon, something to protect myself with. In the room, nothing looks amiss. Other than the massive double king–size bed, there's a large sleek closet set in a wall, and a designer-looking armchair. Slowly—ready to jump back or deliver a kick if necessary—I slide open the door of the closet, but it's empty. Sadie drops cautiously on her hands and knees and peers under the bed, then shakes her head. *Not under the bed.*

Where can the killer be hiding?

"We need to check the rest of the house again," growls Will under his breath. "And we can't let them escape while we're looking, so, Ant, you stand guard downstairs while Sadie and I search these two levels."

That makes sense. I nod and bound downstairs.

But once I'm alone downstairs, all of a sudden, cold apprehension floods me.

Because what if the killer is already down here? Hiding somewhere, just waiting for a chance to kill again?

Suddenly, I can't shake off the feeling that eyes are on me right now, watching my every move. My heart racing, my palms wet with sweat, I spin around, try to take in the ridiculously large and open space all at once. I don't see anyone, but they could definitely be hiding. After all, even though it's an open space—the enormous living area, the dining area, and the massive kitchen spaces all flowing into each other—there are still places where someone can hide.

Behind the couch, for example. Or the huge island in the kitchen. Someone could be crouched there right now with a knife, just waiting for me to let down my guard.

Sweat drips down my forehead into my eyes, stinging them, and I swipe it away with the back of my hand. Now that I think about it, it's obvious the person must be hiding there, and with a weapon. After all, that's what I'd do if I haven't left the house yet. My heartbeat reverberates in my head, and I realize suddenly that I'm afraid. I don't want to die.

But quickly, the familiar rage takes over, floods my veins with adrenaline. How dare this person, whoever the hell they are, come after us? After me. Okay, they may be dangerous, but I'm dangerous too. I'm strong, not vulnerable like Emily, or drunk like Charlie, or naked in a slippery tub like Isla. I can fight back. Whoever they are, can they really overcome me in a fair fight? I seriously doubt it.

Psyched up, I look around for something to protect myself with. The vase is heavier than expected, and hard to get a good grip on. I guess one of the dining chairs will do for now. I pick it up. Finally armed, I approach the kitchen slowly…treading as soundlessly as I can…raise it in preparation to attack as I round the kitchen island…

But there's nobody there.

Feeling a little foolish, I put the chair down. Okay, so there's no one behind the kitchen island. But it would be stupid to let my guard down just yet. I'm not just being paranoid. Whoever killed Isla did it while we were all in the house and has to still be here. And if they're on this level, there's one more place they could be hiding.

The bathroom.

I pick up the big carving knife from the block on the counter. It feels good in my hand, much better than the dining chair. Much less heavy and unwieldy, much more *deadly*. I feel safer already just clutching it.

I make my way quietly to the bathroom. The door is closed. The killer has to be inside. My mouth tastes acrid, and I'm absolutely dripping nervous sweat. I pause just outside the door. Transfer the knife from hand to hand as I wipe the sweat off them on my shorts.

I take a deep breath…then grab the handle and shove the door in hard. It swings, hits the wall at the back with a *bam*.

No one. The bathroom is empty.

Standing in the doorway, panting, my panicked heartbeat finally starts to slow. I wipe the sweat out of my eyes again as my gaze sweeps the entire bathroom. Definitely empty.

The killer must still be hiding somewhere upstairs then. Good luck to Will and Sadie.

God. I can't believe that it's just the three of us left. The stunning speed in which the killer has already murdered three people sinks in as I realize we haven't been on this island for even a full twenty-four hours. Will is right. This entire thing must have been a trap.

But yet, how could it be? How could this all have been a setup? So we don't know which celeb actually owns this island. But I was seeing posts all over social media about this mansion and island for about, what, half a year already? Thousands of people all over the *world* have been salivating to come here. This luxury island is the real thing; you can't fake it.

Which means it has to be someone who saw the opportunity to get us *after* the six of us all decided to come here. It makes sense. Will has to be right. It has to be Elle, who's really Eleanor.

I head back to the kitchen. I'm just about to put the carving knife back in the block when I change my mind. I should hold on to it, just in case. It's good to be cautious. Stay on my guard. I don't want to be defenseless when the killer goes for me next.

Besides, if I put it back, Will or Sadie might take it, and then what would that leave me?

SADIE

After Ant dashes downstairs, Will turns to me. "We need to make sure that whoever it is doesn't slip out from where they're hiding into a room that we've already checked, or from one floor to another. You should stay on the landing and keep watch while I search the rooms."

I nod, because that's very smart. "Be careful," I tell him as he starts to head away. "You don't know what this person is capable of."

Will's mouth twists. "Don't worry, I'm always careful. Besides, they should be worried about what *I'm* capable of."

His words spark a vivid flash of memory. For a split second, I see him crouched over Vera's body on an icy stone floor, brandishing that Swiss Army knife that he brought in his backpack. I shudder before I can suppress it. Will's eyes flicker, as if he guesses what I'm thinking about. I tear my eyes away from his.

But before he turns away, another thought occurs to me. "Wait! What if someone comes out while you're in one of the rooms and tries to attack me?"

"If that happens, just scream for help and run away," snaps Will. "You can do that, can't you? Ant and I will be able to hear you. We'll come running."

Fine. I stand guard at the landing, just by the stairs, as Will enters a room. It will take him time to search all the rooms on this level; this house is so big. *So many possible hiding places for monsters*, my mind whispers. *A monster hunting other monsters.*

I wish I had my Valium.

My legs feel wobbly, so I keep a trembling hand on the stairs' handrail, my back against the wall as I try to stay alert to my surroundings. It's hard to do; Isla's drowned face now joins the others' faces in my head. Her eyes are filmy white; her hair floats dreamily around her head. *Everyone is going to die*, she smirks in my mind's eye.

She's right. We escaped death that time, but now it has come back for us…

"We're going to die," moans Vera, her spider-thin white fingers pulling at her dark hair.

"We're not going to die." Charlie strides back over to her from the door and grabs her hands, brings them calmingly to his chest.

But I can't help but think that she's right. I can't stop thinking that this is where we die. Will, Ant, and Charlie couldn't open the door last night no matter how hard the three of them pushed at it together.

They've been trying again on and off all morning and afternoon, but the door isn't budging. And why would it, since the avalanche has practically buried us almost completely in snow?

I sneak a look at my phone. Twenty-eight percent battery left, and no cell network at all. Being buried under all these feet of snow is probably why none of us are getting any cell network at all, even though the storm has passed.

Buried alive. We're buried alive. And we can't even call for help.

I try not to think about how we all had to go in the corner when we needed to pee last night.

Tom's face is so pale. He's looking at me, his eyes watery with pain. At least, that's what I tell myself, but if I'm honest, I think he's crying. I finally notice that his lips are cracking.

"You should drink more water," I say.

"I'm all out," he whispers hoarsely.

My flask is empty too. But there's no need to panic. I go over to the slit opening in the wall and scrape some snow, collect it in my water bottle. Thank god for this opening. The snow may have trapped us, but at least it has the decency to be as high as this opening. I bring my bottle to Tom and give it to him, and he takes a grateful swallow. Then he shivers. I bring the bottle to my lips and have some of the melting snow too. The cold slithers down my throat, alleviating my thirst a little, but making me feel twice as cold, and I shiver too.

Will is the next one to break the silence. "They'll be looking for us. They must have already started looking for us when we didn't come back yesterday." He looks as confident as his words, and I feel a desperate surge of hope. I want to believe.

"They won't know where to look," says Isla. Her eyes are closed, as if she can't bear to look at us, at our circumstance. *"Lucas initially planned to take us on the other side of the mountain. They don't even know we're here. They'll be looking in the wrong place."*

My hope flickers, dims. Vera whimpers, her eyes large and anxious in her face as she takes in Isla's words.

"Even so, they'll find us soon enough," says Charlie quickly. *"The pilot dropped us off at the top of this mountain, so how hard can it be for them to find us?"*

I'm not sure it'll be that easy, considering we're miles from where we were supposed to be, plus we're buried under all this snow. But I bite my tongue and don't say anything.

"They'll find us," says Ant. *"We just have to wait it out."*

"At least we have water," I say, nodding at the snow in the slit.

Isla roots in her backpack, digs out an energy bar, and tears the wrapping open.

"Better ration out our food," says Will.

She hesitates, bites her lower lip as she stares at the energy bar. Then her lower lip juts out. *"I haven't eaten anything since yesterday's lunch, okay? It's been more than twenty-four hours. I* am *rationing my food. Let's hope they find us quickly, because other than this, I only have a small pack of potato chips left."*

She bites into the bar, chews slowly, obviously savoring it. The sight brings saliva springing into my mouth, and I tear my eyes away.

I have an energy bar too in my backpack, chocolate raspberry flavor, and a Snickers chocolate bar. I'm a chocolate fiend. I also have an apple. I wish I packed more. I'm starving, and it's killing me not to eat them right now, but I should try to make them last. I'll have the apple now, and maybe I'll eat half of the protein bar tonight, the remaining tomorrow night, and if we still haven't been rescued, half of the Snickers the next day. That would be a smart thing to do, stretching my rations out over four days…

Emily is crying quietly.

"What's wrong?" *I ask her.*

"I forgot to bring anything to eat." *She says it in a whisper, her eyes not meeting mine.*

But Isla has overheard her. "You didn't bring any *food?*" *she says incredulously.*

"Maybe we should all pool what food we have together," *says Charlie,* "and—"

"Yeah, that's not happening," *says Isla, cutting him off.* "Why do I have to give my food to someone who didn't bother to bring any? That's not fair."

"Don't worry," *Tom says in a low voice to Emily.* "I'll share some of mine with you."

"Me too," *I whisper to her. The apple is definitely safe for her to eat. Anything else, we'll have to check the label to make sure there isn't any dairy.*

Still, the thought of sharing whatever meager rations I have with someone else pains me.

Because who knows how long they'll take to find us?

"Nothing," spits Will, making me jump. He must have come back while I was distracted. He looks so furious, I can't help but think that if he finds this killer, he very well just might kill them on the spot with his bare hands.

"No one came out?" he asks.

I shake my head, even though the truth is I was so lost in that memory, I wouldn't have noticed even if someone had walked past me. But that would enrage him, so I can't tell him that. Jesus, I need to stop drifting off like this. It's dangerous.

"Upstairs," Will commands. He stalks up, a beast of prey on the hunt, his movements tight and controlled—I can't help but marvel at the danger radiating off him—and I follow.

He doesn't need to tell me what to do. We stick to our earlier MO: me standing guard on the landing as he searches all the rooms on the third level. This time, I manage to stay focused.

But once again, he comes back empty-handed, his fists clenched, his face flushed with rage. "Where can she be hiding?" he rages, frustration ringing clearly in his voice. *She.* He's convinced it must be Elle.

We head back down to find Ant standing in the kitchen, clutching a long, very sharp-looking carving knife in his right hand.

"Why are you holding that knife?" I ask.

Ant ignores my question. "She wasn't upstairs?"

"No," growls Will. "We searched the whole house, and you were down here making sure nobody left. So where is she?"

But the answer to that is obvious, of course, if you think it through. I shake my head. "She must have hidden in one of the other rooms on the second level after killing Isla, and left the house when the three of us were all in Isla's room."

Will curses loudly as Ant smacks his head and says, "You're right."

Will clenches his fists. "She must still be hiding somewhere on the island. There's no way off."

I shudder. "*We* need to get off this island. We can't just wait here like sitting ducks."

Will laughs humorlessly. "You figure? And how are we going to do that? We can't call for help, and it's not like we can swim to shore."

Ant starts pacing, still clutching that knife. "Actually, why can't we? People swim across the English Channel all the time."

I shake my head again. "Aren't there only a few people in history who have attempted to swim across the English Channel and succeeded? And I think they trained for months to do it."

"How do you know that?"

"I saw a documentary about it once. Plus, the distance across the English Channel is around twenty miles, and we're much farther from shore than that. Didn't you check out the island on Google Maps before coming? We're like, almost forty miles out from shore. Even if we wanted to swim to Martha's Vineyard, that's twenty-five miles. Assuming we swim in the right direction, and don't miss it entirely."

We all fall quiet.

"We can take her," says Ant suddenly. He and Will exchange dark looks.

"Wait," I say. "What? You can't be thinking that we should—"

"You said it. We can't just wait here like sitting ducks," growls Will. "We need to find her."

—Wasn't there supposed to be staff? I saw those glossy videos. The island supposedly came with a whole assortment of staff. Housekeeping, even a private chef. Oh my god, was it one of the staff who killed them?

—Oh yeah, I saw those videos too. My girlfriend kept suggesting we rent the island for our wedding. As if we had the money. But no, there was no staff. Apparently they were all alone on that island.

—Wait. That doesn't make sense. If there was no one else on the island, then... who killed them?

ANT

It's a great idea. She's somewhere out there; we just have to find her and put a stop to this bullshit once and for all.

But Sadie blanches and shakes her head. "*Why?* Why can't we just hole up here? Right here in the living room." She holds up her palms, as if begging us to see sense. "We're safe here. There's a bathroom right here, and the kitchen too. We just need to hold out until tomorrow when the helicopter comes for us."

I don't like Sadie's idea. "We can't just let her get away," I mutter.

Will juts out his jaw too, obviously agreeing with me.

"Jesus!" exclaims Sadie. "Do you *want* to get yourselves killed? Don't you two get it? She *wants* us to split up. It's how she gets us! If the three of us stick together and stay here, keep a lookout—be vigilant—she can't. Look, I know you want revenge. But this is the smartest thing to do."

The thing is, revenge isn't the only reason I want to go after them. I mean, it's the main reason. I want to get revenge for Emily. But there's another reason I want to go hunt them down.

Because the idea that someone is threatening me is downright *offensive*. I have to exterminate this threat. I want their *blood*.

"Come on, guys," pleads Sadie. "This is the most logical idea. The safest one."

I grip my knife until my knuckles are white. I want to argue, but Will sighs.

"Fine," says Will reluctantly. "I get your point. We'll stay here, together."

Goddamn it. "Fine," I say between clenched teeth.

Sadie exhales a relieved breath, her shoulders relaxing.

Will hunkers down on one of the armchairs. He sits with his feet planted wide and firmly on the floor, resting his elbows on his knees as he steeples his hands under his chin and stares out of the glass wall at the trees in the distance.

I settle on one end of the couch. From my position, like Will, I have a good view of both the main entrance and the stairs.

Sadie goes to grab a few bottles of water from the kitchen, and throws one to me and one to Will. "So…are you going to put that knife down, or what?" she says, side-eyeing the carving knife resting just beside me on the couch, which I'm still holding on to.

Irritation flickers in my chest. "What's it to you?"

"Umm, that just looks like an accident waiting to happen."

"Listen. I don't tell *you* what to do, so don't nag *me*, okay?"

She rolls her eyes and mutters, "Don't say I didn't warn you when you cut yourself later." She curls up on the other end of the couch, her legs tucked up to her chest and her arms wrapped around them, like she's retreating into herself.

I roll my eyes back at her. She'll be the one sorry later on if she's attacked and she doesn't have anything to defend herself with. The killer is probably hiding nearby, just waiting for an opportunity to finish what they've started.

I check the time on my phone; it's a quarter past five. How the hell are we going to pass the time until the chopper comes tomorrow?

With nothing to do, my thoughts keep wandering back to Emily. The horrible way she died. And Charlie, and Isla…and the jolting realization that we haven't been on this island for even a full day. "Not even twenty-four hours," I say.

Will looks at me. "Huh?"

"I've been thinking the same thing," says Sadie quietly. "This person managed to kill off half of us—three people—in less than a day." She looks at Will, then back to me. "Who's going to be their next target?"

"No one." Will smiles thinly. "The only person to die next will be them, if I catch them."

He seems to feel very confident that he'll be the one to catch the killer. I roll my eyes, then stare at my knife, run my thumb over the blade to feel how sharp it is.

It's not sharp enough. It has to be razor sharp, so sharp it breaks skin with the littlest contact. Maybe there's something in the kitchen for sharpening knives. I go in search.

It isn't long before I find a whetstone in a drawer. The *sssss* the blade makes when I drag it over the whetstone is satisfying, comforting, even thrilling. As I drag the blade over the stone again and again, I imagine confronting the asshole who murdered Emily. Plunging the knife into their belly, or chest, or neck, and how satisfying that would feel. Their blood spurting out a few feet in the air as they beg for mercy, before they collapse in a heap before my feet.

It would serve them right. It would be a just end, a much more gratifying outcome than simply some jail time.

I hold up the knife and admire my work. There's a basket of fruits on the counter: apples, bananas, peaches, a watermelon. I lift the watermelon out and place it on the counter, then stab it with the carving knife. The sharpened blade slices through the rind smoothly, easily. Red juice oozes out of the cut, dribbles onto the counter.

"When you're done murdering that watermelon," Sadie calls dryly from the couch, "maybe you can cut it up into slices so we can eat it."

✗ ✗ ✗ ✗ ✗

After we eat the half of the watermelon I sliced up, Sadie stands up suddenly and heads toward the stairs.

"Where are you going?" I ask.

"To my room. To get a book from my bag."

But she pauses after placing one foot on the first step. Then she turns, comes back, and sits back down on the couch.

"What is it?" says Will.

She shakes her head and flushes slightly. "Nothing. Well, something just occurred to me, that's all."

"What?" I ask.

"Well," she starts hesitatingly. "We think we've checked everywhere upstairs. But…what if…there's, like, some secret hiding place that we don't know about?" Sadie's face flushes an even deeper red, as if she's embarrassed about sounding paranoid or like a scaredy-cat.

But I don't say that, because she could be right. What if there *was* some secret hiding spot, and the killer *is still hiding somewhere upstairs*? I should be afraid. Instead, I feel a hot spurt of excitement in my tummy.

Will is frowning. "I checked everywhere."

"No, I know you did," says Sadie. "Ignore me, I'm just being silly." Still, she doesn't get up again to get her book.

I pick my knife back up. "I'll go with you. I have to go up anyway, wanna grab my phone charger."

She eyes me, her eyes darting to my knife. A strange look floats fleetingly across her face before she carefully rearranges her features into a blank expression. "It's okay. I don't really want to read that book anyway. You go ahead."

I laugh. Could she be afraid of me? Maybe she thinks I'm the killer, and that I'll chop her up as soon as we're alone upstairs. How ridiculous. "Hey, did you know studies say most stabbings are committed by someone close to the victim? *Within arm's length*, to be specific." I chuckle at my own joke.

She just rolls her eyes and ignores me, but her face flushes pink. Wow, I was right. She does think I might attack her. She's really getting paranoid. Whatever. "So…want me to get that book for you, or not?"

She shakes her head.

"What about you, Will? You want me to grab anything from upstairs for you?"

"I'm good, thanks."

Armed with my trusty, freshly sharpened knife, I head upstairs. Although it's all quiet up here, adrenaline is making my pulse race and my senses as sharp as my blade. I'm not afraid like I was earlier on, not anymore, now that I have this weapon. Now that I have this knife, I realize I'm kinda actually *hoping* to come face-to-face with the killer. I wanna deal out my own justice, for Emily. And I'd like to see how they think they can overpower me.

Because if they had a gun, they'd have used it already, right? There would have been no need for all this cloak-and-dagger stuff, all this waiting for us to be alone before poisoning, drugging, or drowning us when we're alone and in a vulnerable state.

Maybe they're even waiting for me in my room right now. I didn't think about locking my door; it didn't seem like I needed to. Now, I step in cautiously, clutching my knife, ready to face the crazed, vengeful killer lying in wait head-on…

But my room's empty. No crazed killer. I chuckle to myself when I realize I'm even a little disappointed.

My phone charger is plugged in the wall socket beside the bed. I pull it out, put it in my pocket. But before I turn back around, my eyes are drawn to a folded piece of paper on the bedside table. My heart stutters in my chest.

I've never seen this paper before. It isn't mine.

I pick it up, unfold it. Stare at the words scrawled on it, in red.

The killer has been in my room.

WILL

"They're messing with us," snarls Ant. He's still clutching that big carving knife, looking like he wants to stab the offensive piece of paper on the coffee table, which we're gathered around. "They literally went in my room just to leave this. Just to screw with my head."

We all read the note again.

WHAT HAPPENED IN THE CABIN?

I crumple it up into a ball and fling it against the wall. "I told you, it's someone who thinks they're out for revenge. It has to be Tom's sister."

Ant starts pacing around. "Yeah, you're right, it has to be her. The *bitch*! Why is she picking on me?"

"She isn't picking on you. The message is for all of us." Sadie has started to cry again. "She knows."

"*She knows shit*," I say, even though alarm frissons down my spine.

"I just can't believe Elle is Tom's sister." Ant runs his hand through his hair. "I mean, I can believe it, but wow, the level of determination and planning is mind-boggling." He looks at me. "Do you know her? Have you met her before?"

"Once. A few years ago. I was hanging out with Tom over at his house, playing video games. Eleanor was back home for the summer from college. But she was in her room the entire time I was there. We only said hi to each other because she came down to grab a drink from the kitchen. That was it. That's how I know how she looked like."

"But *when* did she leave this note?" whispers Sadie. "We searched the house after we discovered Isla in the tub, remember? This wasn't in your room then when Will checked it…" Her voice trails off as she shakes her head uncertainly and looks at me for confirmation. "…was it?"

"I…I don't think so." But actually, I'm not sure either. After all, why would I have taken note of all the small stuff lying around in Ant's room? I was looking for a killer. "I guess it could have been there and I didn't notice."

"So the killer could have left it there either just before or after they killed Isla, while we were in the kitchen," says Sadie. "Before they left the house, when we were in Isla's room. Because there's no way it could have been after that."

Unless the killer really is still hiding somewhere upstairs in some secret hiding spot, I think. *Thanks, Sadie, for putting that thought in my head.* But I don't say that out loud because the two of them are obviously already paranoid enough right now, and it doesn't help to have anyone freaking out further, getting spooked by unlikely possibilities.

Besides, there is no secret hiding spot, I tell myself firmly. I checked everywhere.

No, it's much more likely the killer is hiding somewhere outside on the island right now.

"But why did she leave this?" says Sadie.

Ant makes an impatient brushing-away gesture with his free hand. "She's just messing with us. Trying to scare us."

I nod. That makes sense. "Or she's taunting us. Or both."

"I'm not scared," says Ant. "We can take her, Will."

"Oh no." Sadie shakes her head. "I thought we already agreed that's a bad idea. We need to stay put, ride this out."

"Like the last time we hunkered down in the shelter and rode it out?" says Ant.

Sadie flinches. "You know it's not the same," she whispers.

I look out of the glass walls. It's still light outside, but the sun is low in the sky, the light already starting to bleed out of the day. What happens when it gets fully dark? With the lights on in here, we'll be lit up and in plain view of anyone hiding outside. We, on the other hand, won't be able to see anything, even if someone was creeping around just outside in the dark. We'd really be sitting ducks. The thought makes my skin crawl.

"It's getting dark outside." A pleading note enters Sadie's voice. "We won't even be able to see anything. How would you look for her? It's madness."

"It'll be just as dark for them as for us outside." Ant looks at me. "And I prefer to be the hunter rather than the hunted, don't you?"

He's right. I'm tired of being hunted. Of just sitting around and doing nothing.

"Let's find this bitch and make her sorry she ever decided to mess with us," I say.

Ant grins.

Sadie stands up, her face flushed. "This is stupid. You're both stupid. You two can go and look by yourselves, I'm not going out there. I'm locking myself in my room." She storms toward the stairs. Then she pauses, spins around, stomps to the kitchen, and grabs a large bottle of water and what looks like two bags of chips, an apple, and a bar of chocolate. "Good luck," she calls as she stomps upstairs without looking back. A loud *bang* as she slams her door shut.

Ant shrugs. "She'd just have been a liability anyway. She'd just have needed us to protect her."

"I know."

Ant holds up his knife and grins. "Ready when you are."

"Yeah, well, hold your horses. I wanna get something too."

He waits patiently as I search in the kitchen for my weapon of choice. It turns out I don't have a lot of choice. Other than the carving knife that Ant took, the only other large knife is a meat cleaver. But I'm satisfied with it; the blade is wicked sharp, and I can do a lot of damage with it.

Ant falls in step as I stride to the door. Before unlocking the door, I check through the glass wall first, but there's no one outside that I can see.

Leaving the house has a strange feeling of finality; as if we're crossing some threshold to a place of no return. The evening sun bathes everything in a reddish-orange light. A lone seagull squawks overhead, as if announcing our presence, telling on us. I lock the door and hand a key to Ant, so we each have one.

He scratches his head. "How do we search the entire island? Should we split up?"

Good question. I look around us. Beyond the landscaped lawn around the mansion, we're surrounded by small trees. Other than the pier south of us, there's no other structure on the island. The beach borders the entire island. Where can someone be hiding on such a small island? Under the pier? Behind a tree or a rock? Without splitting up, how would we begin to look? And even if we split up, there are only two of us.

Frustration thrums through my veins. I hate not knowing exactly what to do.

"There's no choice," I say finally. "We have to split up. If not, it'll be too easy for her to avoid us. We can cover more ground this way, increase our chances of finding her. It should work. The island isn't that big. Unless you have a better idea?"

Ant nods. "Yeah, let's split up."

I walk around the house, scan the rest of the island. "We'll each search half of the island. See that large rock in the north?" I point with my cleaver. "Imagine drawing a line from that rock down to the pier; that splits the island in half. I'll cover the entire side west of that, and you the other side. Okay?"

Ant nods. "Okay. We should start from the rock. I'll work my way clockwise down to the pier, and you counterclockwise?"

I see the logic. It'll be like casting and tightening a net, making it harder for her to evade us. "Yeah, let's do that."

We set off toward the big rock. Past the groomed lawn, the grass is tall, almost up to our thighs. The island really isn't big at all; we reach the rock that borders the sparse forest and the beach without coming across anybody hiding behind a tree. The rock turns out to be taller than me, almost as wide as it's high. But there's no one hiding behind it.

"What do we do if we find her?" says Ant.

I give him a thin-lipped smile and raise my cleaver. "We give her what she deserves. She killed three of us first. It's called self-defense."

Ant grins, but then his smile is replaced by a frown. "What if we don't find her?"

"If we don't find her, we head back to the house." I check my phone. "It's five to six. No matter what happens, we head back to the house by seven at the latest. Okay?"

Ant tightens his grip on the handle of his knife until his knuckles are white, and nods grimly at me. And we split up.

ANT

Finally, we're doing something. Fighting back, instead of just sitting around feeling impotent as we wait for this bitch to make her next move. I feel electrified, like there's pure energy flowing in my veins, powering my muscles and my brain. I want to run, to howl. This must be what predators feel like when they're on the hunt, chasing after prey.

I scan the desolate beach quickly. The waves, so angry this morning, now lap dejectedly at the shore. Weathered pieces of driftwood lie scattered like limbs ripped from bodies on bone-white sand. The beach is completely deserted as far as I can see. There's no point going down there because there's nowhere for anyone to hide without being seen for a mile. Will must come to the same conclusion when he glances at it quickly before he heads off west.

After he goes, I start stalking through the tall grass, scanning my surroundings carefully. Some of the trees are certainly big enough to conceal a person behind their trunks. The plan is to zigzag through the trees and back up to the house, then back down to the beach; rinse and repeat to cover as much ground as possible. I keep a careful ear out for any sounds, but aside from the soft rustling my own path through the grass is making, and the occasional squawk of a seagull passing overhead, it's completely silent.

As I skulk through the grass, I fantasize again about using this knife. Ruminate on how it would feel like to plunge it into Eleanor's chest, to twist it in her soft belly. Want to know how you make any salad into a Caesar salad? Stab it twenty-three times, ha.

No, actually, I'll make her beg for mercy first. Make her get down on her knees before I give her a taste of her own medicine. I'm the only one who hasn't seen her before, but my imagination begins to fill in the details of her appearance: She's tall, almost as tall as Tom was, her straight brown hair dyed blond. Freckles dotting her face, which is bloodless and thin like a rat's, her cunning eyes hazel like his. I can't wait to rearrange her face for her, teach her the lesson she deserves.

I look up, take stock of my position. I'm almost halfway to the pier already. Still no sign of anyone, but I'm not worried. It's still early and I'm only getting started.

It's boring, tiring, work, though, trudging up and down this hill. After a while, my adrenaline starts to wear off. Maybe she's hoping to wear us out like this, so that by the time she makes her move, we're too tired from all this hiking to fight back.

If she thinks that this'll give her an advantage, though, she's wrong. I may not be an athlete like Will, but it'll take a lot more than this to wear me out.

Okay, but what if she also has a weapon? nags my brain.

I brush that aside. Even if she does, Will and I can easily handle that. It's clear the reason her attacks are so sneaky is because she knows she can't take us on in a fair fight and win.

Sneaky little rat. Maybe I'll bash her head in with a rock instead. Actually, no. She deserves to die as slowly and as painfully as possible. Emily's monstrous, swollen purple face flashes before my eyes, and the red-hot rage that reignites in my stomach and surges up my throat tastes like bile. What I need to do is to first incapacitate her with a quick gut stab, and then I can take my time with her. Make her feel at least as much—if not more—pain than Emily felt when she died. I want her to grovel, to apologize and beg Emily's ghost for forgiveness, to beg for her life. "I'm doing this for you, Em," I whisper.

Eleanor's entire plan is so stupid. She thinks she's fighting the good fight, taking revenge for her little brother. She knows shit.

Vera went mad. She was ranting and raving. We were just trying to stop her, get her to calm down before she hurt herself, or someone else. What happened next was an accident. As for Tom, he was already on the verge of death with that infected, broken leg. He'd been running a fever for days. It was an act of mercy.

It's easy to pass judgment when you weren't there going through what we did. All I did was what I had to do to survive. I can tell you one thing: when you haven't eaten for two weeks, all lofty ideals and notions are stripped away. You're left with nothing but the animal inside. The animal that knows only one thing: that it's *hungry*. You either go mad, like Vera did, or you do what the rest of us had to do to survive.

This bitch really picked the wrong people to mess with. We're survivors. After what we had to do to make it out alive that time, she must be delusional to think that she can take us on and come out on top. She's going to learn that we're really hard to kill.

Yeah, well, she's already managed to kill three of you, nags my treacherous brain again.

Okay, that may be true, but Emily and Charlie weren't like us. They only survived the last time because of us, because we made the hard decisions and carried them out. They were easy targets. Isla was mentally stronger, but still physically weaker than Will and me. Sadie would have been an easier target, but Sadie locked her door and Isla slipped up and forgot, which was too bad for her.

If Eleanor comes for me, she'll soon learn I'm made of something much tougher.

As I stalk through the grass, snatches of some old nursery rhyme drifts into my head. "Here comes a chopper to chop off your head," I sing. "Come out, come out, wherever you are. Come out and let me kill you."

It's time to put an end to this. I hope it's me who finds her.

SADIE

I throw the snacks on the bed and lock the door. And then check it to make sure that it's really locked.

It's a relief to finally be alone again in my room. It was starting to turn bad down there with the two of them. It's clear that Ant and Will are starting to lose it. Ant is dying to use that carving knife, and Will is just as bloodthirsty, vowing to kill this person if he finds them. This isn't the behavior of normal people. Normal people would want to stay hidden—to stay safe. And if the killer is somehow caught, to turn them over to the police. The way Will and Ant are acting, it's clear being around the two of them is becoming as dangerous as being hunted by a faceless killer hiding in the shadows—perhaps even more so.

I get on the bed, take a gulp of water, and tear open one of the bags of chips. As usual, whenever I start to feel anxious or trapped, the irrational fear of starving grips me, and I feel an overwhelming urge to eat. Will and Ant are messed up, but so am I, in my own way, in more ways than one. Food trauma, Dr. Armstrong called it, but I didn't need a four-hundred-bucks-an-hour therapist to explain it to me. Knowing what it's called doesn't help to reduce it. Oh, Dr. Armstrong and the registered dietitian that my mom found tried to help me, with their therapy sessions and diet plans. But nothing worked. How could they help, when I couldn't even tell them what really happened? What they did? What we all did, in the end?

All of us, crouched on the ice-cold stone floor, gnawing on the bones...

I retch a little, bile burning my throat as I run to the bathroom. But once I'm done puking, the awful compulsion to eat returns, and I finish the bag of chips. Then I start on the apple. It's only when a fat wet teardrop splashes my thigh that I realize I'm crying as I stuff my face...

We ran out of food by the end of the third day. It's now day fourteen. Or is it fifteen? It's getting hard to keep track.

We didn't have a lot of food to begin with, only the few bags of chips and chocolate and energy bars we'd packed for a light lunch break on the slope. But we should have made them last longer.

No one believed that we could really die here. At sixteen, the possibility of dying is the furthest thing from one's mind, impossible, a bad joke. Now, however, dying no longer seems like such an impossible outcome. Now, it's all I can think about. This is where we die. In fact, now that I've come to accept this, I feel calm, more at peace than I've been since we were trapped here all those weeks ago.

Still, it's hard to just lie down and give up. There's the gnawing hunger, and the cold, and the thirst. At least the thirst we can do something about, alleviate it somewhat. We've been scraping the snow at the opening in the wall for water, and we've managed to clear a large hole. Before our last phone—Tom's—died, though, there was still zero service, even when we held it out of the hole in the snow at the opening. There must just be no network in this area.

I'm so sad about Tom. I think he will be the one to go first. He's been refusing to let any of us take a look at his leg, keeps insisting he's going to be fine. But I think it's bad. Even though I never saw any blood, the middle of his shin is bulging in a horrible way. Obviously I'm no doctor, but it makes me think there might be internal bleeding in addition to the bone being broken. He's stopped talking, but it's obvious he's in severe pain. If only there was some way to take his pain away, to let him die peacefully. His face is pale and waxy, the skin drawn tightly over the bones in his face, and he shivers nonstop. I touched his forehead when he was asleep, and I think he's starting to run a fever. He must have an infection, or something worse. The thought is frightening, and I push it away.

Sometimes, I find myself starting to hope again, to think that we will get out. To hope that they'll find us, and Tom will be okay, that we'll all be okay. And then the moment passes, and black despair crashes on me again, crushes my chest so I feel like I can't breathe.

And then there's Vera. She's not physically injured, not like Tom, but it's clear there's something inside her that's broken or hasn't mended well, and right now in this living nightmare that we've found ourselves in, it's coming to the surface. In between crying fits, she mumbles to herself, and her eyes are restless, skittering from floor to ceiling, from wall to wall, from one of us to another. Listening intently, I manage to catch a few words of what she's mumbling: a dream…stuck in a dream…monsters at the end. *But she's not dreaming, not talking in her sleep. Her eyes are wide open.*

I can't think about it.

No, stop. Don't think.

Millions of dollars in my trust fund, and not even a scrap of bread to chew on.

Maybe our guide, Lucas, was the lucky one. At least he got to die quickly.

I wish I could google how long someone can last without food. Wasn't there some Irish protester who went on a hunger strike for, like, two months or something before dying? How long would it take for us to waste away? Then again, do I really want to know? Would knowing make a difference? How long would it take for all this snow to melt?

A low wail breaks into my dark thoughts. It's Vera. Charlie tries to calm her down, but it's not working this time. "They can't find us," *she moans.* "No one is coming. Don't you all get it? No one is coming!"

Despair courses through me as she voices what we're all thinking. What we've all been thinking since the sound of the helicopters stopped coming back. What no one has dared to say until now.

A low laugh burbles out of her, warping into a scream as she pulls her hair and scratches her own face.

"Vera, no—someone help me!" pleads Charlie as he grabs her arms to try to stop her from hurting herself.

Ant gets up to his feet slowly, wearily. I go over too, but I only stand beside them uselessly, wringing my hands. What else can I do to help? "Gonna die gonna die gonna die—" she moans as she bangs the back of her head on the stone floor.

"No," rasps Isla suddenly. "We're going to survive. I'm not dying like this."

"No one's going to die," I manage to say. I even manage to sound like I believe it. "We have water. We'll be fine as long as we have water; we can survive until they manage to find us. I heard that people can live without food for…"

Isla stares wordlessly at me, and my words die in my throat as a terrible feeling of foreboding floods me.

Charlie manages to calm Vera down so that she's back to only whimpering and rocking back and forth on her heels, arms wrapped around herself.

But something is in the air this evening. In their corner, Isla and Will have been whispering to each other for the past hour, and now Ant has joined in their little group. It almost feels like they're plotting something.

I must just be being paranoid. It's easy to descend into hopelessness and paranoia when it's so cold you can't sleep properly at night, when the constant gnawing hunger makes it feel like your stomach is eating itself.

When it gets dark, I somehow manage to drift off into an uneasy sleep, a half sleep where monsters lurk in dark corners, waiting, biding their time to come out, to devour...

A shriek startles me awake. Have the monsters in my dream gotten out? Are they in the room with us? I cry out in fear. A warm—too warm, much too warm, burning hot—hand reaches out to me—it must be Tom—and I grab on to it. Was he the one who shouted?

No, it was Vera who screamed. I can make them out now in the faint moonlight drifting into the room from the opening in the wall, Vera wailing as she twists and struggles in Ant and Will's hold. "Stop it," Will is saying. "Calm down!"

"Stop," I shout. "Why are you fighting?" And how do they have the energy for this?

"She's gone crazy! She's going to hurt us!" shouts Isla from one corner of the room.

Charlie is scuffling with Will and Ant, trying to pull them off Vera. "Let go of her!" he shouts.

"Your girlfriend is out of control!" says Will, letting go of Vera and giving Charlie a hard shove.

Ant screams. Vera has bitten his forearm. I watch in horror as he pulls his arm back and gives her a hard slap, hard enough to snap her head back as she falls. There's a terrible crack *as her head hits the stone floor.*

Tears stream down my face, but even then, I can't stop stuffing my face with chips from the second bag. Vera's and Tom's faces haunt my head. The Valium usually helped to dull the memories of the final week, but now that it's gone, they're back, and knife sharp.

The worst thing is I can't really remember what Tom and Vera used to look like anymore. All I can recall of them are how they looked in the final days: greasy hair, dull eyes, cheeks sunken in. Emily's, Charlie's, and Isla's faces now crowd my head too, jostling and fighting each other for attention. *Doomed*, they chant. *We're all doomed, and so are you.*

Creak...

Startled, I drop the bag. The chips scatter all over the bed. What was that sound? Did I imagine it, or was it someone coming up the stairs? They said they were going out to look for the killer. Why would someone be coming up the stairs now? My heart freezes, then picks up again double time in my chest. I tiptoe to my door, press my ear against it.

When I hear the voice, I know this is it. It's finally my time to die...

WILL

The sun is low in the sky now. The trees cast long ominous shadows, skeletal branch fingers stretching to grab my feet as I make my way carefully over my half of the island.

I take my time, but even though it's not a lot of ground to cover, it's still too easy for the killer to evade the two of us. There are just too many damn trees. Where the hell is she?

I hack uselessly at the grass in my path with the cleaver, my muscles and head tight with frustration. Panting, I stop in the middle of a grove of trees and force myself to take a deep breath. I need to calm down. I can't let this person get the better of me.

This is impossible. She could be hiding behind any one of these trees. I can feel eyes watching me—my every movement—right at this very moment.

There must be a way to flush her out. I think...and an idea comes to me.

"Hey," I call out in my friendliest, most reasonable voice. "I know you're out there. Listen. Can we talk?" No reply. "Why don't you come out? I just want to talk."

I fall quiet and listen. A rustle in a tree makes me jump and spin around to face it. But it's only some damn bird that flies out.

When my breathing slows, I call out again, "I know it's you, Eleanor. I get why you're mad. You think I don't beat myself up every day that Tom died?" I slink closer to the nearest tree as I talk. "He was my best friend! Not a day goes by that I don't wish he were still here. That he didn't break his leg." I check behind it, but she isn't there. Nor is she hiding behind the other trees beside it.

I keep moving and checking, all the while keeping a lookout for any sign of movement. "You know that's how he died, right? He broke his leg real bad, and it must have gotten infected because he started running a terrible fever. There was literally nothing any one of us could have done. I tried so hard to help him. I did everything I could. We could have left him in that crevasse, you know, but we didn't."

We should have though. If we'd just left him, none of what happened next would have happened. We should have skied down to the nearest village and called for help there. He would have probably been dead from exposure in that blizzard by the time a rescue helicopter went back for him. But one person dead was still better than three, right? And the rest of us wouldn't have had to suffer the way we did.

Still no sign of Eleanor. I can see hoping she'd be reasonable isn't going to work. I'll have to change tack. "He was the reason we were all stuck there, you know. It was all his fault. He went off by himself, instead of staying near our guide like we were supposed to. If he hadn't done that, he wouldn't have fallen into that crevasse and broken his leg. And our guide wouldn't have died going down there trying to rescue him. If it weren't for him, we could have all skied down the mountain, instead of getting trapped in that avalanche. It was his fault they died!"

There. That should enrage her enough to draw her out. I hold my breath and look around. Steel myself. But if I expected her to dash out—gnashing her teeth, screaming in anger, nails poised to gouge out my eyes—I'm disappointed. She doesn't take the bait.

Well, either that or she's not here, so I keep moving on.

As I continue my search, uncertainty starts to creep in. What if *this* is also part of her plan? To draw us out into the open. To separate us. Have *we* fallen into *her* trap?

It can't be. She isn't capable of taking me on in a fight. Or Ant either. Unless…

Unless she has an accomplice.

Fuck. Why hasn't this possibility occurred to me sooner? Why did I assume that she's working alone? If she has an accomplice—a hired thug, for example—I could be in real danger right now.

The more I think about it, the more I realize this is completely possible. Suddenly, I realize that I might be the one being hunted instead.

Shit! We should have just hunkered down together and waited it out until the helicopter came for us tomorrow, like Sadie said. I should have listened to her. I wanted so much to teach this bitch a lesson that I wasn't thinking straight. It was Ant's fault too—him and his knife—goading me on to come out with him on this wild-goose chase against my better judgment.

I have to get back in the house. I'm safer inside, with a wall behind my back. It must be nearly time anyway, right? I check my phone: 6:45. Thunder rumbles in the distance. I look up; the sky has gotten much darker than what should be normal for this time in the evening. The sun has disappeared behind black storm clouds. It looks like it's going to rain, and by the look of those angry clouds and the way the wind is picking up, it's going to be a hell of a storm, just like last night.

Screw this. Even though I haven't finished searching all of my half of the island yet, it's definitely time to start heading back.

Being out here feels stupidly dangerous now. I can practically feel the target on my back. I head back up to the house at almost a run. Is Ant still searching the grounds, or has he already returned? If I had any service, I'd call him, tell him to abandon the search. But since I don't, he'll just have to fend for himself. I'm sure he's more than capable. I need to watch out for myself first.

My hand is shaking as I fish the key out from my pocket and unlock the front door. *Not from fear, from the adrenaline*, I tell myself as I look over my shoulder to make sure no one's sneaking up on me.

Once I've slammed the door shut behind me and locked it, I start to feel better. Wiping the sweat away from my eyes, I look around, but Ant doesn't seem to be back yet. Or if he is, I don't see him. But he could be in his room. "Ant?" I call. There's no reply. Whatever. If he isn't back yet, he will be soon.

Don't think about Isla, Emily, and Charlie dead in their rooms upstairs.

I grab a cold Coke from the fridge and gulp it in big swallows. It helps to cool me down, make me feel better. It's then that I realize I'm starving. I should have something to eat. Keep my strength up, just in case.

There's lots of meat and vegetables in the fridge, and even more frozen meat in the freezer, but I have no idea what to do with them. I guess I could make another ham and cheese sandwich, but I already had that for lunch. Or I could boil some pasta and heat up a jar of sauce. That seemed easy enough when we did it yesterday—Jesus, was it only yesterday that we arrived?—but that seems like so much trouble. God, having to prepare all my meals is getting old real fast. I should have known having a private chef was too good to be true. Nothing about this weekend turned out to be what we were promised.

In the end, I take a page from Sadie's book and just open a bag of chips. Maybe Sadie will feel up to cooking something for all of us. Okay, maybe not since she's already having all those snacks in her room. With a private chef at home, she probably doesn't even know how to cook either. Maybe Ant then, when he's back.

I'm eyeing the bowl of fruits dubiously when the sound of a key scratching at the lock in the door makes me jump. The door swings open; it's just Ant. I can tell that he's in a foul mood from the way he stomps in. I guess he didn't manage to find Eleanor either.

"You're back early," he says. "I thought I'd meet you at the pier."

Right, the pier. "Did you check under it to see if anyone was hiding under there?"

Ant raises one brow. "I did, but why are you asking me? Thought you'd have checked it for yourself."

"Lock the door." Hopefully, the curtness of my reply will put him off asking me any more questions.

He frowns but does as I say before he turns back around. "Why are you acting so weird?"

I don't want to tell him how freaked out I got out there, but I can see he doesn't want to let this go, so I sigh. "I just realized that it could have been dangerous looking for her out there, that's all."

He snorts as he strolls over to join me in the kitchen and grabs a can of Coke from the fridge too. "Dangerous? For us or for her?"

"Have you ever considered that she might not be acting alone?" I blurt out.

Ant stares at me. "What makes you think that?"

"Just a thought, that's all."

He eyes my chips. "Is that all you're having?"

"Hey." I gesture at the kitchen around us. "The fridge is fully stocked. Knock yourself out if you want to cook."

Unfortunately, he just sighs and grabs a bag of chips and a candy bar. "Shit. I miss my mom's cooking." He stares morosely at the candy bar. "I wish we never came here."

"Thank god we'll be outta here tomorrow."

"I can't believe they're dead."

I nod. But I don't want to talk about it. There'll be time to grieve later, when we're safe, away from here. Not now.

Ant slams his knife onto the counter. "I just want to get revenge for them!"

"Me too, buddy."

We sit and eat in silence. I grab a candy bar too, but I'm still hungry after I finish that, so I give up and get an apple.

Ant just rips open another bag of chips. "Sadie still holed up in her room?"

"I guess. I came back just five minutes before you."

"So…what do we do now? With that psycho still out there."

I shrug. "I guess we have no choice but to stick to Sadie's initial plan. Safety in numbers and all that."

"Why don't we just each stay in our rooms and lock our doors?" says Ant.

Because something's been lurking on my mind ever since we found Isla dead in the tub. I've been trying to understand why she didn't lock her door. It just seems like such a stupid and careless oversight, especially when I specifically reminded everyone to do so just before.

Turning it over and over in my mind, I can only think of three possible explanations.

First, that Isla really did just forget to lock her door...but I still find it hard to believe that she'd be that careless with her own life. It's just not the kind of mistake the person I knew would do.

The second possibility is that she did lock her door but unlocked it later on. Maybe she did it because the killer somehow managed to trick her into thinking that they were one of us. Maybe Eleanor convinced Isla into thinking that she was Sadie, for example. This scenario seems unlikely though, since we found Isla naked in the tub. I highly doubt she would have gotten out to unlock the door for anyone.

The third explanation is that she did lock her door...but the person who killed her unlocked it.

This is the scariest possibility of all, because it would mean that when we're locked alone in our rooms, thinking we're safe, we actually aren't at all. We're actually just sitting ducks.

But I can't be bothered to explain all of that to Ant. He never was the sharpest tool in the shed. So I just say, "It's safer if we all stick together. We should go get Sadie to come back down."

"If she even wants to. She didn't seem too thrilled with my knife. Bearing arms is my *right*," he mutters. "The Second Amendment says so."

"Let's go get her." I hop off my stool.

But Ant just reaches for a banana from the fruit bowl.

"Hey, come on."

"Why do I have to come too? The main door is locked," he says in a way that seems to be saying, *Wow, you're getting really paranoid, dude.*

"We should stick together," I repeat, resisting the urge to snatch the banana from his hand and whack him over the head with it.

He rolls his eyes, but even though he starts peeling the banana, he slides off his stool too.

But before we even reach the stairs, the vague, uneasy churning in my gut finally bubbles over when we walk past the picture. Out of what I guess is habit by now, my gaze slides over the damn picture, and I automatically start counting the number of red *X*s crossing out the figures in it. One, two, three, four, five, *six*.

My heart sinks to my stomach as I stare at the new, sixth X crossing out yet another figure.

Beside me, there's a small *plop* as Ant drops his banana.

ANT

My head is spinning as I stare at the new *X*. There are only two figures left unscathed now. Will and I exchange horrified looks. "Sadie." My voice comes out as a hoarse croak, creaky and grinding.

This time, we don't run. We climb the stairs slowly, step by reluctant step. It's hard to get my legs to move, to work properly. Sadie can't be dead. She can't be. She locked herself in her room… didn't she? She was already so spooked just now—much more spooked than Will and I were—so she must have. So how did the killer get her?

Arriving on the third level, I see immediately that the door to Sadie's room is open. My legs freeze in place at the top of the stairs. Will walks slowly over, looks in. It's only when horror seizes his face that my body unlocks and I go over to join him. Because

I have to see just how horrific the scene is. I have to see what provoked such terror in him.

But nothing could have prepared me for the sight of Sadie. Even when I'm staring right at her, it takes a while for the image to fully sink in.

Sadie is lying on her bed, on top of the bedcover, which is all mussed up. Scattered around her are the empty bags of the snacks she brought up, and crumbs. From the extreme disarray, it looks like she put up a fight. That isn't the horrible part.

The horrible part is her face.

Her face is blue, dotted with small dark purple spots; her eyes wide open, staring at the ceiling, the whites of her eyes red, filled with blood. Her mouth is open, lips stretched wide open in a frozen scream, or probably a last desperate attempt to draw breath. Her hands are claws. She almost looks like a reenactment of Emily, without the swelling. And she's most definitely dead.

"How did she die?" I gasp.

Careful not to touch her, Will points to Sadie's neck—at the purple bruises forming a ring around it. The bruises are uneven, the shape of them clearly formed by fingers. "Looks like she was strangled to death."

"Jesus." A maelstrom of thoughts is swirling in my head. I stumble out of the room. Sadie's air-starved face looks too much like Emily's, and I need to get out, need to not be looking at it anymore.

Will comes out too, closes the door shut behind him. He looks like he's either deep in thought or distracted by something. Either way, he doesn't meet my eyes.

That's alright, because I've got lots to chew on myself.

The killer is getting more and more violent. Emily and Charlie's murders were sly, subtle, nonviolent; made to look like they could have just been tragic accidents. And even though it was clear when Isla died that that couldn't have been an accident, it still didn't require much strength for the killer to simply hold her down in the slippery tub until she drowned. The ways Isla, Emily, and Charlie were murdered—all not requiring much physical strength—made me think the killer was female.

But now, strangulation. It isn't easy to strangle someone to death. It takes a *lot* of strength to maintain that kind of grip for so long. Maybe if a woman had a rope or a belt or something to help her, okay. But most women, they're not going to be able to strangle someone to death just with their bare hands.

I snap out of my brooding thoughts to find myself standing just outside my room. Subconsciously, wanting to be alone, I've made my way down to the second level and back here. Yes, it's better to be alone in my room. Screw this *it's-safer-if-we-stick-together* shit. Why does Will keep insisting we stick together anyway? No, something is wrong, and until I can figure it out, I don't want to be anywhere near him anymore.

Because things are starting to make sense. I'm starting to figure it out.

Damn it, I left my knife in the kitchen. I want to go get it, but

I'm already standing in the doorway to my room. If I go down now to grab the knife, that'll let Will know I'm on to him now, put him on alert. He'll know the game is up. Jesus, he's just behind me. "I'm going to sleep," I say.

He doesn't say anything, just nods stiffly and turns to go. I move slowly, slow enough so I see him going into his own room just before I shut my door. Quickly, I lock it.

I sink shakily onto my bed.

I don't know for sure, of course. There might still be someone else on this island. Someone still in hiding, someone we didn't manage to flush out. All this time, I bought into Will's story that it must be Tom's sister. It made sense: the new PA—so coincidentally named Elle—had the best opportunity to sabotage all of us. It made complete sense...except, where is she? When, and how, did she arrive on the island? Where can she be hiding? How could she have put cheese in Emily's food? There were only the six of us at the dinner table.

Only us.

Maybe the killer has always been one of us all this time.

And now I know the killer has got to be a guy. Only a guy would be strong enough to strangle someone to death with his bare hands.

Eleanor could still be behind all this. She's still the only person who could have dismissed the staff that were supposed to be here, got us stranded on this island, and made sure the rest of our graduating class wasn't coming. She could still be here on the island right now with us. She could have arrived before us, and maybe the reason she's been able to hide from the rest of us so well is because someone else is helping her to stay hidden.

Oh my god. Why didn't this occur to me sooner? It all makes sense now. Eleanor organized all this, but she needed someone else to help her carry out the murders. Someone who was part of the group, who had access to us. Someone none of the rest of us would have ever suspected.

Someone like Will.

Have you ever considered that she might not be acting alone? he said so cryptically just now. He was sounding me out, testing to see how much I've guessed.

Jesus. All this time, *the call was coming from inside the house.*

But why? Why the hell would he do this? Maybe he's gone mad. Or maybe…

Maybe Tom's sister has something on him. Maybe she threatened him with it, because she needed help, couldn't do it all on her own, and he agreed to help her kill all the rest of us so that she'd stop blackmailing him.

I think back over all the deaths, see now how Will had the opportunity to kill them.

He was the one who suggested doing the tequila shots, and he was the one who poured them out. He could have easily dropped some cheese in the bottle of tequila. None of us would have seen or tasted it, yet that would have been enough to kill Emily.

He was the one who "found" the red pen in Charlie's room.

He could have stolen Sadie's Valium, and he was the one who held on to the key for Charlie's door. After we all went back to our rooms, he must have gone back to Charlie's room last night and made Charlie swallow the pills.

And the lunch. He volunteered to make lunch for us, but when I went down after my shower, all he'd done was put some bread and other stuff on the counter and told us to make our own sandwiches. That's an awful lot of time. Instead of cooking, he must have knocked on Isla's door. It would explain why her door was unlocked. She must have let him in, not suspecting anything.

And then he tricked me into going on a wild-goose chase while he snuck back into the house. He must have convinced Sadie to open her door and murdered her. It was why he was acting so strange just now. It's why he didn't look under the pier. He didn't bother to search the island at all.

All these realizations hit me one after the other, like blows to my head, *bam bam bam bam bam*. The treacherous, backstabbing, double-crossing snake. I thought we were *buddies*. Whatever Eleanor has over him, it must be something really bad.

The betrayal cuts, but the more I think about it, the less it surprises me. Will has always—will always—put himself first.

So now Sadie is dead too. But at least I've figured it out now. I gotta focus. I gotta think. Because now that it's just the two of us left, I'm obviously the final target.

When I thought it was just Eleanor, I felt confident in my ability to dispatch her. But if she's got Will with her, I'm in serious danger. It's the two of them against me, and like me, Will is physically tough. Probably tougher and fitter than me, though I hate to admit it.

What should I do?

I could stay locked in my room all night. But what am I going to do tomorrow when the chopper comes back for us? I need to be down there when it comes, but going out there and waiting for it before it's here seems like an extremely dangerous idea. They could get me easily while I'm out in the open.

What if I keep an eye and an ear out for the chopper? A clear image of myself making a mad dash for it forms so clearly in my mind that my heartbeat picks up and my palms go sweaty, of me unlocking my door, running down the stairs—just like last night when I ran back down to Emily but was too late, far too late to save her. Out the front door, the mad dash down the hill to the bottom where the pilot is waiting. How will I tell him that we need to leave right now, *tout de suite*, to shut up and not ask any questions until we're safely in the air? I don't even remember his name. He would never listen to me, would never leave without Sadie. How will he react when I tell him that she's dead?

Also—and I hate to even acknowledge this doubt; it makes me ashamed, makes me want to punch someone—but would I even make it down there to begin with? Will might be right outside waiting to attack me as soon as I open my door.

If none of us are there when the pilot arrives, what will he do? Will he come looking for us? Or will he try to call Sadie and, having no network, just assume that we're not there because we've all decided to go back by boat instead, and simply leave?

The thought of being stranded here for who knows how long with Will leaves me cold.

If it comes down to a death match between the two of us, who would win?

—*Could the killer have escaped by boat?*

—*I suppose that's possible, but there's something off about the whole thing.*

—*Off? Like how?*

—*Like the way the police don't seem to be looking for a killer.*

—*I heard one of them died from her allergies. Was that an accident?*

—*It could have been, except for some of the other deaths being a lot more…*

—*Gory.*

—*Yeah.*

—*So definitely murder then. Wait, so…you think the killer was…one of them?*

WILL

Now that the sun has set, with the rain obscuring whatever moonlight there might have been, the room is pitch-dark. I reach out automatically to turn the light on…but stop just before my fingers hit the switch.

Do I really want to flood my room with light, let anyone who could be outside looking in at this very moment see my every move? Yeah, maybe not.

I pace the room in the dark as I wrestle my racing thoughts into coherence.

Ant must have realized I'm on to him, the way he beat it back to his room so quickly, pretending he was going to sleep. But I went along with it because I needed time to think and work out what to do now that I know.

I started to realize earlier that Eleanor must have an

accomplice—that she couldn't have done all of this by herself—but it wasn't until I saw those marks on Sadie's neck that I finally realized her accomplice had to be *one of us*. It makes sense. She needed an inside man, someone close enough to the group to carry out the rest of her plan.

She must be paying Ant to be her hit man. He's always been desperate for money, willing to do anything for it. With him here, doing her dirty work, she probably isn't even here on the island herself. There's no need for her to be.

No wonder he was so eager, kept pushing for us to go outside to look for her. He needed me out of the house so he could finish off Sadie.

It was how he did Tom, and—I remember now—he attacked Charlie the same way last night. If he had a signature method, that was it. What a brute.

Incandescent rage simmers in my belly as I realized how I've been played. And I always thought he was simple. He had all of us fooled, especially the way he seemed so distraught over Emily's death. I should have realized that if he really cared for her, he wouldn't have treated her the way he'd been treating her, wouldn't have been as cruel as he was to her.

I also realize now how easy it was for him to kill the others.

He was the one who got the shot glasses and put them on the counter. He must have added the tiniest amount of cheese to every one of them. No matter which glass Emily took, she would have died.

I have no doubt now that Eleanor must have handed him spare keys for all the rooms. He must have been the one who swiped Sadie's Valium, then returned to Charlie's room that night after the rest of us went to bed, and got Charlie to swallow those pills and OD. That's how he must have gotten into Isla's room too, with a spare key.

As for Sadie, he must have snuck back to the house, murdered her, and went back out again before I came back.

He must think that Eleanor will really pay him, that she'll let him live after he's finished the job. He must be really dumb if he believes that. Because if she were smart, she wouldn't let him stay alive to potentially blackmail her, to give her away anytime in the future. If he manages to kill me, he'd be the next one to go. I know that if I were her, that's what I'd do. But then again, like I've said, he's never been the brightest bulb in the box.

He must be plotting a way to kill me now, if he doesn't already have a plan. He can't be planning to take me on in a fair fight, and he probably knows I'd never trust anyone enough to fall asleep in their presence while they "*keep a lookout*," so he's going to try and trick me in some way, drug me, or get me drunk.

Shit. What should I do?

He must have a spare key for my room too, so keeping myself locked in here isn't a solution. My heart sinks further as I realize that even if he doesn't try to force his way in, I can't stay in here anyway, because he could just set fire to the house while I'm trapped in here. That would be such a beautiful solution, wouldn't it? Burn the house down along with the other bodies inside, and tell the authorities everyone died in the fire, everyone except him, such a terrible accident. No one would even know that we were really murdered. (Is he smart enough to think of this? Maybe not, but Eleanor could.)

I keep pacing my room, feeling more and more like a rat trapped in a cage with every passing moment. No, it's clear I can't stay in here, waiting to see what move Ant or Eleanor will make next. The smartest thing to do would be to get out. Stay in hiding somewhere else on the island until the chopper comes tomorrow. It'll be tough. Not only will I have to stay alert and keep watch the entire night—make sure I don't fall asleep—but also the rain is really beating down outside now.

It would be so easy to stay in here, in this luxurious room with the door locked, giving me a false sense of security, and this warm, dry, comfortable bed. Outside, I'll be cold, wet, and miserable. But I only hesitate for a second before I make up my mind.

I need to be careful. I need to be smart. I need to move fast. Shit, I left the meat cleaver in the kitchen, and there's absolutely nothing in here that I can use as a weapon.

In front of the door, I get down on my knees and press my face against the floor, look under it to make sure Ant isn't standing in wait outside. Once I'm certain there's no one outside waiting to stab or bludgeon me, I unlock it. Opening the door, I peer cautiously around it, make sure he isn't on the landing waiting to ambush me.

It takes every single ounce of my self-control not to run across the landing and down the stairs. I tell myself not to panic. Even though he can hear me going downstairs, he wouldn't be alarmed just yet. I could be going downstairs for any reason, to get a drink or more food. I could just have decided to hang downstairs because I couldn't fall asleep. But if I run, Ant will know I know it's him and the game will be up. So even though every single cell in my body is screaming to make a dash for it, I force myself to walk at a normal pace. Step by never ending step down the stairs, turning to check over my shoulder every few excruciating seconds.

When I'm finally downstairs though, I allow myself to run quietly to the kitchen to grab my cleaver. It's then that I notice, with a soaring feeling of glee, the carving knife that he's carelessly left on the counter. I grab that too. Then I'm out the front door and into the night, into the pouring rain.

ANT

The unmistakable sound of a door being unlocked drifts faintly under my door.

I'm unable to move, rooted to my bed as I listen intently, cold dread gripping my guts. This is it. Will is making his move now. He's coming for me. What is he going to do? The sound of his footsteps grows louder…then fainter as he continues walking past my room toward the stairs. The steps creak.

What's he doing? Where's he going? Upstairs or downstairs? And why?

There's nothing upstairs, nothing except Charlie's and Sadie's stuff…and their bodies, of course. He can't possibly have any reason to go in their rooms…can he?

I mean, it's not like there's no food downstairs.

Maybe he's trying to lure me out. That must be what he's

doing. Maybe he's gone downstairs to cook something, to tempt me out with the promise of a hot meal. Any moment now, he'll come and knock on my door, and say he changed his mind and cooked us a real dinner, tell me that we should eat to keep our strength up. Or he's going to try and persuade me to have drinks with him, in memory of our fallen friends, or some crap like that. Or maybe he's just going to insist again that we really should stick together in the living room downstairs because that's safer.

I wait to see which lie he's going to use…but the knock on my door never comes. I press my ear against the door, but I can't hear anything. If he went downstairs, he doesn't come back up. I check the time on my phone as I stay pressed against the door listening.

The minutes go by.

Ten.

Twenty.

Half an hour.

Is he going to stay downstairs the whole night?

What is he doing?

I shouldn't go out. I'd just be falling into his trap, whatever his plan is. But staying in here, not knowing what he's doing, isn't the solution either.

I'm getting a very bad feeling about this. Something is wrong. I can feel the certainty that he's up to something crawling up my spine. Something I haven't managed to guess at. Something that will end up killing me.

I have to know. I need to find out.

I should be able to hear the stairs creaking if he comes back, just like when he went down (or up). I can peek out and have a quick look. If he starts coming back, I'll just dash back inside and lock the door again before he makes it to my room.

I unlock my door quickly and peer outside. He's not on the landing. Holding my breath, I listen. It's dead quiet in the house; the only sound I can hear is the rain lashing against the glass walls, and the wind howling like some demented animal. Like the way it howled during that blizzard. *Like the way Charlie howled after Vera died*, my brain whispers, before I shove away that memory.

I take a tentative step out, then another one, and look over the banister, but there isn't much I can see of downstairs from here. All the lights are on downstairs. But that doesn't mean anything, because we didn't turn them off earlier. *Do NOT go down; this is a trap!* my brain yells, but my feet seem to move of their own accord, and I find myself moving stiffly down the stairs. Because there's nothing worse than not knowing what he's up to, and I have to know.

But he isn't downstairs. Not anywhere that I can see, anyway, unless he's hiding behind the kitchen island or in the bathroom. A sickly sensation of déjà vu washes over me. It was only a while ago that I just did this—come downstairs and searched the entire place for the killer—and now I have to do it again.

I should check the kitchen first, so that I can grab my knife. Just like before, I steel myself and make my way cautiously, slowly, quietly over there. If he jumps out from behind the island, I'll kick him in the face.

To my relief—and slight puzzlement—he isn't here. My muscles start to relax…but then I notice what else isn't here.

My knife. He's taken my knife.

WILL

The rain lashes down on me like icy daggers from the sky, and within seconds, I'm completely soaking wet. Despite the earlier heat of the day, it's surprisingly cold. The rain is also making it hard to see anything out here, except when the occasional lightning strikes and illuminates this drowned world for a glaring second. My mom's voice rings in my head: *When thunder roars, go indoors!*

I can't go indoors right now, Mom.

All of a sudden, a wave of homesickness hits me so hard my breath catches in my throat. What I wouldn't give right now to just be at home; nagging mom, grumpy dad, annoying little sister, and all. To be on the couch watching the Red Bulls play Inter Miami.

Instead, I'm stuck on this miserable island of death, hiding from a killer, on the verge of being washed away like a drowned rat, or fried by lightning.

At first, I think about going down to the pier and taking shelter under it. But that would be too obvious since it's the only place on the island where someone can shelter from the rain, and one of the first places Ant would look.

Besides, maybe it's better to stay near the house. This way, I can keep on eye on him and be ready for whatever he gets up to.

I settle on the grass near the tree line, in the shadows beyond the reach of the light from the house. This is a good spot to keep watch. For the first time, I'm grateful for how this entire side of the house is made of glass. In fact, I can see Ant right now, sitting on the bed in his room. Unlike the house, which is fully illuminated, it's pitch-dark out here where I am. If he looks out, he won't be able to see me, even if he looks straight at me. The predator has become the prey, and he doesn't even know it yet.

I watch as Ant finally stands up. I knew it wouldn't take him long before he made his move. Too bad for him, I'm one step ahead of him now. He goes over to the door and presses his ear against it, listening for me. Watch as he unlocks it and goes out.

Predictably, he heads straight to the kitchen. The shock that comes on his face when he discovers that I've taken the carving knife too—what a terrible rookie mistake he made, forgetting it on the counter—is priceless. His head whips around, scanning the space for me, features contorted in panic and black fury. I can't help but laugh as I watch him yank open the drawers and rummage for another weapon that he can use.

What is he going to do now?

ANT

I tell myself not to panic, but my heartbeat pounds in my head, *boom boom boom*, as rage, fear, and despair surge through me, all fighting for dominance. The meat cleaver is gone as well, so he's taken the two largest knives. I should have known he'd take them first chance he got.

Fear trickles coldly down my spine as Will's plans become clearer. I still can't quite believe that he intends to use those knives on me. He must have realized he can't trick me, and that it's going to come down to a one-on-one fight.

I need a weapon, but there's nothing else that comes close to those two knives. The steak knives are sharp, so better than nothing, but in a knife fight I won't have the reach he'll have.

I manage to find a rolling pin. I feel a bit silly as I lift it up, but it feels solid enough. I suppose this will give me reach. Maybe I can bash his head in with it.

In the end, I grab both a steak knife and the rolling pin. So this is what it finally comes down to. It's going to be either him or me. In the end, there can be only one left standing; our very own reboot of *Highlander*. Well, I'm ready for him.

With the knife in my left hand and my right firmly gripping the rolling pin, I tread silently over to the bathroom. The door is slightly ajar. I brace myself…and kick it open.

But there's no one inside.

I don't understand. Where is he? Did he head back upstairs after grabbing the knives? He couldn't have, because I would have heard the stairs creaking. So where can he be hiding?

Maybe he did sneak back upstairs somehow without me hearing him. After all, the way the rain is really beating down now, it could have drowned out any sounds he made going back upstairs.

The thought of him hiding somewhere upstairs—that I may have passed him unknowingly—that he may have been near enough to strike me just now—turns my blood cold. I should go back in my room, where I can at least lock the door. I shouldn't have come down at all. Too late, the feeling that I'm playing right into whatever twisted trap he has for me floods me.

But he may already be waiting for me in my room; I didn't lock the door when I left. Maybe it's safer to just stay here. Besides, if I spend the whole night here, it would be so much easier for me to run down to the lawn when the helicopter comes back tomorrow.

Clutching tightly to the steak knife and the rolling pin, I sink into an armchair facing the stairs. I just have to stay awake and alert until tomorrow. I still have no idea what I'm going to tell that pilot tomorrow to convince him to take off with just me, but that's a problem for future Ant.

I just have to stay awake and alert.

WILL

To my surprise, instead of coming after me, Ant settles into one of the armchairs.

He must think that I won't last the night outside here in this storm. He thinks I'll give up and come back in the house eventually, so he's content to just sit there and wait.

Well, he can wait all he wants. I'm made of much tougher stuff; I'm not going to melt. A little bit of rain isn't going to hurt me. I can stay out here all night if I have to.

Ant pulls out his phone and starts tapping on it. What's he doing? Does he…does he secretly have Wi-Fi? Oh my god, he must have. He must be communicating with Eleanor. I creep right up to the glass, look over his shoulder at his screen. He's…playing Solitaire.

Gritting my teeth, I head back to my spot in the shadows and settle in to wait it out.

X X X X X

I have no idea how much time has passed, but I've gravely underestimated the challenge of spending the entire night outside out in the open in a thunderstorm like this.

The rain is just so *relentless*. It keeps getting in my eyes and my nose, so I almost feel like I'm slowly drowning to death. The grass is flooded; I'm practically sitting in a pool of water. And the last time lightning struck, it hit a tree close to where I'm sitting. I could smell the freaking ozone, sulfur sharp. It stung my nose, brought tears to my eyes.

And the storm shows no sign of ending. If anything, it seems to be growing even wilder. The wind is picking up even more, so now it's howling in my ears, eerily just like that day on that mountain when we got caught in that blizzard.

And all this while, as I'm suffering outside, Ant is sitting nice and warm and cozy in there. As I watch, he gets up, goes to the kitchen…and starts making himself what seems to be a cup of coffee, for god's sake. I have to stifle a scream. He probably guesses that I'm nearby, keeping an eye on him, because all this—playing Solitaire on his phone, making himself a nice hot drink—can't possibly be anything other than intentional provocation. *Hey, Will! Don't you wish you were nice and warm and cozy in here like me? You stupid asshole.*

I've made a terrible mistake. While I'm suffering out here—having my senses assaulted by the storm, being weakened by the cold with every passing minute, probably on the way to catching pneumonia, and running the deadly risk of being killed by lightning—Ant is fortifying himself, staying alert, caffeinated, and strong for our eventual, inevitable confrontation. He's probably biding his time until the early hours of the morning—when I'm half-drowned and completely exhausted—to strike.

I need to rethink my strategy. I think about all my possible options, but it's starting to become clear that there really aren't that many left to me at all. Being out here the entire night isn't a solution. I'll be at a physical disadvantage when he comes for me after I've been weakened by staying out in the storm all night. And he will surely come for me before the helicopter comes. When the sun rises, there is nowhere I can hide from him on this tiny island.

I can't delay this confrontation. If I have to fight him eventually, it's better to do it right now, while I'm still strong.

I stand up. No more messing around. It's time to head in.

It's time to end this.

ANT

The armchair was way too comfortable. Even with the game, I found myself starting to doze off, so I got up to make myself a cup of instant coffee. Because if I know one thing, it's that it would be deadly to fall asleep. It would probably be the last thing I do. Gulping the coffee down while it's still scalding hot helps; the drowsiness starts to dissipate.

And then something happens that obliterates any last traces of sleepiness completely.

I'm staring out of the glass wall while drinking my coffee, when a flash of lightning streaks across the sky, for a split second illuminating the outside world as bright as day.

And in that split second, I see Will standing outside in the rain staring at me—thirty feet from the house—a long knife in each hand, looking like a fucking psycho in one of those horror slasher flicks.

Icy fear stabs me in the chest. It feels like my heart stops beating, before it starts up again in triple time. I barely notice the cup slipping from my hand and smashing on the floor as I snatch my own laughably small steak knife and rolling pin from the counter.

Thunder booms so loud it's like I can feel the sound in my skull, but it's pitch-black outside again, and I can't see a bloody thing beyond the glass wall. Can't tell where he is or what he's doing, if he's sneaking up to the door or not. He must have gone out as soon as he took the knives, just before I came downstairs. But that was more than two hours ago. Has he been standing outside like that, in the rain for over two hours, *watching me the entire time?*

Why?

My god, Will is insane. I realize this now. Maybe there is no Eleanor. Maybe it's just always been him all this time. How long has he been off his rocker? Maybe he got a sick kick from what we did in that mountain shelter, and he's been plotting to kill off the rest of us ever since.

The handle on the door starts turning, and all thoughts scatter from my brain. Shit, I've been frozen for too long. Finally, my body starts reacting. I sprint to the door, but it feels like I'm running in slo-mo, like in one of those nightmares where you're running away from some monster or demented clown, but the air around you has turned to glue, or molasses, and you can never run fast enough to escape.

The door swings open just as I reach it. Instinctively, I bring the rolling pin smashing down right on Will's face. But it was just a glancing blow. He staggers and takes a step back but doesn't fall. I should have dropped this stupid little knife and swung the pin with both hands.

His right arm swipes at my belly. I barely manage to lean back in time. The tip of his knife grazes me, ripping a tear in my T-shirt. A long line of heat erupts on my skin where it managed to slice me.

I bring the rolling pin down hard on his hand. The cleaver drops on the floor with a metallic clang. He swings at me with the knife in his left hand. It slices my right arm. The pain that explodes in my arm and shoots up to my shoulder is incredible, and I scream. I've dropped the rolling pin, and he kicks it away.

Blood is gushing out of my right arm. It's all but useless. All I'm left with is the small steak knife in my left hand. I kick out at him with my right foot. It connects with his left knee with a popping sound, and it's his turn to scream. His leg gives out, and he drops onto his knee.

I raise my left hand. But before I can plunge the knife down, he hacks the carving knife in my right thigh. The pain is excruciating, and I fall. I swing out with my knife, but I don't connect with anything but air. He hacks at me again and again and again. There's nothing but pain, blinding pain. I've dropped my knife. My hands are empty, slick with blood as I hold them uselessly in front of my face, lying on my back on the floor staring up at Will.

His face is hideous, deformed with bloodlust, features stretched in a grotesque sneer.

No. This can't be it, I manage to think before he brings his knife down on my face.

WILL

It's a while before I can move again.

That asshole was hard to kill. But I win in the end, of course. I'm an athlete who spent hundreds, thousands of hours doing strength and endurance training. He spent those hours playing video games, partying, and screwing girls. My victory was an obvious, foregone conclusion. He should have stuck to his sneaky, underhanded attacks instead of trying to take me on face-to-face. But I didn't give him a chance, did I? No, not after I figured out what was really going on.

It takes a while for the adrenaline to ebb. When it does, I'm drained and utterly exhausted, but also giddy with triumph.

Everyone is dead. Everyone except me. Once again, I have survived. Bested, outwitted, *outlasted* everything and everyone determined to end my life. Finally, I can rest. I drop the knife, dripping with Ant's blood, down on the floor beside his mutilated face.

I'm so tired I can barely think now. All I want to do is fall in bed. Obviously, I can't, not dripping wet and covered in blood and gore like this. I have to take a quick shower first before I can rest. As for how to explain all this to the pilot when he arrives tomorrow, I can think about it in the morning when I wake.

I stand up, but he must have busted my left knee because the pain that shoots up my leg is excruciating. I can barely stand up. This is bullshit. Of all the things he could have done, he went for my knee.

Maybe it isn't so bad. Maybe it just feels worse than it actually is. Most injuries are. Many pro athletes bust their knees, have them fixed with surgery, and continue to have great careers.

I limp toward the stairs. Before I reach it, I stop in front of that picture of the people trapped in the blizzard, the art print of the Donner Party. Look at the six red *X*s crossing out the six figures, leaving two unscathed. That's not correct now. There's only one person left standing—me. It has to be fixed. No problem, I can do that. I look at the blood on my hands. With a finger, I cross out one more figure with Ant's blood.

There. Now it's right.

I start to pull myself up the stairs. It's not easy with one busted knee, being completely exhausted, and my hands and shoes slick with blood and rainwater. I have to be careful—imagine how stupid it would be if after everything that I've been through, I fall and break my neck now.

I'm so focused on the steps as I climb that I don't notice, until I'm almost at the top, the feet standing on the highest step.

Small feet clad in white trainers. Eleanor.

Time seems to slow, as if in a nightmare, as my gaze travels up. Slim legs. Cream linen shorts. A plain white tee. And finally… Sadie's ghoulish purple face, staring back at me.

Not possible, my mind shrieks. *What the hell is this?*

Before I can react—to run or even to scream, *But you're dead*—her hands stretch out and give my chest a hard shove.

I fly backward. I hear a sickening crack as the back of my head hits a step. Stars explode in my vision like fireworks. Pain everywhere as I tumble down the stairs like a rag doll.

As I lie in a crumpled heap at the bottom, the last thing I see, before everything goes black, is Sadie floating down the stairs toward me.

SADIE
THREE HOURS EARLIER

I press my ear against the door. *Ant*, Will's muffled voice calls questioningly. He's back early. I need to hurry. Finally, it's my turn to die. For all of us to die. The two of them are so predictable. I put on a show going on about how we should stick together—hole up in the living room and hold out until tomorrow—because that's what they would have expected of me. They would have suspected something was wrong if I hadn't. But I knew it was always only a matter of time before they'd ignore me and go hunting for the killer. Because they haven't changed a bit.

I needed to get them out of the house in order to carry out the next step.

Why do some people get to live while others don't? What gave them the right to decide that Vera and Tom had to die so that they might survive?

Poor Tom. We had to keep our relationship a secret because my dad didn't approve of us dating. He never did tell anyone about us or let anyone on to the fact that we were together, even in the final days. Maybe we still held out hope that we were going to be rescued, even after weeks of being trapped. That everything was going to be alright, and then we'd go on being secretly together until the entirety of my trust fund was released to me, and we could finally run away and *be* together, without my father to keep us apart.

Even now, thinking about Tom makes me want to cry again.

And the baby. The miscarriage was inevitable, of course. I knew, after the starvation began, that it was never going to survive. Still, I hoped. It was why I finally decided to eat. I was desperately hoping that if I did, I wouldn't lose it. At least I'd still get to keep a part of Tom.

But it was too little, too late. A week after we were rescued and "safe" back home, the bleeding started. And went on, and on, and on. The nights were full of the same recurring nightmare—dreams that always, always had monsters at the end that devoured. The days were strange, numb blurs, connected only by all that blood. Blood that made the horrors of everything that happened real again.

The miscarriage was nobody's fault except mine, for being persuaded to go on that stupid ski trip. Okay and, I suppose to be fair, Tom's too, for venturing too far against instructions and falling into that crevasse.

But I can 100 percent blame Isla, Ant, and Will for everything else.

It was almost half a year after we returned—half a year after we murdered Vera and Tom—half a year of continuous nightmares—that I realized dying was the only way to escape this never-ending torment. The only way to stop the nightmares.

For a while, I contemplated different ways in which I could kill myself.

But then I realized one more thing. I couldn't just go like that. I wasn't the only one who did this gruesome, terrible thing. I wasn't the only one who was now a blight in this world.

The six of us were monsters, and every one of us had to die.

It was the only way to right what had gone wrong. To wipe the slate clean. I could make amends. Make things right. It was the best thing I could do. The only way to make it up to Tom and Vera.

I need to focus now, stop slipping into memories of the past. There's no putting it off any longer. It's time to end this.

When they left the house just now, I grabbed the other red marker—the twin of the one I planted in Charlie's room—from my makeup bag, rushed downstairs, and crossed out one more figure in the picture.

It's a funny story, this picture. I came across it in a historical archive a few weeks ago. I'd already worked out most of how I was going to carry out the plan, but as soon as I saw it, I realized how perfect it was. It was creepy. It was poetic. It would fit so beautifully. What better way to rachet up the paranoia and panic? No idea who the artist was, but it was easy enough to order a canvas print of it.

Convincing my parents to let me hang it in this house a few weeks ago was the difficult part. Obviously, they were puzzled as to why on earth I wanted to do this. They didn't want to have to look at such a "distasteful horror" every time they spent a weekend here. In the end, I managed to persuade them to let me do it by telling them that it was Dr. Armstrong's idea, part of his advice that I come to terms with my past trauma by facing it in a safe space…and that if they didn't let me hang it here, that I'd hang it in our house instead, and they'd have to see it every day. Quite astonishing, really, that they fell for that ridiculous bullshit that I pulled out of my ass.

They let me come alone with the chopper the previous weekend to hang the picture. That was also when I cut out the satellite cables in the wall downstairs. And that was it. Thirty minutes of work was all it took to set the scene and cut off all contact with the outside world.

Now, I rummage quickly in my bag until I find what I'm looking for: the box of theater makeup that we use for special effects.

When I first joined theater freshmen year, I had some kind of half-formed dream about learning how to act and moving to Los Angeles to become an actor after high school. Even then, all I wanted was to get out from under my dad's thumb. To live my own life—even if it was a broke one. At least I would be my own person.

It soon became clear to me, however, that that was just a child's dream. I was too self-conscious onstage, and I had the worst stage fright. Oh, I learned enough to be a good enough actress, if I wasn't acting in front of an audience of hundreds or thousands of people, or if I wasn't auditioning for a role—just look how useful all that acting training turned out to be this weekend. But I was never going to make it as a real actress.

I couldn't be onstage, but I made myself useful with backstage work, helping out with makeup and costumes. I thought I'd move to LA, be a makeup artist. It still meant getting away from my family, still meant freedom.

It's incredible what you can do with makeup like this. You can make someone look like a zombie, or create wounds or bruises that look so realistic nobody can tell you're not actually injured.

It takes me exactly eight minutes to make my skin the exact same shade as Emily's when she suffocated to death. Although objectively that's already fast, I'm jittery as I work because it's still much too slow. Ant could be back at any moment, or Will could spot the new *X* on the picture and come investigate by himself.

As I'm creating the bruises around my neck, I hear the front door downstairs slam shut.

Ant must be back too.

Sure enough, I hear Ant's muffled voice say *You're back early*. My hands are trembling as I finish up painting the bruises, and I have to force myself not to panic and to take all the time this requires and not do a shoddy job. They'll be looking closely, so it needs to be perfect.

I'm just finishing up the last of the bruises when I hear Will say *We should go get Sadie to come back down.* They'll notice the new *X* on the picture soon; there's no more time to waste. I pop the red colored contacts in, then hurry to the door and unlock it quietly. Then I get on the bed and into the position I'll have to maintain. When they come in, I'll have to breathe as inconspicuously as possible, even hold my breath when they get nearer for as long as their eyes are on me. Holding my breath isn't going to be the hardest part though. The hardest part will be keeping my eyes open without blinking or tearing up.

But I can do it. Because I'm doing it for Tom, and Vera, and the baby. I'm finally making things right. We should all have died then, instead of committing the atrocities we did.

Finally, the nightmares are going to stop. I can't take the nightmares anymore. Because what made them truly horrific was that at the end, when the monsters came out to devour, I was one of them.

WILL
NOW

My head is pounding like the worst hangover I've ever had, as if someone has hit it with a sack of bricks.

My eyelids peel open, but my vision is blurry. It's hard to focus on anything when the pounding pain in my head drowns out everything else. And *Jesus*, everything hurts, like I fell down a flight of stairs or something.

Oh, right.

I finally realize that I'm sprawled at the bottom of the stairs and that there's someone standing in front of me.

Sadie, who's supposed to be dead.

Is she a ghost?

A zombie?

Panic surges through me, but I can't get up. It hurts too much everywhere. Not only my busted knee, but especially my head. The slightest motion brings on a wave of nausea. I also can't move my right hand. Turning my head, I discover my right wrist is shackled to the staircase's handrail with…one of those fluffy pink novelty sex handcuffs. The cuffs are so ridiculous that I stare at them for a moment, trying to make sense of what's happening.

Okay, Sadie can't be a ghost or a zombie, then. A malevolent spirit or the undead wouldn't be shackling me with pink fluffy handcuffs.

But she was *dead*. I turn back to look at her. She *still* looks dead, her face that ghastly purple shade, bloodshot eyes, and those bruises around her neck.

"It's makeup," she says, as if reading my thoughts.

Understanding dawns sickeningly in me. "It was you, wasn't it? All along, it was you. You killed everyone."

"Not everyone. Not Ant. Thanks for that."

Horror clamps its icy fingers around my throat. She's played the two of us. "You crossed out that figure, made us think the other snuck back here to kill you."

She shrugs. "The two of you are so predictable."

She manipulated Ant, manipulated *me*, pulled our strings, and pitted us against each other. Probably laughing the entire time while I was suffering out there in the storm. Listened, maybe even watched us hack at each other. Anger pulses darkly through my veins. Ant was innocent, and she made me kill him.

I want to wrap my hands around her throat and strangle her to death for real, wipe that smug look off her face once and for all. I jerk my right arm, try to pull free, but the cuffs—ridiculous as they look—hold tight, and I only succeed in hurting my wrist.

Another emotion creeps in, like poison spreading through my body, makes me cold all over. Fear. Because it's then that I fully appreciate just exactly how fucked I truly am right now.

But if she was going to kill me, she'd have done it already, right? Why cuff me and wait for me to regain consciousness? Is there something that she wants from me?

Maybe she's doing this to draw it out, like a cat toying with a mouse, enjoying the final moments before it makes its kill. Because she wants to draw out my fear to the maximum, make sure I know exactly what's happening, before I die.

I need to buy time. Get her to talk. Maybe if I find out why she's doing this, I can persuade her to stop. I blurt out the first thing that comes in my head. "So, you're the one behind it all. It wasn't Eleanor at all."

"Tom's sister?" Sadie laughs softly. "Nah, my dad's PA isn't Eleanor. Elle is just Elle. But I knew you'd think she was, the way I made it look like she was the one who arranged everything."

"How did you stop the others from coming? We all heard you ask Elle to arrange the boats."

She nods. "I did. And then when you all wrangled a ride on the helicopter like I knew you would, I told her to cancel the boats. When I was back home, just before you all arrived."

It was that simple. The others were never coming. It was a trap all along, designed just to lure the five of us here. I could kick myself. "And you got rid of the staff that were supposed to be here too."

She laughs softly. "There were never any staff here."

What does that mean? Nothing made sense. "How could you have plotted all this in the few hours after we decided to come here? How did you manage to set all this up so that we'd decide to come in the first place? How could you have known that the owner of this island would rent it, and that we'd know about it?"

Sadie tilts her head and gives me a pitying look. "Haven't you worked that out yet? This island isn't owned by some celebrity at all. It's owned by my family. The entire ad is fake, Will. I've been planning this for a long time."

The entire ad is fake. The words echo in my head, making me dizzy.

She continues. "Months ago, I paid a whole bunch of influencers to post about it, seed the rumors that it's owned by various celebs. Then a few weeks ago, I paid them to post about it again, put out that it's available for rent. It was only a matter of time before someone from school saw it. I got so many emails from people everywhere wanting to rent it. It was almost funny."

It's mind-boggling. "How did you kill Emily?"

"I rubbed a bit of cheese on all the lime wedges, while I was cutting them."

"So it was really an immediate allergic reaction when we had those tequila shots? You didn't poison her during dinner? But why did she puke then?"

Sadie shrugs. "She must have just had too much of that champagne."

I shake my head. "And you were the one who went back to Charlie's room that night and made him OD on your Valium. You pretended to lose it to make it seem like someone else took it."

"Actually, I did lose it. It must have fallen out of my pocket when we arrived. It was Isla who took it. I found it in her room, just before dinner."

Oh. That doesn't surprise me at all, now that I think about it. No wonder Isla seemed so giddy during dinner. I thought then that she was just thriving off all the attention Ant was paying her. She must have just been high from Sadie's Valium. "How did you get Charlie to take the pills?"

"He was so drunk. At first, he thought I came to let him out. I told him I couldn't, but that I wanted to give him my Valium to help him sleep. I told him that it would stop all the pain. I told him to take all six of the remaining pills, which he did without question. His judgment was a little impaired by then." Her face twisted with the memory, and she looked genuinely sad about what she did. "Poor Charlie. He was so tormented. Losing Vera like that really destroyed him." She looked at me, her eyes hard. "Especially after what you all got him to do after."

"He didn't have to. Nobody made him."

Sadie sighs and looks even sadder. "No. Nobody made me either."

"And you had spare keys for all the rooms, of course."

She nods.

"But why? Why do all this?"

"Why?" Her voice is a whisper. "You really don't know why?"

I can roughly guess from the picture of the Donner Party, but I still don't understand. "Because of what happened when we were trapped in that shelter?"

"*What happened.* As if it was something that just happened, and not something that we *did*."

I clench my jaw. "All we did was what we had to do to survive."

"You didn't have to kill them!"

"It was an accident that Ve—"

"That's not true and you know it!" shouts Sadie.

I try to speak calmly. "What are you talking about?"

"The three of you. You *wanted* her dead. And then she was."

I shake my head, still keeping my expression calm even as my palms start to sweat. "It was an accident. She was hysterical. Freaking out. It's understandable you don't believe it because you were still sleeping, but she lashed out at Isla when Isla was only trying to get her to calm down. We were just trying to stop her from—"

"Hurting herself?" Sadie says mockingly. "Yeah, and then you 'accidentally' killed her. Sure. And Tom's was a 'mercy killing'."

"He was in a lot of pain and already dying," I whisper.

Tears well in Sadie's eyes until one trickles down her cheek, followed closely by another one on the other side. "We shouldn't have survived. Not if it meant doing what we did. Turning into monsters. Tell me, who would have been next? If we hadn't been rescued. Who would you all have chosen to die next?"

I shake my head again, but she's not done talking. "How do you just go on? How do you continue, as if nothing happened? *How do you not feel any guilt at all?*"

Because it was a tragedy, but it wasn't our fault. And we did what we had to do to survive, like I said. Why should I feel any guilt? What does she want me to say? "It was an accident. You have to believe me—"

"*Shut up!* Vera and Tom didn't have to die," sobs Sadie. "We could have lasted until the search party rescued us. Don't you understand? They didn't have to die. It didn't have to happen that way."

"We'd been trapped for two weeks," I snap back at her. "It's not like we had a crystal ball and knew they'd find us a week and a half later. Also, how the hell do you know we could have lasted without any food at all till then? It was so fucking *cold*. I think we *would* have died if we hadn't done what we did."

"*I would have preferred to die!*" she shouts.

"You could have just chosen not to do it," I point out.

Sadie closes her eyes for a while. When she reopens them again, her face is calm. "Yes, I could have. But I was too weak. And I've been paying the price for it ever since. Unlike you, I've been having nightmares every night. But it's okay, the nightmares will stop soon."

She walks off over to where Ant is lying, and panic swamps my chest. "This is all so overly dramatic," I call out frantically. "What's the point of all this? If you're not coping, why don't you just get more therapy?" With all her money, she could have a therapy session every day. Heck, twice a day. And if that still doesn't work, I don't know, just spend her money on ridiculously expensive stuff. Like another private island. If I had her kind of money, I wouldn't have a care in the world.

Sadie looks down at Ant. "Look at what you did to him." She shakes her head. Then she bends and picks up one of the knives.

No. No no no. I need more time. I have to keep making her talk. "What do you mean by the nightmares will stop soon?"

She doesn't answer, just comes slowly nearer and nearer, the bloody meat cleaver clutched in her right hand.

"Wait," I cry. "But why did you kill Emily and Charlie?"

She closes her eyes. "Emily and Charlie had to die because we all have to die after what happened. Don't you get it? What we did… We're abominations. Monsters. We should have all died there in that shelter. At least I let Emily and Charlie die first." She opens her eyes, raises the meat cleaver.

"*Wait!*"

Her hand freezes at my cry.

"You keep calling us monsters. But we're not. We're just people who did what we had to do to survive." I babble the words out. Sweat trickles down my forehead, stinging my eyes. "You don't have to do this, Sadie. I understand that you've been trapped in this nightmare for a long time, and you want it to stop. But you don't have to do this. Nothing you do will change what happened. It won't bring Tom back."

Her mouth twists. Her raised hand, still frozen in the air, is trembling.

Hope surges in me. "Please, put down the knife." This time, it's me who starts crying. "Please, Sadie. I don't want to die."

She closes her eyes again. Tears are streaming down her face now. Slowly, she begins to lower her hand.

Before she can make another move, I grab her wrist.

SADIE

I gasp as Will's hand grips my wrist, twisting my hand so hard I drop the knife. It clatters on the floor. I reach for it, but he snatches it up first and slashes at me. The blade splits the skin on my thighs. I see it happening before the searing pain catches up.

A scream escapes my throat as I crumple, landing on my butt with a bone-rattling *thump*. I try to scramble away, but his hand clamps around my left ankle. He's transferred the knife to his cuffed left hand and is yanking on my leg with his right, trying to pull me back to him. He must want the key for the cuffs, which is in my pocket. I kick at his hand with my right foot and get free.

"Sadie!" Will shouts as I pull my legs to my chest so he can't reach me. "Stop this!" He's furious and scared.

I hesitated once, and he grabbed his chance immediately. I cannot hesitate again. I cannot stop to think. I must finish this.

He has this knife, but there's the other long knife by Ant's body. It doesn't matter that Will is much bigger than me and has a longer reach.

It doesn't matter because I don't need to survive this.

I just have to make sure he dies too.

I crawl over to Ant's body. My thighs are burning where Will slashed me. I've never felt such pain in my life. I realize I will feel more before it's over.

That's okay. It will be over soon. I can rest then, because I'd have made things right. I just need to rid the world of us.

The knife is in a pool of Ant's blood. When I pick it up, it's cold and sticky. I manage to get up on my feet and hobble back toward Will, knife clutched in my hand.

But I make a detour, stop first in front of the picture. It feels important to cross out the last figure too. I cross out the final figure with the blood on my hands. There. That's all of us.

"You fucking crazy bitch," Will spits, knife back in his right hand.

"That's offensive and perpetuates harmful stereotypes," I tell him as I hobble back to him.

He lunges forward, sticks the knife in my thigh. I fall on my knees. He's pulling his knife back out when I plunge mine in his neck.

His mouth gapes open, his eyes rolling to look at me. Blood bubbles and spurts from his neck as I pull my knife out. He manages to pull his out from my thigh and stick my belly with it. I stick mine in his at the same time.

We both crumple over. Will's eyes stare accusingly at me. *Look what you've done*, they seem to be saying.

It's finished. It's over. I did it.

The room is a blur through the tears.

Finally. No more nightmares.

No more guilt.

—*So one died from asphyxiation by anaphylaxis, from her allergy…*

—*One died from a fatal overdose from a mix of Valium and alcohol…*

—*One was found drowned in a bathtub…*

—*And three were brutally hacked to death in the living room. Jesus. And nobody really knows what happened?*

—*There was no suicide note or anything. Like I said, just that picture of the Donner Party on the wall, with the eight figures all crossed out. Six with red marker, two with blood. And if the police know anything more, what really happened, they aren't saying.*

READ ON FOR A SNEAK PEEK OF CINDY R. X. HE'S
PERFECT LITTLE MONSTERS...

HIDE AND SEEK
NOW

The soft, tuneless whistling drifts over to where she's hiding, as she crouches in the dark closet, peeking through the slats.

She hadn't known how loud simply breathing was. Surely the person hunting her can hear her panicked, shallow breaths—and her too-loud heartbeat, thumping against her ribs like a frantic trapped bird. To make things worse, it's so dusty that she's going to sneeze. She pinches her nose, fights the deadly urge. Sweat trickles down her back, like the faint caress of ghostly fingers.

Her eyelids droop closed…but she snaps them open again. She focuses her eyes on the narrow line of light pooling under the closed bedroom door. She must not fall asleep. Absolutely cannot sink into the darkness that is threatening to engulf her. But she can feel how heavy her limbs are, heavy and clumsy with the drug slushing through her bloodstream. She pinches her left arm hard, twists the tender skin to keep herself awake.

A nightmare. That's what this is. Even so, she can't quite believe that this is happening, that someone is trying to *kill* her. Surely, she'll wake up soon in her queen-sized bed with its eight-hundred-thread-count Egyptian cotton sheets. The muscle in her right calf seizes in a painful cramp from crouching for so long, and she stifles another sob.

It's so unfair. She doesn't deserve this, no matter what she did. The punishment is too harsh! She could cry from the injustice of it. A sob bubbles up from her chest to her throat, and she clamps her shaking hands over her mouth to keep it from escaping. Her mind is shrieking, but she mustn't make a peep because the smallest sound would give away her hiding place in a second. And then this game of hide-and-seek would be over. *The end. You lose. Time to die.*

Soft, deliberate footsteps now, in the corridor. That insane, tuneless whistling. The footsteps grow louder…and louder…until they stop just outside. There is a shadow under the door. She watches through the slats as the knob turns slowly…

But she's locked the door from the inside! The knob stops turning, and she's almost giddy with relief. She starts to smile…

But then there's the unmistakable *scritch scratch* of a key entering the keyhole. The bedroom door swings open, and that horrible whistling starts up again. She tears herself away from the slats, scrambles backward into the darkness at the back of the closet.

Shrinks into a small ball, her knees pressed against her chin. *Nonono, I can't die like this can't die like this can't—*

The closet doors open. She looks up at the person standing over her trembling body. The whistling stops.

"Found you."

Those empty eyes.

That awful smile.

The dull gleam of the carving knife.

She opens her mouth and screams.

DAWN
TWO MONTHS AGO

The bell for the first class is going to ring soon. But I'm still sitting on the closed lid of the toilet in a stall in the girls' restroom on the second floor of Sierton High. I can't seem to make myself get up. My head is lowered almost to my knees as I try not to hyperventilate.

I'm still safe for now in here, where no one can see me. But once I step out…who knows what might happen? Not for the first time, the feeling that my being here is a mistake rears its head… but I push it away quickly. *I'm a new person. Nobody knows me here.* I try to focus on what my mom told me—her warm brown eyes crinkling in the corners like they always do when she smiles— before I left the house with Aunt Maddy this morning: *Everything will be fine, you'll see. I know you'll do us proud.*

I try to take slow, even breaths. Okay, I think I'm okay now. I get up, unlatch the door.

I've just taken a step toward the sinks when the door swings open and hits the wall with a loud *bang*. Three girls enter: one with hair so blond it has to be very expensive and high maintenance, her waist-high shorts showing off her long coltish legs; the second a pretty Latina girl with long-lashed dark eyes and black hair flat-ironed to shiny perfection, in a trendy cropped top and lululemon leggings; and then possibly the prettiest one of them, half-Caucasian, half-Asian, with caramel doe eyes and impossibly perfect glowing skin, in an expensive-looking minidress and cashmere cardigan. I recognize them. I know them because I'm like them.

They stare at me, and my heart starts beating triple time as I walk self-consciously past them to the sink and start washing my hands. I can see them checking me out in the mirror out of the corner of my eyes. Their eyes travel over my appearance too, taking in my hair, my face, my clothes, my bag. They're curious because I look like them, like I could be part of their clique. I could be their friend…or a possible rival.

Thing is: I might look like them, and once upon a time, stuff like being popular or being part of this friend group was important to me too. But not anymore.

Luckily, they soon lose interest in me. The Latina turns her attention back to the girl with the white-blond hair. "What's wrong with my leggings?" It sounds like a continuation of whatever conversation they were having before they entered the bathroom.

ACKNOWLEDGMENTS

Thank you to:

My editor, Annie Berger, whose enthusiasm for this book helped me overcome the dreaded book-two fears. The draft I turned in was so rough, but once again, your thoughtful, painstaking edits helped shape this into a much better book. Thank you for loving and championing this story. Huge thanks to the team: Gabbi Calabrese, Aimee Alker, Thea Voutiritsas, Deve McLemore, Tara Jaggers, Karen Masnica, Lia Ferrone, Delaney Heisterkamp, Stephanie Gafron, and Stephanie Rocha for all your hard work and Nicole Hower for the stunning cover. I can't imagine a more perfect home for this book than Sourcebooks Fire.

My wonderful agent, Michael Bourret, for your never-ending kindness, patience, enthusiasm, and belief in my writing. I am so lucky to have been adopted by you.

Librarians, booksellers, teachers, BookTokkers, 'grammers, and early readers who have found a place for this book in your hearts. I'm so grateful for your support and enthusiasm for this story.

Early readers Joanna Farrow and Lindsay Chubak, who read the terrible first draft. (When am I ever going to get to pay back the favor, Jo??)

Amelia, Elizabeth, Beatrix, and Greg. I love you.

ABOUT THE AUTHOR

 Cindy R. X. He is the author of *Perfect Little Monsters*, a finalist for the Killer Nashville Claymore Award and the Daphne du Maurier Award. Born in Singapore, she now lives in the French Alps with her husband, children, and rescue cat, where she skis in the winter and hoards books all year round.

cindyrxhe.com
Instagram: @cindyrxhe

sourcebooks fire

Home of the hottest trends in YA!

Visit us online and
sign up for our newsletter at
FIREreads.com

....

Follow
@sourcebooksfire
online